"This is the story of a mixed-race professional young woman who looked for the best in others while modeling kindness and love in her interpersonal relations while fighting a virulent form of blood cancer. Through it all, she gains considerable understanding of the meaning of life and the power of love. This book contains romance, spirituality employing the medium of meditation, the gifts and limits of modern medicine, and the importance of a dedicated family facing down the haunting specter of excruciating medical procedures. It is an instructive story for all of us who must, in the end, confront our own mortality."

—Albert P. Melone, PhD
Author of *Mezzogiorno in Chicago* and *Political Culture in the Age of Trump*

"In these pages, a mother reverently recounts an experience every parent fears the most: losing a child. Yet the story she shares—of her daughter Vashti's joyful life and heroic journey toward her death at age thirty-four—is uplifting. Vashti's full-on embrace of life, even during her difficult two-year battle with cancer, inspires her to say without hesitation, 'I've done everything I wanted to do in life, and I have no regrets.' This re-markable book will open your heart and enlarge your spirit as it gives witness to the power of a bright and beautiful light."

—Beverly Miller, licensed professional clinical counselor

"From the start of *Autumn Gold*, I was enthralled. This story of a family navigating the illness of an adult child caused me to experience the full range of emotions. Lesley Lowe's storytelling is well worth the time it takes to read and reflect on family love and loss."

—Charles Perkins, counseling psychologist

"A loving, well-rendered chronicle bearing witness to the value of living life fully while we can. The author paints an indelible picture of the highs of her daughter Vashti's life, full of love and compassion, and the lows of the final phase of her journey. Her parents walk by her side as Vashti battles her terminal illness with grace, humor, and concern for those she will leave behind, including the young man she loves."

—F. Sowers, director, Board of Veterinary Medicine, New Mexico

AUTUMN GOLD

A RENDEZVOUS WITH CANCER, KNOWING DEATH IS NOT FINAL

LESLEY LOWE

33 Greyhound Press

ALBUQUERQUE, NEW MEXICO

Published by:

33 Greyhound Press
8124 Curry Avenue NE
Albuquerque, NM 87109
www.33greyhoundpress.com

Editors: Ann Mason, Ellen Kleiner
Book design and production: Angela Werneke
Front cover design and illustration by Dave Arcade

First Edition

The contents of this book are for educational purposes only and not intended as a replacement for diagnosis or treatment of any medical or psychiatric ailment. Individuals with such an ailment should first see their physician or psychiatrist for treatment and make use of alternative therapies only as an adjunct to such treatment.

Printed in the United States of America

PUBLISHER'S CATALOGING-IN-PUBLICATION DATA

Names: Lowe, Lesley, 1951– author.

Title: Autumn gold : a rendezvous with cancer, knowing death is not final / Lesley Lowe.

Description: First edition. | Albuquerque, New Mexico : 33 Greyhound Press, [2022]

Identifiers: ISBN: 979-8-9850508-0-6 (paperback) | 979-8-9850508-1-3 (ebook) |
    LCCN: 2020911771

Subjects: LCSH: Cancer—Patients—Fiction. | Man-woman relationships—Fiction. |
    Multiple myeloma—Patients—Fiction. | Cancer—Patients—Psychological
    aspects—Fiction. | Cancer—Treatment—Fiction. | Bone marrow—
    Transplantation—Fiction. | Cancer—Patients—Family relationships—Fiction. |
    Women lawyers—United States—Fiction. | Women lawyers—United States—
    Family relationships—Fiction. | LCGFT: Autobiographical fiction. | Romance
    fiction.

Classification: LCC: PS3612.O8835 A98 2022 | DDC: 813/.6—dc23

1 3 5 7 9 10 8 6 4 2

Acknowledgments

My utmost thanks go to my husband, Rusty Lowe, at 33 Greyhound Press. For over thirty-seven years you have been the better half of our partnership, giving me endless love, support, and encouragement.

Many thanks to my wonderful editors, Ann Mason and Ellen Kleiner, who cast a professional eye on the manuscript and improved the clarity of the story.

A special thank you to Dave Arcade, aka David Bunnell, who created the cover art, which both honors the protagonist Vashti and portrays the special relationship he had with her. Thank you to Angela Werneke for the interior design.

Heartfelt gratitude to Vashti's comrades and friends who journeyed through life with her and willingly shared stories that now appear in this book. There are too many to name. You know who you are.

Exceptional gratitude to Jeff, who loved Vashti beyond measure. I will hold you forever close to my heart.

A deep bow to my dear friends Beverly Miller and Cheryl Moats for believing in me and supporting this work when it was just an idea floating around in my head.

Finally, eternal appreciation to my wonderful greyhounds, Lola and Bimba, whose eyes show the depth of feeling and wonder that Vashti exuded every day.

Prologue

WALKING INTO THE PSYCHIATRIST'S OFFICE, Vashti selected a chair by the window, where she sat silently in anguish peering out the glass to a freer place than the emotional confines created by struggling with her diagnosis.

Dr. Miller finally broke the silence, asking, "Vashti, would you like to start the conversation?"

Vashti stared at her face for a long time before responding, "No."

Dr. Miller gently continued, "Then why don't we sit in silence for a few minutes while you see if you can confide in me about your feelings or suggest ways I might be able to help you."

Again gazing out the window for a momentary escape from her agony, Vashti noticed the beautiful color of the autumn leaves. She thought it odd and paradoxical, yet exquisite, that in the natural process of their imminent death they displayed such bold, vibrant hues, especially the vivid gold that reminded her of royalty, victory, value. After several minutes, realizing she had nothing to say to Dr. Miller, she made her way slowly across the office, opened the door, then, in disbelief that it had come to this, whispered before disappearing, "My soul is shattered."

CHAPTER 1

A few years earlier Vashti, an energetic, upbeat, twenty-six-year-old assistant district attorney in a busy DA's office in Albuquerque, New Mexico, was arguing cases every day in court with expertise admired by judges. However, as she was more than occasionally tardy, she was admonished by them as well.

One day at the office, as she scrambled to stuff papers into her briefcase, she realized that even if she ran she would probably be late for court again. Opening the door, she saw her secretary, Cathy, looking perturbed, holding files she needed in court that morning. She dropped her briefcase, hugged Cathy, and said, "What would I do without you? I love you even if I drive you crazy because I'm always late. You know they give us too many cases to handle sanely. Sometimes I want to tell the district attorney how overworked the assistant DAs are, but I'd just be told to buck up." Vashti then grabbed the files and ran down the hall toward the front door, muttering under her breath, "Another day in paradise just living the dream."

Cathy smiled slightly as she watched Vashti disappear through the doorway. Cathy had worked at the district attorney's office for several years, but Vashti was new to its Community Crimes Division. She had worked her way up from being a prosecutor in Metropolitan Court in downtown Albuquerque, handling misdemeanors, to a prosecutor in District Court, focusing on felonies. Cathy remembered the day the supervisor of the Community Crimes Division, David Chambers, had announced that they would be getting a new attorney from Metro Court. The Metro Court evaluation of Vashti had been glowing, saying she was intelligent, quick on her feet, a team player, and had a positive attitude that led to success in her work. Later they found out that even defense attorneys had good things to say about her because they felt she was always fair to their clients. When

David had asked for volunteers to be Vashti's secretary, Cathy had raised her hand. Cathy's life had been a whirlwind ever since.

When she had first met Vashti, she was surprised at how short she was, given her reputation for effectiveness as a prosecutor in court. But Cathy had soon discovered that Vashti camouflaged her short stature by wearing the highest heels. She had big hair made up of beautiful curls in several shades of brown, which accentuated her flashing brown eyes and radiant, youthful face. Cathy thought she looked sixteen instead of twenty-six.

Vashti had injected new, uplifting energy into the Community Crimes Division. Now laughter could be heard every day in the hallways, and more pranks than ever before were pulled on people working there. Cathy re-called how Vashti had once given a young attorney in the office, who had continually boasted about his legal victories and sexual prowess, an attitude adjustment. That day he had left for court to try a big case, telling everyone that he expected a victory celebration when he returned. Before his return, Vashti had strategically placed a stink bomb purchased at a gag gift store just inside his door so that he would have an odiferous surprise when he entered. A few minutes later she had overheard him ask a group of young attorneys to come into his office so he could tell them his most exciting victory story to date. Then she had heard groans of disgust and fleeing footsteps. Of course, Vashti had realized that when he discovered the iden-tity of the prankster she would get payback, but she had confided in Cathy that it would be worth it. Part of the fun of working in the DA's office was interacting with young attorneys who enjoyed good times together along with acquiring ample court experience.

As Vashti entered Judge Sanchez's courtroom, she glanced at her watch and saw that she was five minutes late again. "Your Honor, you know that I drive a very old vehicle," she remarked in an effort to excuse her tardiness.

Judge Sanchez slowly looked up from the bench and replied, "Don't bother telling me, Ms. Warner."

Vashti quickly took her place at the podium and declared, "I'm ready to start arraignments, and I promise you we will get out of here on time."

Judge Sanchez gave Vashti a stern look, but after several seconds she noticed a slight smile on his lips before he stated, "The prosecutor may proceed."

Vashti flashed him her usual smile. Judge Sanchez was her favorite judge in District Court. Despite his reprimands for her tardiness, he was fair and reasonable, and appreciated her professional style and expertise.

The arraignments went smoothly, and Vashti finished on time, as promised. After court, Vashti returned to her office and, as she did every day, called her mother, June, who was also a lawyer. "Mom, what are you doing?"

"What does any attorney do in the Civil Division of the attorney general's office? I'm giving an agency advice that they don't want to hear, about things they want to do but legally can't. Vashti, remember you promised you would come for dinner tonight? We will eat around six o'clock, and we're having your favorite pork chops."

"I'll be there," Vashti responded. "There is a case I want to talk to you and Dad about, and I always look forward to your awesome pork chops. I may be a few minutes late, though," Vashti added, "because I'm planning a bridal shower and have to stop at a couple places after work to make some arrangements."

"This must be the hundredth shower you've planned for friends over the years," June commented. "Many wedding showers and baby showers, but none of them for you."

Vashti laughed and replied, "Mom, don't go there. It will only depress you. See you tonight."

After hanging up the phone, Vashti thought about her close relationship with her parents, wondering if it was because she was an only child and they were both talented lawyers in their own areas of law. Since they made a good living, life had gone well for her growing up. They had spoiled her in some ways, but not overly so. She remembered asking them to buy her a BMW when she was in high school because other kids had them, and seeing her mom give her an incredulous look and say, "Why would we ever do such a thing? Even if we can afford it, buying those kinds of gifts for kids is crazy. Where would it end? Next you would probably ask for your own house. And why would you ever get a job after finishing your education when you have nothing to work for?"

Instead, her parents had helped her buy a used Land Rover a few years ago, but she had paid for all repairs. Now she was proud to have gotten it running perfectly and knew she would never have had any such feelings of accomplishment if her parents had bought her a new BMW and handed her the keys. As she thought more about it now, she didn't even like BMWs or care for a lot of the people who drove them. She knew that if her parents had bought her things like expensive cars she would not be the person she was today, a public servant practicing law in a district attorney's office for a meager salary.

After she had graduated from college with a degree in English, her parents had encouraged her to pursue a graduate degree in English so she could teach it at the university level and write poetry, believing she was a talented poet and such a path would align with her aspirations. Ultimately, however, she had decided to go to law school no matter how her parents felt. Sometimes she wondered what it would be like to have time to write poetry; summers free to travel the world, even though she had seen much of it already on family trips; and be able to do volunteer work for causes about which she felt passionate.

She recalled how her parents, rather than initially supporting that decision, had insisted she fill out the law school application on her own, which had made her think deeply about her self-image as a biracial woman and question society's perception of ethnicity.

"What do I put down for race?" Vashti had asked her parents while completing the application.

"How does the question read?" her father had responded over the history book he was reading.

"Circle the one that most closely identifies your race—white, black, Indian, Asian," Vashti had replied, handing her mom the page.

After reading it, June had said, "This won't be easy given your family background. You are white *and* black *and* Indian *and* Asian, but predominately white and black. I'm white; my grandmother was a Canadian First Nation Indian; your biological father was half black; and his mother was part Chinese. None of these choices really fits you. There should be some way to indicate your mixed-race identity, reflective, as it is, of an unusual and interesting heritage."

Vashti had thought about it for a couple minutes then marked all four choices, determined to give the most honest answer and, at the same time, make officials aware that they had not provided an option for people who, like her, were of mixed race and proud of their diverse ancestry. In fact, Vashti was not only proud of her multiracial background but certain that it had helped her feel empathy for the people of many backgrounds that she encountered.

Today Vashti felt confident that pursuing a legal career was the best decision she could have made. She loved practicing law and the fact that being in this line of work had a positive impact on society, often helping the disadvantaged of various races, a realization that made even the ugliest cases bearable.

As these thoughts faded, Vashti returned to preparing for a trial to begin the next morning. When she had first started working at the DA's office, trials had made her nervous. No matter how long she prepared, she worried about questions coming up that she would not be able to answer. But with a few trials behind her she realized that good preparation was more than enough to competently litigate, and she began enjoying it.

There was a loud knock on the door. "Brittney!" Vashti exclaimed as she opened it and gave her friend a big hug. "What are you doing in town, girl?"

Brittney's eyes flashed deviously as she replied, "I needed a break from work, hubby, and all of Las Vegas, so I came home to play."

Brittney, having grown up in Albuquerque, had been good friends with Vashti for years. Vashti had encouraged her to try anything once and never give up playing, because in Vashti's view play was as important as work. As a result, some of Brittney's best times were with Vashti. Both gifted athletes, they had participated together in many sports, including a women's rugby team called The Atomic Sisters. The minor injuries they had sustained during games had been insignificant compared with the passion and mayhem of the sport they both loved. After the rugby games, they had enjoyed the wildest parties imaginable when the men's and women's rugby teams got together. Now that she was a few years older Brittney knew she could no longer dance and drink until dawn, stumble home, then get ready for a day of work. Still, she lived in accordance with Vashti's insistence on play.

After graduating from college, Brittney had moved to Las Vegas, found work as a photographer, and married a handsome man. Although she missed her hometown and Vashti, she didn't often get the chance to come back as being grown up took more time than she'd ever imagined. It was no wonder adults got grumpier as they aged since they often stopped playing, she thought.

"Want to take our boards and skate downtown for old times' sake? Then we could hit a few clubs," Brittney asked enticingly, with a gleam in her eyes.

"That sounds positively liberating, but tonight I have dinner plans with my parents and then I must prepare a case for court tomorrow. How about tomorrow night? It'll be Saturday, so the clubs should be fun. You're staying until Sunday, right?"

"I have to catch a plane early Sunday morning so I can have brunch with hubby and his parents. Then I have to get ready for a shoot on Monday."

"Sit down for a minute so we can catch up. Anything new and exciting going on in your life?" Vashti asked.

"We are thinking about starting a family," Brittney said with a mixture of joy and fear in her voice. "I want to have kids, but I had planned to wait until I was thirty. Since my husband is older than me, he is ready to start a family. I guess I am, too. But it is a huge decision, leading to so much responsibility."

"The hugest," Vashti replied. "This calls for a celebration! I'll take you out for an exquisite dinner tomorrow night, followed by skating, dancing, and drinking."

"Deal," Brittney responded, smiling and endorsing Vashti's plan. Her friend never failed to make her feel good while facing difficult decisions. And they always had a wonderful time together when they went out.

Brittney then asked, "What about you? Any interesting new men in your life? Please tell me there are and that you have forgotten about Jeff."

"Many guys ask me out, and sometimes I go. I have fun, but it never gets serious. I think I have been single and independent too long. I like my life the way it is," Vashti asserted.

"I don't believe a word of it," Brittney responded as she got up and opened the door. "You haven't forgotten Jeff. He is married now. Moved on with his life. You have to get over him and find another man you can seriously love."

Vashti pushed Brittney out the door, saying, "I'll call you tomorrow and set up our play date. Love you."

Vashti's thoughts turned to Jeff, aware that Brittney's words had touched a nerve. She had met Jeff in college. He had been stationed at Kirkland Air Force Base in Albuquerque, and they had fallen in love almost instantly. They were the same age. In fact, their births had occurred just a few hours apart. Several years earlier her mom asked an astrologer to do their charts, and the results reflected contrasting extremes, indicating that they would either share a beautiful, once-in-a-lifetime love or clash like titans to the end.

Jeff was very much like Vashti. They were both athletic and active. Her passion was running, and his was lifting weights. One of the first things she'd observed when they met—after noticing his handsome face, radiant smile, and expressive eyes—was how well-proportioned and muscular his body was. She had a small body but strong as well, capable of great endurance from her years of running competitively. As a couple, they'd had great times. They liked all kinds of sports and games, traveling, camping, dining at marvelous restaurants, and partying with friends, yet were also happy staying home and cuddling as they watched movies. Though Vashti had always had lots of friends with whom she was comfortable talking about many things, with Jeff it was different. They talked for hours, and she was able to tell him everything about her life, including her dreams, goals, and aspirations, as well her faults, mistakes, and failures. Talking about sex had never been easier. Making love had never been better. She had to confess that she still remembered every little detail about him—how he smelled, laughed, kissed, and made love.

Looking at her watch, Vashti realized she had to stop thinking about Jeff and run a few errands before dinner with her parents. She might be a little late, but her parents would understand since she was always late. In fact, arriving on time might throw them into shock since they were getting up there in age, she thought, amused at how she rationalized her tardiness.

After locking her office door, she noticed her boss, David Chambers, whom she affectionately called D-Chappy, standing in his doorway, just beside hers. She knew that most people would detest having an office next to their boss's, but she really liked him. She was grateful that he had helped her navigate the waters when she first started working at the DA's office, and because of their mutual love of Jameson whiskey, she enjoyed having an occasional drink with him to decompress after work.

"Want to have a shot before you head out?" he asked.

"Would love to, but this evening I'm off to plan a shower for a friend and then have dinner with my parents," Vashti explained.

As he watched her disappear down the hallway at the speed of light, he shook his head, thinking that her upbeat energy, playfulness, and willingness to help others made her irresistible.

CHAPTER 2

"OKAY, I WANT TO TALK TO YOU GUYS about this case that bothers me," Vashti announced after raving about June's pork chops at dinner. In this household, the conversation was almost always about law. The debates Vashti and her parents often engaged in were monumental, convincing Vashti that her upbringing had honed her litigation skills.

"Nothing too gruesome at the dinner table, I hope," her dad, Conor, said softly. Conor's mother had forced him to read books on manners when he was growing up, stating that certain topics were off limits when people were eating, like gory medical issues, religion, and politics.

Vashti responded, "Not gruesome, but troubling. There was a group of five young men downtown one night just hanging out. They came up with the idea of looking for a homeless man to hassle, and in this town they're easy to find. Their victim was a middle-aged man sleeping in an alley. When they started trying to wake him up, he got angry, and a fight ensued. They ended up beating him to death, and now they're being charged with murder. Each was over twenty-one and looked like a hardened criminal except one, who was a few months shy of the age of majority."

Her father commented, "No problem for a prosecutor. He should be tried as an adult."

"Normally I would agree, but this kid has no criminal record and a beautiful, cherubic face that makes him look like a teenager. God only knows what he was doing with those punks that night," Vashti stated.

"But he took part in beating a helpless man to death," Conor reminded her.

"Yes," Vashti said as she stared out the window lost in thought. "It was horrible, Dad, but what lies ahead for this angelic-looking young man is horrible, too, if he is sentenced to an adult men's prison. He might have a chance to get his life on track after this terrible experience, but it won't happen in an adult prison."

"Still," June interjected, "they killed a vulnerable, innocent man. I don't know what happens in prisons, and I'm sure it isn't good, but the young man helped commit a murder."

"Mom, prison isn't good at all, especially for this kid."

"What options are there for someone so close to the age of majority who has participated in such a heinous crime?" June inquired.

"I don't know, but I can't stop thinking about this kid," Vashti replied in a troubled voice as she walked to the back door to leave. She had always had, as June well knew, a natural empathy for people who were struggling in life. While opening the door, she muttered under her breath, "Knowing what I know, if I were his sister I would tell him to end it all if he gets sentenced as an adult since death would be merciful compared to what he would face in there."

"I heard that, Vashti," June said quickly, ready to challenge her about such an extreme view, even if it did show that Vashti's heart was in the right place. But Vashti had already disappeared.

The next evening Brittney and Vashti enjoyed a delicious dinner downtown at one of their favorite restaurants and then skated leisurely among the people shopping in the little eclectic shops by the university.

"I haven't been on a skateboard in more than a year," Brittney shouted over her shoulder. "It feels wonderful!"

"Remember how we used to go to the parking garage in the tallest building in town and skate down the ramp going a hundred miles an hour?" Vashti asked.

"Yes, and I remember that you were the only girl I knew who could make it to the bottom," Brittney said in a disgusted voice.

"I can still make it to the bottom, and sometimes on nights when I can't sleep I take my board and sail down the ramp in the wee hours of the morning. It clears my head, and I go home and sleep like a baby," Vashti confessed. "Hey, you want to check it out?"

"Sure, let's see if you can still get to the bottom, old lady," Brittney challenged, laughing.

They went to the parking garage a couple blocks away and took the elevator to the top.

"Who's going first?" Vashti asked, teasing Brittney.

"I'm going first because I'm the guest here," said Brittney as she sped off.

Vashti listened to the sound of Brittney's board gaining speed, hoping she would make it to the bottom. Then Vashti jumped on her board and started down. She always made it to the bottom, so while it was no longer challenging it was still fun. She passed Brittney about three quarters of the way down the ramp and gave her the high sign.

Watching her fly by, Brittney shouted, "You go, girl!" Then Brittney heard a terrible scream. Concerned, she ran toward the sickening sound. When she rounded the corner, there was a man standing over Vashti as she lay crumpled on the ground crying in pain.

The man explained, "I was working late. I opened the door to the parking garage, and there she was coming right toward me like a bat out of hell. She swerved sharply to avoid hitting me and crashed."

Brittney bent down and asked her friend, "Are you okay?"

Vashti attempted a smile and clumsily pulled the right leg of her jeans up to reveal a knee already the size of a grapefruit. "Take me to the ER," Vashti requested, weakly.

The frazzled man immediately said, "I'm so sorry. Can I help in any way?"

Vashti quickly replied, "It wasn't your fault. Don't worry, I'll be fine."

Brittney implored him to stay with Vashti until she got her car. In minutes she returned with the car and, with the man's help, lifted Vashti into the back seat.

As Brittney drove toward the hospital, to give Vashti some comic relief she teasingly said, "At least you weren't skating topless."

"Shut up," Vashti replied. "It hurts even more when I laugh." She knew Brittney was referring to the hot summer night when the two of them had been out dancing then had come up with the idea to skate the neighborhood at 3:00 a.m. topless to cool down, a crazy but fun experience, Vashti thought.

When Brittney sped into the hospital's driveway, the ER staff rushed outside with a cart and wheeled Vashti to X-ray after the doctor quickly looked at her knee. Then they took her to get an MRI and returned her to the ER, where the doctor delivered the bad news, saying, "Unfortunately, you have completely torn the ACL in your knee. Surgery will be required; a cadaver ligament will need to be attached to repair the injury. I have arranged for you to see an orthopedic surgeon tomorrow at three o'clock, but in the meantime I'll place your right leg in an air splint and send you home with some pain medication." Vashti, while concerned about how this might interfere with her heavy work schedule, was glad she had not injured anyone else in the accident. And she couldn't honestly be sorry that she had skated with such passion and speed.

When they reached Vashti's apartment, Brittney asked if Vashti wanted her to spend the night or call Vashti's parents.

Vashti replied, "I'll be fine, and I'll call Mom in the morning."

The next morning sunshine poured through the window onto Vashti's splinted leg, instantly reminding her of the accident the night before. She groaned in pain as she phoned her parents.

When June answered, Vashti mustered the cheeriest voice possible and said, "Mom, I need a favor. Can you take me to a doctor's appointment at three o'clock?"

"Sure, what's wrong?" June inquired.

"Don't be mad, but I fell off my board and hurt my knee."

"You fell off your skateboard?" June asked, in an exasperated tone. Then, flooded with compassion, she added, "No problem, honey. Listen for the horn when I pull up out front."

Vashti hesitantly replied, "Ah, I think you'll need to arrive early and come inside and get me."

With apprehension, June agreed, realizing that this could only mean her daughter needed help moving around. She looked upward and muttered, "Please, Lord, tell me she still has a leg."

Her daughter did little skateboarding these days and hadn't fallen since first learning the sport, so June was worried about what had caused her to fall. But Conor took June's hand and said, "Don't get mad at her or be too worried. To her, skateboarding is like surfing in the desert. She taught herself to skateboard, excelled at it, and still loves doing it. And you know that when Vashti loves something she never gives it up."

June shook her head and muttered, "Like never letting go of Jeff."

Conor hugged June and replied, "We all loved Jeff. He became family—the perfect son we never had. We haven't forgotten him. Imagine what it is like for her."

"But it's been years since they were together," June responded. "It is time for her to go on with life and find someone else, and maybe even time she stopped skateboarding."

After calling her mom, Vashti faced the grim task of phoning her boss. She had no idea how long she would be absent from her job, requiring the other overworked attorneys in her division to take over her cases. However, she reminded herself that she'd had an accident—something people have all the time—though mention of a skateboarding accident at her age might raise some eyebrows, she conceded.

Still, she pondered what to tell David. The truth? No, it would be better to just explain she'd had a fall. When David answered the phone, Vashti said, "D-Chappy, it's Vashti."

"What's up?"

"I'm calling because I need sick leave."

"Oh, too much vino with Brittney?" he asked, accusingly.

"I wish," Vashti replied, then paused. "I fell and hurt my knee."

"You fell? Where?"

"In a parking garage downtown."

"Okay. Will we see you tomorrow?"

"No. I need surgery on my knee."

"Stop and back up. I want the whole truth," D-Chappy insisted.

Vashti didn't know what to say. She figured that if she told the truth the DA would be livid hearing a request for extended sick leave for a skateboarding accident. But she wanted to tell her good friend David the truth, so she took a chance and said, "I was skateboarding and fell. We were in the Telstar Building parking garage, and it was late. I was flying down the ramp when a man suddenly came out a side door. I had one second to decide between running over him, possibly breaking his leg, or bailing. I bailed."

There was a pause as David tried to absorb the image of Vashti skateboarding down the parking garage ramp of one of the tallest city buildings. He had not been aware that it was a sport she loved and didn't know any other women her age who skateboarded. Then, realizing that such spontaneity and craziness was what he loved about Vashti, he replied, "Don't worry about it. Just concentrate on getting well and getting back. I will tell the DA that you fell and will need surgery to fix the injury to your knee; what you were doing when you fell is your business. Keep me posted."

"Thanks for understanding. Mom's taking me to see the surgeon today, and I'll call you when I know more," Vashti promised and hung up. She thought about how lucky she was to have a great boss. They had gotten along from the minute they'd met. She found him very attractive. In addition to sometimes sharing Jameson whiskey after work, they had gone to dinner a couple times, though just as friends.

After David hung up, he thought more about why, amidst the division's busy workload, he wasn't furious about losing a staff attorney because of a skateboarding accident. But after reflection, he knew that it was precisely because Vashti was wild, wacky, wonderful, and made no bones about it that he liked her so much. She was a tough woman, and he thought she would be able to recover sooner than most other people.

When Vashti and June got to the doctor's office later that afternoon, Vashti was in agonizing pain, though she tried to keep a brave face. No one in her family ever cried unless they were experiencing the worst pain imaginable. However, this was the worst pain she had experienced. God help her if she ever had to endure more than this, she thought.

Finally, Dr. Moss examined her and explained, "Vashti, you have a severe injury, but I think we can repair it surgically. You will have some down time, though."

"How much down time? My boss needs to know," Vashti quickly asked.

"A few weeks at least. Then you'll be on crutches," he replied.

She said, "I can handle that. I ran track in high school for four years, and I have been on crutches more than once."

"What did you run?" he asked.

"The hundred-meter dash and the hundred-meter relay at La Cueva High School," Vashti answered. "We had a great girls' track team."

"Her best time is still posted above La Cueva auditorium's main entry," June boasted as she grabbed her daughter's hand. "She loved the sport, and we were so proud of her." Vashti appreciated the fact that her mom was always her most enthusiastic cheerleader.

The doctor looked at Vashti and asked, "Do you still run?"

"Every day," Vashti replied. "I tried to run to work, but I got too sweaty for court."

"Well, you won't be able to run after your surgery until I clear you to do so," the doctor said sternly. "And, speaking of restrictions, you are approaching age thirty, so it shouldn't be too much of a disappointment that you'll have to give up skateboarding."

Vashti replied passionately, "Wait. When I am completely recovered, why wouldn't I be able to use my board?"

Dr. Moss looked confused, wondering why this was so hard for his patient to understand. "Well, as I said, you're almost thirty. You are an attorney, and it would seem to me that you would not want to take unnecessary risks. If you tear this ligament a second time, I don't know that we can repair it."

Vashti looked him straight in the eye and bluntly stated, "You don't know anything about me except for a few facts in my chart. Why would you assume that because I'm almost thirty years old I would want to quit boarding when I'm fully recovered?"

Without waiting for Dr. Moss to respond, June wrapped her arm around her daughter and said to him, "We will see you in a few days for the surgery. Thank you."

On the way to her parents' house, where Vashti knew she would have to stay until recovered enough to return to her apartment, she heard her mom say, "I'm so proud of you for speaking up. You're right. People tend to make assumptions based on their own sometimes narrow perspectives, and often they're wrong. It didn't make sense to me that just because you grow older in years you automatically have to give up the fun, playful things you used to do, as long as you can still do them and enjoy them. The doctor's attitude seems to be a recipe for growing old fast."

Vashti replied as she stared out the window, "Thanks, Mom."

June nodded in agreement, then, knowing that Vashti must be disappointed about having to slow down for quite a while, she squeezed Vashti's hand and said reassuringly, "Hey, we'll get through this."

Vashti smiled and replied, "That's what you always said when I was growing up and faced disappointments and setbacks. I always believed you, and you were right. Speaking of track records, we have a pretty good one."

Before they knew it, the day of Vashti's surgery arrived. They checked into the hospital, where Vashti was prepped for the procedure.

"Are you feeling lucky?" June asked her.

"It depends on what you have in mind," Vashti replied.

"Not an escape. We wouldn't get very far with your bad leg," her mom said, teasingly. She then pulled out a deck of cards and asked, "How about letting me beat you at a little gin rummy?"

Vashti won all but one game, all the while appreciating the distraction from her pain.

When the nurses wheeled Vashti down the hallway toward the operating room, she shouted loudly, "I love you, Mom!"

June shouted back, "I love you too, and I'll see you soon."

After about three hours, June spotted Vashti being wheeled out of the recovery room to a patient room. Without opening her eyes, Vashti gave her a thumbs up, and June's heartbeat returned to normal.

"She's been talking to a Jeff ever since she started coming out of the anesthesia," the nurse told June. "She was acting as if he was with her, taking away her fear and making her confident that everything would be all right." June was glad Vashti's memory of Jeff had helped support her but was also concerned about Vashti's apparent reliance on a former boyfriend who was no longer in her life.

Vashti was resting when the doctor arrived and reported, "Miss Warner, the surgery went well. I expect you to have a complete recovery. You will have some pain the next few days, but it should decrease each day. The harder you work in your rehabilitation program, the faster you'll recover. I'll recheck your knee in one week and then two weeks after that."

Vashti flashed him a weak but heartfelt smile. Her knee felt like it was on fire. The pain was excruciating. Years before, while playing rugby, she had watched a male athlete from Australia suffer many painful injuries in silence, but with the most severe injuries he'd shouted out at the top of his lungs, "Rat fuck!" Remembering the expression, she said it over and over in her mind, which made Vashti feel better.

CHAPTER 3

When Vashti was given her doctor's blessing to return to work, she knew the DA's office would be as busy as usual, but she was so glad to be going back she didn't care how much work was waiting for her. Still, as she entered her office on crutches she groaned at the sight of her desk buried in files. Her spirits lifted as co-workers shouted greetings and Lettie, Rose, and Ann, her three best female friends at work, came by to welcome her back. She told them what her surgery had been like and how hard she had pushed herself in rehabilitation, but purposely omitted her crying out in pain when the physical therapist had pushed her too far. They started calling her Cadaver Woman because of the cadaver ligament used in her surgery, and they promised her a freedom bash the day she could throw her crutches away.

She looked for David, hoping he'd ask her to have a shot with him after work, but couldn't find him. She wanted to thank him in person for covering for her and to enjoy some downtime with him as she had missed their conversations. She thought he most likely loved her, but she didn't behave in any way that reflected feelings for him. She found him attractive and thought having a relationship with him would be easy because they were great friends already, yet a little voice in her head told her that her life wasn't going in that direction. When she was completely honest with herself, she had to confess that her feelings for Jeff, the one who got away, could be holding her back. But by now he'd been married for years, probably had children, and surely wasn't thinking about her, she figured.

For hours she worked through the mountain of files on her desk. When she finally looked at the clock, it was 4:45 p.m. Just then her phone rang, and Megan, a secretary with whom she had worked in Metro Court, said urgently, "Vashti, I really need your help. I was picked up for a DUI, and I'm in jail. I gotta get bailed out. My kids are alone at home."

"Oh, that is terrible," Vashti replied.

"Can you bail me out?" Megan pleaded.

"Don't worry," Vashti said. "I'm on crutches, but I'll be right there. I've got to get you released before five o'clock or I won't be able to until tomorrow morning." She grabbed her crutches, bolted out the door, and practically ran into Adam, an older attorney in the division who several years earlier had worked with her mother at the attorney general's office.

"Where are you going so fast?" Adam asked.

"Adam, I don't have time to talk now. I have to get to the jail before five o'clock. One of the secretaries from Metro was arrested for a DUI and called to see if I would bail her out."

"Stop right there, Vashti," Adam responded in a stern voice. "You can't bail out a DUI. The DA has been in several ads lately taking a firm position against drunk driving. You'll probably lose your job if you do this."

"Dammit, out of my way!" she demanded. She contemplated assaulting him with a crutch but instead pleaded, "Adam, she is single with three young kids. They are poor, barely making it. If she stays in there overnight, the kids might have to spend the night alone."

"They surely have a relative or someone else to call, but whether they do or not I am not letting you go," Adam replied calmly but firmly.

"Fuck you!" Vashti shouted, lunging toward Adam with such force that she fell, screaming in pain as her leg hit the ground.

Adam slowly sat beside Vashti, feeling terrible that he'd made her fall, and stated emphatically, "I'm mad at you because you're not using your head! You are a prosecutor, dammit! We prosecute DUIs here not bail them out of jail!"

They sat in silence until Adam noticed it was after 5:00 p.m. and offered to help Vashti up. She refused, so he quietly walked away. When she, too, realized it was after 5:00 p.m., she began to groan, knowing she didn't have Megan's address and, with Metro Court now closed, would not be able to get it and go check on her kids.

Finally, a janitor helped her up and out to her car. While driving home, Vashti decided she had to clean up her language. While a swearing assistant DA was common, her mom had told her that people who swore had limited vocabularies; and Vashti herself felt she was showing weakness when she swore. But she didn't regret opposing Adam in her effort to help Megan. She vowed to contact Megan the next day for an update and to explain what had happened. She believed that from a humanitarian viewpoint it was almost always right to help people in distress, especially friends, even if you didn't condone their behavior.

A few days later Vashti looked at her calendar and realized it was almost Christmas and she hadn't made the usual holiday preparations. Normally, Vashti and her parents delivered holiday care packages before leaving on a trip a week or two before Christmas. The previous year they had purchased several cases of spring water and delivered them to homeless shelters, clinics providing medical care to the poor, and women's shelters for victims of domestic violence. This year they would not be traveling, so Vashti came up with an idea for a charitable activity they could do together on Christmas Eve and called her mom to ask her opinion.

"Mom, I have a plan for Christmas Eve. I know how much you love playing your portable electric piano. Since we enjoy singing carols, why don't we load it in Dad's truck, drive downtown to where the homeless people hang out, and treat them to Christmas carols while handing out our pooled money?"

"I love it," June replied. "I'll call Dad to see what he thinks, and tonight I'll start practicing carols for our special gig."

"Great! This will be fun!" Vashti replied enthusiastically.

Vashti sat on her couch remembering the years before, when her family had begun its tradition of giving holiday gifts to less fortunate people since they themselves had almost everything they wanted. They had made a list of their favorite charities and written checks to several of them before going to Mass.

Attending Christmas Mass was a family ritual, even though they each had different religious beliefs. Conor enjoyed the Anglican Church Mass because of the beautiful music, though he claimed no specific religion as his own. His father had been a Catholic and his mother a Lutheran, but by the time he was thirteen he had rejected both denominations, preferring instead to commune with nature in a beautiful grove of cottonwoods, peacefully sitting with his face tilted toward the sun and listening to the wind blowing through the leaves, as if it were whispering uplifting messages to him.

While growing up, June was forced to go to Mass every Sunday. While this routine had given her a solid moral foundation, there were many things about it she had not liked, such as getting up early and putting on her Sunday clothes. That had led her to rebel when she was in college, but she later resumed going to church. She now believed that people came to God, or the Great Spirit, in their own ways, including in a grove of cottonwoods. June was open-minded about religion and, having read many comparative religion texts, borrowed from various faiths concepts most meaningful to her, though she still enjoyed attending Mass, especially on holidays.

Vashti had an untraditional belief system and considered herself a spiritual person. Her most powerful spiritual experiences occurred in nature, especially when she was near the ocean or hiking in the mountains. Vashti and June agreed that spirituality was of greater importance than organized religion.

The next day at work, as Vashti unlocked her office door and hobbled on crutches to her desk, she heard Rose yell from the hall, "Vashti, come help us get this office decorated for the holidays!"

"I'm an invalid on crutches. How can I help string lights?" Vashti shouted back.

Rose entered her office and thrust a sack of paper snowmen in Vashti's arms, saying, "No one likes a party more than you, so start taping these snowmen on doors. We'll handle the ladder and the lights." They soon had the place looking very festive.

Afterward Vashti worked on case files until dark. Suddenly she noticed David standing in her doorway.

"I've got a great idea," he said. "We're the last two standing, so why don't we shut off all but the Christmas lights and sip some good scotch."

"I'm in," she readily agreed.

Sitting next to him on the comfortable couch in his office felt heavenly. Her neck and shoulders were hurting, so she started doing slow head circles to relieve the pain.

He slid closer to her and said, "Here, let me rub out the knots."

The massage felt so good that she remarked, "I'll give you two hours to stop that."

He moved closer and whispered in her ear, "God, I missed you."

She pulled his hand from her neck and said, "You're just feeling sorry for Cadaver Woman on crutches. Admit it!"

She tickled his ribs, and soon they were both tickling each other and laughing. Then he gently placed his hands on her face and kissed her lips softly. When she didn't pull away, he kissed her again. His hands moved slowly down to her breasts, and he started to caress them, but Vashti pulled away, softly saying, "Walk me to my car. I have so many things to do tonight that I'd better get on the road." They walked slowly through the parking lot to her car. Before they said good-bye, he kissed her one last time.

Driving away, she was angry with herself, wondering why she hadn't let things unfold naturally. His kisses were heavenly, and because they were good friends it would be easy sharing intimacy with him. But lately when men wanted to get close to her she turned things into a joke or made a quick getaway. She knew it was because of the little voice in her head advising her that her future wasn't going in that direction. She knew it also

could be partly because of her inability to forget about Jeff. But she sensed
something more was involved: that in the future she would encounter a
challenge requiring all her strength. Wondering if it would involve her parents, she concluded that if they faced a life-altering situation she would
want to focus completely on them.

After Vashti arrived at her parents' house, the family began practicing
carols for their Christmas gig downtown for the homeless. "Mom, let's not
start with 'Silent Night.' We don't want to put the audience to sleep,"
Vashti advised.

June looked at her questioningly and said, "Okay, Missy, what song
do we start with?"

"'Jingle Bells,' of course. 'Joy to the World' next, and 'Silent Night' for
the finale."

When June asked Conor for his opinion, he responded, "I don't sing,
remember. I'm merely the designated truck driver."

On Christmas Eve, they loaded the truck and drove downtown. They
didn't have to worry about rounding up other singers because June's piano,
at the touch of a button, had a choir that accompanied her as she played.
When they reached an alley where homeless people were gathered, June
started playing and singing along with Vashti.

It filled Vashti's heart with joy to see the faces of homeless people
brighten as they heard the music, and she wished them Merry Christmas
as she handed out bottles of water and cards containing twenty-dollar
bills. She wondered, as she had a thousand times before, how in such a
rich country there could be so many with so little and why people couldn't
share some of their bounty with the less fortunate.

During a pause between songs, she recalled how her mom had taught
her as a little girl to live from a perspective of abundance, saying that

generosity and love would then flow freely between her and the people who shared in her bounty. Next her mom had gathered her in her arms and explained that having two pieces of bubble gum in her pocket meant she had an abundance because she could chew only one piece at a time, so she had one piece to share with someone who didn't have any. She had always remembered that important advice.

When Vashti and June were too hoarse to sing any longer and the water and cards had all been handed out, the family returned home in festive spirits. Then Vashti announced, "Now, for our holiday treat!" Pulling a bottle from a bag she had left on the kitchen counter, she explained, "The last year Jeff and I attended the wine festival I tasted the most exquisite port and bought a bottle to share on Christmas Eve with him and both of you." Pausing for a moment as she realized what she had just said, she concluded, "Oh well, it's time that the three of us share it."

"Good choice," her dad stated as he filled glasses and handed them out. Vashti raised hers for a toast and said, "Happy Christmas. I love you both so much." Then they clicked their glasses, shouting, "Salute!"

As they sat around the Christmas tree talking about the people they had seen, they tried to think of a solution to the homelessness problem. Conor always ended such conversations, or those after sightings of homeless people, with the phrase "There but for the grace of God go I." Vashti knew he often went to lunch with other lawyers from the firm he worked for downtown, where they frequently encountered homeless people, and that saying this phrase made the other lawyers uncomfortable, which he rather enjoyed. But she was proud of him for acknowledging and having compassion for homeless people.

After sharing much good cheer, Vashti said, while hugging her mom and giving her dad a mock pained look, "*Mamacita*, I will be back early in the morning to start the jigsaw puzzle." June maintained an old family tradition of doing a Christmas puzzle, and while Vashti and her mom loved putting them together, Conor did not, though, being a good sport, he would put a couple of pieces in place.

Then Vashti hugged Conor and added, "What would I ever do without you guys?"

Conor looked her in the eyes and replied, "Why do you always get that backward? What would we ever do without you? You keep us young. You are a ball of positive energy, more powerful than the sun, with a heart filled with love."

She smiled and, just before disappearing into the night, said, "You're buttering me up because you know I'll be the one selecting the nursing home you end up in when you're old as sin and crazier than a loon."

As Vashti drove slowly through the quiet streets to her apartment, she thought about how happy they had been spreading holiday cheer among homeless people and how special her parents were, full of love for others and support for her. She remembered her mom telling her how she had married Vashti's biological father, William, a brilliant man who had received a scholarship for a PhD program at Harvard University but had struggled to get through it because of alcohol addiction. June had been thrilled when Vashti was born, naming her Vashti Aisha, which meant beautiful life. June loved Old Testament names and chose the name Vashti, the queen of Persia prior to Esther, because the biblical Vashti had shown an independent spirit, defying the orders of the king, her husband, to dance for men at a gathering and later had been cast out of the kingdom for her disobedience.

But when Vashti was less than a year old, June had left William in Boston because of his alcohol addiction as well as other issues. After their marriage had failed, June had never planned to marry again until Conor had swept her off her feet during her first year of law school. When he had asked June to marry him and she had accepted, he had asked Vashti, who was five at the time, if she would like to have him as her father. She had told him that she would like that, feeling more special than she ever had before. After June and Conor had married, the judge for whom her mom clerked at the time had conducted Vashti's formal adoption proceeding, after which he unzipped his black robe, came down from the dais, and asked Vashti if she was happy having Conor as her new father. She was and told him so. Only years later, however, did she realize just how happy it had made her to have Conor as a father.

Vashti recalled how her parents had not initially told her she had been adopted on grounds that her biological father had abandoned her. Later she had learned the truth while studying domestic relations in law school. One day when lunching with June Vashti had said, "Mom, you know I'm studying for a test in my domestic relations class. During class I thought about my adoption, and I realized that my biological father, William, was not in court during the proceeding. Was he properly served with the petition?"

June had replied without hesitation, "He was served but didn't respond. We didn't know for sure where he lived, so we sent the documents to his parents, who had lived at the same address in Chicago for over fifty years, so I'm sure he must have been aware of the proceeding." June took a sip of water before continuing. "He didn't really abandon you. I left him when you were less than a year old. He had serious issues, was struggling in the PhD program, and his alcohol addiction was getting worse."

Vashti also remembered asking her mom about William when she was young. June had praised him for his accomplishments and not focused on his faults, telling Vashti that William was a brilliant man but, lacking common sense and having fallen prey to alcohol addiction, would likely waste his talents if he did not get help.

June had further explained that when she left William, Vashti was only a few months old and had not been adopted by Conor until she was almost five. During the intervening years, it had been just June and Vashti making their way in the world. Having grown up in Fargo, North Dakota, June had taken Vashti back to her hometown after the divorce and practiced nursing in a local emergency room there. William had visited them in Fargo only once after the divorce, while traveling through the Midwest on vacation when Vashti was a year old. June had been so thankful to have gotten full custody of Vashti that she had never pressed William for child support, nor had he raised the issue. And while she and Vashti didn't have a lot of money they had a life filled with fun and adventure.

As time passed, June had explained, she realized that raising a child on her nurse's salary was not going to be easy. So she had enrolled in evening classes to pursue another degree in liberal arts in preparation for studying law. Early in her nursing career, June had been a witness in two court cases. One case involved the chain of custody of a blood sample she had drawn after a drunk driving incident, while the other entailed helping an intoxicated orthopedic surgeon set a young child's leg late one evening in the ER, which unfortunately led to the necessity of another surgeon re-breaking and resetting the leg a few months later. She had found both cases so interesting that several years later she decided to study law. Less than two years after starting the evening classes, she had received a degree in political science/public service, written the law school entrance exam, and been accepted into law school. To attend, she had to relocate with Vashti to Grand Forks, North Dakota.

June had told Vashti how they had loved their new apartment on the University of North Dakota campus and enjoyed decorating it before the start of school—kindergarten for Vashti and law school for June. She had described walking an excited Vashti to school on her first day of kinder-garten and insisted her daughter had nothing to worry about because she was a rock star. Vashti had laughed, hugged her mom and, sensing June's nervousness, said, "Don't worry about law school because it can't be that much harder than kindergarten." To this day, she reminded herself, they both still laughed uproariously about that special memory.

Vashti recalled a picture in her mom's photo album of William and his parents standing in front of their home in Chicago. His mother was part Chinese, with the most beautiful face; his father was a dark-skinned black man; and William was somewhere in between. Vashti had never seen much resemblance between William and herself, but she had inherited his big nose. Although she didn't know the man and didn't consider him her father, she was grateful to him for having contributed to her mixed-race heritage.

These thoughts receded when Vashti arrived at her apartment. She quickly undressed, realizing she had to get to bed soon so she could participate in the family ritual of claiming her stocking from the fireplace mantel and then putting together the communal Christmas puzzle. But before retiring she went out the back door in her robe to feed Bertie, her African tortoise, whom she loved dearly and had raised since he'd been the size of a quarter.

"Bertie, Mom's got your favorite dinner, yummy bok choy!" she called. Because of his reactions, she believed he not only recognized her voice but understood what she was saying, even though scientific books didn't attribute such abilities to tortoises.

Sure enough, Bertie ambled slowly out of his house to greet her. Her dad had helped her construct Bertie's house with good lumber, insulation, and heat lamps so Bertie wouldn't get too cold during the winter. Then she had painted crazy multicolored art all over it. He seemed to love his pad.

"Merry Christmas! You get extra bok choy to celebrate," Vashti said, looking into his eyes as she spread his food on the grass. "I can't believe how big you've gotten. You were the size of a quarter when I first got you, but now you weigh almost fifty pounds. Don't think for a minute that you'll ever get too big for me to pick you up, even if you reach two hundred pounds. You have one strong mama." Vashti always talked to Bertie, wanting to be in harmony with nature's creatures, which she believed were all connected. Vashti especially felt good entrusting Bertie with her secrets, where she knew they would be safe. When Bertie finished his dinner, she carried him back to his warm house. "I love you, Bertie," she said softly, pulling down his door flap. If that turtle could talk, she would be in serious trouble, Vashti thought.

One day following the beginning of the new year, Dr. Moss assured Vashti that her leg had healed well and she no longer needed to use crutches. That evening, thrilled to finally be rid of her crutches, Vashti shouted, "So long, suckers!" as she tossed them in the dumpster beside the restaurant where she and her friends had gathered to celebrate her liberation.

"Good riddance," Ann chimed in.

"Freedom, freedom," Rose and Lettie sang.

After enjoying several glasses of wine and delicious entrees, they ordered desserts and then another bottle of wine to drink while sharing stories about their work at the DA's office. They finally left sober because they had stayed at the restaurant so long. Vashti ran toward her car jumping and screaming with joy, "My cadaver leg works, and I'm free." Her friends laughed at her display of pure glee, realizing that in the new year Vashti could once again be her spirited self.

CHAPTER 4

AT HIS HOUSE IN SAN DIEGO, CALIFORNIA, Jeff stalked Vashti on Facebook before leaving for work, as he had been doing for several years, mostly by reading her friends' posts—since she herself rarely posted—to keep up with events in her life. While driving down the San Diego Freeway to his office at NCIS, he recalled how determined they had been to succeed when they were together. His dream after getting out of the air force had been to become a forensic investigator at NCIS in California; and he had thought her dream was to practice law in California. But things hadn't turned out that way.

One of his favorite memories of Vashti was celebrating with her when he received notice of his acceptance into NCIS. "Vashti," he had shouted excitedly from the mailbox in front of his house near the air base. When she had come running to the door, he had lifted her in the air and swung her in circles, exclaiming, "I got in and can start work in San Diego in a couple months."

She had given him a long, sensuous kiss, then pulled back and said softly, "I never doubted you would make it. I'm so happy for you, Cookie. I love you so much."

Thrilled as he always was when she called him Cookie—a nickname she had given him when their relationship had become serious—he had carried her to the bedroom effortlessly since she had seemed light as a feather in his ecstatic mood. Making love with her that day while sharing his success had been so passionate that he could still feel it deep in his soul.

But after they had made love, reality had set in, and Vashti had asked in a troubled voice, "What are we going to do? I still have three months left of law school here in New Mexico."

"Don't worry, I will go to San Diego, start the job, and find us a wonderful place to live," Jeff had responded.

"By the ocean, Cookie. This desert girl can't wait to live by the ocean," Vashti replied.

He had agreed and added, "You'll finish law school and then move to California to study and write the California bar exam. Then we'll live happily ever after."

"But I'll miss you!" she had replied.

"Don't worry," he said, drawing her close and looking into her beautiful brown eyes, "it won't be for long."

Those memories still haunted him. Despite being married now to Karen, he knew in his heart he still loved Vashti. He felt pain not being with her to express his love. He wondered how something so right could have ended so wrong.

He remembered vividly the events that had led to his breakup with her. Some conversations he recalled word for word.

"Jeff, you won't have any problem getting back for graduation?" Vashti had asked.

"Of course not," Jeff had replied emphatically. "I love my new job, and I don't have a lot of vacation time, but you know I'll be front and center no matter what."

"I thought that, because of our fights about my decision to stay home and write the New Mexico bar exam first, maybe you wouldn't want to come," Vashti said hesitantly.

"Listen, I don't know about you, but I was under the impression that the minute graduation was over I could steal you away to the ocean," Jeff had answered.

"It will be much easier for me to prepare for the biggest exam of my life at home with my parents, who you know are both lawyers. They have agreed to help me take the prep course," she had said, defensively.

"Whatever," he had responded, ending the conversation.

Jeff had become aware that both Vashti and their relationship seemed to be unraveling. Maybe he had been unreasonable because he'd wanted her with him so badly. Although recognizing that she had her own goals and dreams, he hadn't been able to understand why she couldn't, or wouldn't, study in California. Yet when being honest with himself, he knew that she wouldn't study as well if they were living together.

These memories of conflict were immediately swept away when he remembered their glorious reunion following Vashti's graduation ceremony. An old friend who was on assignment overseas had offered his house for their private graduation party. After making love to her for what seemed like hours, he had looked in her eyes and said, "Vashti, I can't live without you. I'm sorry I have been so crazy about all of this, but I can't stand being so far away from you."

"I feel the same way, Cookie," she had replied, kissing his lips.

"You will come to San Diego as soon as the bar exam is over, right?" he had asked.

"Nothing could keep me away from you and this!" she had replied in a sexy voice, after which they had made love again.

He remembered how happy he had been when he'd left a few days later feeling that he could wait a couple more months to have Vashti in his life forever. After his return to San Diego, they had talked at least once every day. Vashti had studied hard and taken several practice tests. At this point his patience had begun to wear thin. Unaware of the stress Vashti was experiencing facing the three-day bar examination, he had just wanted Vashti with him in California. He was young at the time, horny, and every day they were separated was agony.

Then came the last straw. A law school friend with whom Vashti had been studying had accepted a law clerk position with a prestigious firm in New Mexico and recommended Vashti to the firm to fill an additional clerkship. Knowing how hard it was to find clerkships, Vashti had requested an interview and been amazed when they offered her the position. She would only have to work a few hours each week until the bar exam was over. Then she could increase her hours for the next couple of months until learning whether she'd passed the bar and was finally a "real" lawyer. After that, she could pack her things and move to California to be with Jeff.

Jeff remembered Vashti's call when she had explained her good luck in getting the clerkship. She had told him how she needed something like this on her résumé. She had further explained that she'd gotten this opportunity because many people in her hometown had given her leads about legal positions and she wanted to have money in the bank to tide her over until she could get a permanent position in California since she didn't want to have to depend on Jeff. Upon hearing her thoughts about working in Albuquerque another few months, he had lost it. She had tried to assure him of her love and that it would only be a few more months, but Jeff, overcome with anger and hurt, had told her they were finished. She had pleaded with him to think it over, but he had hung up, shattered by the deepest agony he'd ever known.

After he and Vashti had broken up, Jeff had gone home to Boston for a long week, hoping to ease the pain. There he had run into an old friend, Karen, in a pub. They had grown up in the same neighborhood but hadn't seen each other in years. That night one thing had led to another, and they had ended up in bed at her place. Karen was beautiful, smart, and single. She had done well in the real estate business during the past few years. Their fathers had both been realtors and knew each other. Jeff and Karen also shared an interest in real estate and, as native Bostonians, had a natural understanding that facilitated their connection. There had been only one problem: Karen wasn't Vashti.

Jeff and Karen had soon started seeing each other every night, making his pain tolerable. He had tickets for a cruise that he'd originally purchased for himself and Vashti to celebrate her passing the bar exam, and one night, while partying with Karen, he had spontaneously asked her to join him on the cruise without taking much time to think rationally, and Karen had immediately accepted. Despite his misgivings, they'd had an exciting time on the cruise, and Karen's love and attention had felt good to him after his stinging breakup with Vashti, making it seem like his wounds were healing. When the cruise had ended, it was time to pack up for the journey to San Diego, at which point Karen had decided to go with him to start a new chapter in her life.

After living in California for only a few months, they had become engaged, then married shortly thereafter. Their marriage had been solid for a couple of years. They had pooled their money and bought properties they could fix up and rent for additional income. They had both worked full-time and focused on their properties in the evenings and on weekends. But as their business relationship had become successful their personal relationship had started to flounder. It was then that Jeff had begun searching for Vashti on Facebook. He had thought about contacting her and talked to Karen about getting a divorce, but had ended up simply staying in his comfort zone.

CHAPTER 5

JUNE'S OFFICE PHONE RANG, and she bent forward to answer it.

Vashti excitedly exclaimed, "Mom, I've decided to run my first marathon!"

"That's a strange declaration from my favorite sprinter."

Vashti explained, "I know, but I heard about the Rock 'n' Roll Marathon in Texas that sounds awesome. I'm getting older now, and I want to have at least one marathon to my name. I'm going to join a running club and train well, so you have nothing to worry about, *Mamacita*."

"I think it's a great idea if it's something you want to do. But I wonder if your heavy schedule will allow you to take the time for all the practice runs the club requires," June replied, feeling enthusiastic about Vashti's aspirations but concerned that she may be spreading herself too thin with her demanding work schedule.

"I hear you, and if it gets to be too much I'll drop out," Vashti assured her mom.

Vashti had six weeks to train, and she was determined to be well prepared. But about halfway through the training her right foot started to hurt. She had injured that foot in track years earlier, so, thinking she'd aggravated the old injury as the practice runs got longer, she started icing the foot after practice, which helped alleviate the pain.

As the marathon date drew closer, she gained endurance. She had two long practice runs left before her departure for Texas. After both runs, she was in agony, and ice no longer eliminated her foot pain, but she didn't tell her parents for fear they would dissuade her from participating in the marathon.

When her parents took her to the airport and saw her limping from the car toward the terminal, June jumped out, caught up with her, and said, worriedly, "You're limping."

"My foot aches a little, but it's only because we've had such long practice runs. I'll be fine. They have doctors at marathons, Mom," Vashti insisted. "Just wish me luck!"

"Good luck! I know you'll complete the race!" June said encouragingly, then walked back to the car with a knot in the pit of her stomach.

"Conor, why don't you ever help me reason with her?" June asked after getting in the car.

"Stand in front of that determination? I would be mowed down," Conor replied. June knew she would worry until the next afternoon, when Vashti would call to tell them how it went.

The next day the phone rang around noon, and June answered with trepidation.

"Mom, it's me, and nothing is wrong," Vashti said, struggling to catch her breath. "I'm running the race right now. My time is horrible, and I can't seem to get into my rhythm. Talk to me for a minute and I'll see if it helps."

"This is your first marathon, so don't focus so much on your time. Just focus on seeing that finish line," June advised.

"Thanks, Mom," Vashti replied and hung up.

A few hours later Vashti called home again and shouted, "I made it!"

"Oh, Sweetheart, I'm so happy for you," June gushed proudly then asked Vashti how her foot was feeling.

"I can't even feel it. My whole body is numb. I have ice on my foot, though," Vashti responded.

"We'll be at the airport in the morning to pick you up," June assured her. "It's best to keep it iced and elevated until then."

Vashti didn't have the heart to tell her mom that she planned to go out for a spaghetti dinner with her running friends, followed by dancing at a club if her foot allowed for it. What actually happened was that, due to the excruciating pain in her foot, halfway through the spaghetti dinner her friends had to take her to the emergency room, where the doctor informed her that her foot was broken, and had been for at least two weeks.

The next morning, when Vashti landed at the airport, she noticed the frightened faces of her parents as she hobbled toward them on crutches. Although they had always told her to take care of her body if she wanted it to go the long haul, that advice had never meant much to her because she felt part of living life was taking risks, and she never really believed she would live a long life. At that particular moment, though, Vashti's focus was not on the injury but on the satisfaction of having completed a marathon. While being a sprinter in track, she had been teased that sprinters couldn't run an honest mile without collapsing. Her response had been that she didn't give a damn about miles but cared only about running one hundred meters in under ten seconds. Even so, deep down she admired distance runners and, when track ended, had promised herself that she would run a marathon someday. Now she had fulfilled that promise.

As her parents greeted her, Vashti explained that she had seen a doctor who had told her that her right foot was broken. Her parents shook their heads in disbelief that she had completed a marathon with a broken foot, seeing it as a testament to Vashti's determination to succeed even when faced with great challenges. While they sometimes wished she would be more cautious, they had to admit that they admired her spirit.

The following Monday, when Vashti returned to the office, her friends were surprised to see her back on crutches. She assured them that it was nothing serious and she didn't have to take any sick leave.

When David walked up behind her, she turned and exclaimed, "I finished the marathon, D-Chappy!" and gave him one of her "monster squeeze" hugs.

He lifted her off the ground and said, "I knew you would do it! But why the crutches?"

"Oh, it's just a little thing. There is no immediate surgery or sick leave required," Vashti replied.

He followed her into her office, where she showed him her medal and her pictures taken at the finish line. Then she confessed, "I have a broken foot. I injured the same foot in track years ago, and the last two long practice runs did my foot in."

"Are you telling me you ran a marathon with a broken foot?" he asked, incredulous. Vashti nodded. He shook his head and walked back to his office thinking how crazy Vashti was and yet how her daring, off-beat way of living was what he loved most about her. He then recalled how he had tried for months to get past just being friends with Vashti. She had told him that she just wanted his friendship, but he knew he couldn't be happy just being her friend, especially while working in such close proximity to her every day.

Vashti rushed through work that day because she was leaving early to have her hair trimmed with her mom. One of her oldest friends, Deb, owned a hair salon, and they both loved having Deb do their hair.

When Vashti walked into the salon, Deb was coloring June's roots.

"Have I missed any remarkable stories?" Vashti asked, giving them each a hug.

"We were just trying to figure out what insanity makes you race through life, doing a million things a day, as though you would never have another chance to do them," June replied.

"*Mamacita*, you know I've always been this way. I thought you were supposed to go for the gusto in life, as if there were no tomorrow!"

"But then, tomorrow always comes. Right, Sweetheart?"

"So far," Vashti replied.

Deb and Vashti chatted while Deb cut Vashti's hair, which was long and curly but not an afro. June had straight hair, and Vashti's biological father had an afro. Together they had created Vashti's unique hair. Vashti had never met anyone with hair like hers, though she knew several biracial people.

She always had Deb just trim the ends of her hair because, having often been told it was one of her best features, she couldn't stand it short. Her insistence on preserving its length had begun when she was a little girl. June had taken her to a beauty shop when she was about seven years old to get her hair cut short. As Vashti had looked in the mirror and seen her short hair, she had been horrified and had the biggest tantrum of her life. It had taken months for her to forgive her mom after screaming many times that she would never, ever have short hair again.

When Deb had finished cutting Vashti's hair, June looked at the floor and asked, "This was a haircut?"

"That is a Vashti Special," Deb replied, smiling as she pointed to the tiny amount of hair on the floor.

As Vashti looked at it, she exclaimed, "Good lord, I feel bald!" Then she gathered up her things and rushed out the door to shop at a nearby bookstore while her mom finished having her hair colored.

Deb and June shook their heads, laughing. Then, reflecting on Vashti's childhood, June asked Deb, "Your mother's Japanese, right?"

"Yes. She married my father after he got out of the service."

"You must look like your father, then, because physically there is no way to tell that you are half Japanese," June observed. Deb nodded in agreement.

"Vashti had a Japanese friend from kindergarten named Ryuu with whom she walked to and from school," June continued. "Imagine a midwestern kindergarten class of twenty-eight blonde, blue-eyed children plus Vashti and Ryuu, who looked quite different from the others. One afternoon as Ryuu and Vashti walked home from school they passed a playground where a boy from their class emerged from a hiding place and threw a brick at Ryuu's head, causing him to collapse, with blood gushing from his wound. Amazingly, Vashti carried Ryuu in her arms and dashed across a parking area to his mother, who lifted Ryuu from Vashti's little arms and took him into their apartment. When Ryuu opened his eyes and started to cry, Vashti breathed a sigh of relief, knowing he was alive. His mother gave Vashti a big hug and thanked her for helping Ryuu.

"A few hours after Vashti got home, Ryuu's mother called to let us know that Ryuu didn't have a concussion but now had six stitches in his scalp. Both she and I were in awe that Vashti had been able to pick him up and carry him so far when he weighed only about ten pounds less than her. Later, when I asked Vashti how she had done this, she told me that when she saw blood streaming down his face she automatically picked him up and ran, without noticing how heavy he was. That evening Vashti and I had our first real conversation about racism. I explained as best I could that certain people had bad feelings about individuals who looked different from them and, rather than examine their feelings, would bully or lash out at the individuals. Still, Vashti couldn't understand why anyone would hurt Ryuu, the nicest boy she knew.

"Another challenging thing to explain to a five-year-old was why she couldn't retaliate the next day. I told her that revenge was in God's hands and advised her to stay away from the boy who had thrown the brick and take a different route home from kindergarten. I remember being thankful that I had explained to Vashti who Jesus, Buddha, angels, and spirit guides were. I told her that these wisdom teachers taught us how to behave toward others. Jesus had taught us that everyone was divine, created in the image of God; Buddha had taught us about kindness and karma; and angels and spirit guides protected and watched over us. I also explained, as well as I could, the legal implications of committing acts of revenge. Vashti learned that night about the crime of battery and the punishment for an adult who committed it. She seemed to understand that if a young boy committed such a crime, the resolution was not for her or Ryuu to commit a crime in return.

"I had never thought about Vashti's life journey being riddled with difficulties like this at such an early age," Deb replied. "She doesn't really look black or white, but I guess the real issue is that she doesn't look all white. It's regrettable that Vashti has had to deal with racism all her life, particularly living in the Midwest. What amazes me is that she doesn't have any hatred in her heart as a result. She's kind and loving to everyone, regardless of their skin color, and she always watches out for the poor, the vulnerable, and the homeless. In fact, she is the only friend I have who knows the names of homeless people wandering around downtown. I used to worry about her living in the downtown area, but now that she's an assistant DA who carries a gun, I guess she's reasonably safe."

"I wasn't worried even *before* I carried a gun," Vashti interjected as she stepped back into the salon. "You both seem to forget that I can run like the wind, so they'll have to catch me first." June and Deb looked at each other and smiled at Vashti's spunkiness. Then June paid for the haircuts and walked Vashti to her car, where they said good-bye.

When June got home and found Conor starting dinner, she told him about her talk with Deb. They recalled how Vashti had found out many years later that Ryuu had returned to Japan and was now a university student and successful model for a well-known Japanese clothes designer. Vashti had commented that the brick-throwing bully had probably ended up in prison, while Ryuu had become a remarkable success, illustrating how karma was a bitch.

"I didn't tell Deb about that other kindergarten child," said June as she helped Conor with dinner, "the friend Vashti waited with one day after school until she was picked up by her mother. Seeing Vashti's brown skin and features, the mother forbade her daughter from ever playing with Vashti again because she was black."

"Who could forget that?" Conor replied. "The next day, Vashti ran home crying her eyes out when the girl ignored her. At least our daughter was persistent enough to ask why the girl didn't want to be her friend anymore. The girl told Vashti that because she was black her mother thought Vashti was not good enough to play with her. When Vashti asked her friend what that meant, the girl shrugged and ran away."

"Why would hardworking, Scandinavian midwesterners teach racism to their young children?" June asked, as she had many times before.

Conor took her in his arms and whispered, "Who knows."

They were both unable to comprehend how people could not see that all individuals, regardless of their skin color, were human beings deserving of respect and equal treatment—a belief they had taught Vashti.

CHAPTER 6

Vashti was busy at her desk when David walked into her office and began telling her about a case he was assigning to her.

"Why are you ignoring me, D-Chappy?" Vashti asked, a question she had been thinking about for several days.

"I'm not ignoring you."

"Your invitations to do things like go to baseball games, lunch, or have shots in your office after work are steadily declining."

"I've been busy," he said.

"Fine," Vashti replied. "Tonight after work let's have a couple of shots of Jameson, because if you're that busy you need them."

"Okay," he said, as he put the file on her desk and left.

While walking back to his office, he thought about the many times he had tried to hook up with Vashti. The first time he had kissed her, after a baseball game on a beautiful summer evening, he had known he loved her. Since that night he'd never been able to accept just being her friend, and it was impossible to forget about her because they were together every day at work, with each encounter becoming more difficult for him. She was beautiful and fun to be around. They had great conversations while hanging out after work. He was able to talk to her about anything, and she seemed comfortable telling him whatever was on her mind. He was always moved by her compassion and big heart, her humor and zest for life, her tremendous strength and conviction, and her honesty. One day when his mother had stopped by the DA's office, she'd asked David what race or nationality Vashti was. That had annoyed David, and in response he'd told her that race and nationality made no difference to him, that everyone was part of the human family—something he hoped always to remember when working in the legal system.

Vashti had previously told him about her ethnic background while discussing her participation in track during high school and crediting her speed to DNA from her black biological father. She had further explained that she was black, white, yellow, and red because her biological father had a black father and an Asian, primarily Chinese, mother, while her mother was white and had a paternal grandmother who was a First Nation Anishinabe Indian. When he had asked Vashti whether this ethnic mix had created hardships for her, she admitted it had been challenging while growing up but she had refused to let racism rob her of happiness. She went on to share how she hadn't been black enough in high school track to hang out with the black athletes and hadn't fit in with the white athletes either. While confessing that this had hurt at the time, she also revealed that it had prompted her to do a lot of soul searching to find her own way of dealing with her unique ethnicity and, encouraged by her parents, to maintain perspective on her mixed-race heritage and other people's prejudices.

Vashti had added that even at a young age she'd realized she could hate all racists, whether black or white, or she could try to befriend and respect everyone without feeling a need to belong to any one group. In the long run, she had said, this had led to having friends of all races, which made her life remarkably interesting and happy. When David watched Vashti's actions, he was certain she had no hatred in her heart and would help anyone, feeling that if one person went down in this life, everyone went down since every human was connected to every other human in the world. This perspective had made working with Vashti in the DA's office inspiring because he had been able to observe firsthand its impact on the lives of people caught up in difficult situations.

Later that day Vashti appeared at David's door and said, "I think you need to run with us." In the past, they'd run a relay a few times in the Albuquerque Marathon with two other lawyers from the office.

"Run what? When?" he asked. "Tomorrow is the Red Dress Run, and you should join us."

"What the hell is the Red Dress Run?"

"Well," she announced with a mischievous look in her eyes, "it's a charity event in which every runner has to wear a red dress and every bar participating has to hang red balloons outside its door. For any red-dress runners stopping in and ordering drinks, the bars will give half the proceeds to charity."

"I can't run in a red dress, Vashti," David protested.

"You mean you *won't* run in a red dress," Vashti corrected him. "You have no idea how much fun you will miss."

"Maybe I'll go downtown and order a drink at an outside bar decorated with red balloons and cheer you on as you pass by," he said, hoping to appease her.

Vashti collapsed on the couch in his office, and he poured them a shot. "What are you doing tonight?" he asked.

"I'm going to meet Gabby for pizza, so I can't stay here long. Even though Ted and I broke up, I could never break up with his daughter Gabby. I love the girl as if she were my own," Vashti said. She had long before told David about her involvement with Ted, a police officer, a few years earlier and how they had eventually agreed breaking up would be best for both of them. Vashti continued, "Ted, who never married Gabby's mother, ended up raising Gabby because after high school her mother became a flight attendant and spent most of her time away from home. I met Gabby when she was about eleven and quite vulnerable. I went through all the biggies with her, like how to fix her curly hair, what kind of makeup she should use, and boy problems. We became so close during that time that she will always have a place in my heart."

"Yes, I can see that. I've noticed a picture of that beautiful girl in your office, next to the picture of your parents," David responded.

During the lively conversation that followed, Vashti suddenly looked at her watch and said, "Hey, walk me to my car. I don't want to be late meeting my favorite date for pizza."

They walked to the parking lot arguing about the best pizza topping.

While he liked pizza with everything on it, she insisted that pepperoni with lots of cheese was far better. She turned toward him before saying good-bye and kissed his lips. "You are such a good sport, D-Chappy, that I can't help but love you to death. I also know that you will always order pepperoni pizza when we're together because it is so much better than pizza with everything on it," Vashti said before getting in her car and driving away.

Left standing in the parking lot, David could taste vanilla on his lips and still feel Vashti's arms around him. He smiled, remembering the many hugs she had given him. She never did anything half-assed. When she hugged someone, she gave them a big, tight embrace they would never forget.

While driving down Central Avenue, Vashti could hardly wait to see Gabby, who was now a busy high school senior. As she parked her car close to Saggio's Pizza Shop, she heard Gabby shout, "Vashti, over here!" Vashti ran up to her and gave her a hug before they quickly disappeared inside.

After ordering, Vashti asked, "Gabby, how is everything going for you in school?"

"Okay, but I have to study my ass off to keep straight A's," Gabby answered. "The only way I will ever be able to go to college is by getting a full scholarship."

"You don't have to worry about it, Gabby," Vashti assured her. "You are smarter and get better grades than is required to receive a scholarship. You are so good in math and the sciences that the pre-med program you want to be in may not even challenge you. Have confidence, Gabby. No one doubts you or your abilities. Are you staying out of trouble?"

"You'll be happy to know that I haven't been grounded in several months and my dad's hair isn't turning gray."

"How is he doing?" Vashti inquired.

"He has a new girlfriend, who has two daughters about my age."

"Do you get along with them?"

"In a way."

Just then the waiter delivered their pizza, so they grabbed a piece before continuing to talk between bites.

"Gabby, are you happy?"

"I guess. I miss you, though."

"Well, that means you and I have to make more dates to get together," Vashti said, grabbing her hand. "I miss you, too. Even though Ted and I broke up, that doesn't affect our relationship. I am always here for you and only a phone call away. Remember, even if we don't get to see each other like we used to, I think about you every day and love you."

"I love you, too," replied Gabby.

After they parted outside the restaurant, Vashti walked back to her car thinking about Gabby and her father. She had clicked with Gabby the first day they had met. She had loved Gabby's father, Ted, and for a long time thought their relationship might last. However, it hadn't. She couldn't remember pushing him away; they had just drifted apart until deciding one afternoon to stop seeing each other. Vashti had told her mom later that she felt terrible about breaking up yet knew in her heart that it was best. But she hadn't revealed that she'd heard a little voice in her head saying, "Such a relationship is not the direction your life will be taking." She had heard that little voice many times before and, years earlier, had started calling it her spirit guide. She believed her spirit guide knew she was fiercely independent and liked living alone so it guided her on a path that both protected those desires and made her aware of favorable directions.

As Vashti drove back to her apartment, she tried to remember whether her spirit guide had whispered in her ear when her relationship with Jeff had ended more than ten years earlier. No, it hadn't. But at least her spirit guide had helped her start healing, a process that she knew was still going on as she continued to reflect on the tragedy of such a wonderful relationship ending so abruptly, without a good reason. Although Jeff had been impatient with her wish to accept a clerkship in New Mexico before joining him in California, she wondered if they could have averted the breakup by discussing their individual needs and finding a way to compromise. She thought it sad that many people suffered due to an unwillingness to compromise—something she saw every day now in her job.

When Vashti pulled up to her apartment, she immediately shifted her focus to the present and called her friend Lia about running together in the Red Dress Run the next day. The two had met years before, when Lia had been bartending at one of Vashti's favorite places. Lia was also a talented artist, and they both enjoyed sharing their ideas about creativity and adventurous activities.

"Lia, it's Vashti," she said. "What's up, girl?"

"I'm painting and relaxing after mixing a million drinks last night," Lia responded.

"Glad to hear you are finding time to paint. And if you were that busy at work, I hope you came away with lots of tip money," Vashti replied.

"As a matter of fact, I did."

"I called to see if you wanted to do something adventurous, like join me in the Red Dress Run on Central Avenue around Nob Hill tomorrow after work. Every runner, regardless of their gender, must wear a personally selected red dress, and the bars in the area that hang red balloons by their front doors give half the proceeds from drinks to charity. I asked my boss, D-Chappy, to join us, but he told me he couldn't run a race in a red dress," Vashti explained, laughing.

"Finally you have called me about a fun event for charity rather than a work-your-ass-off-in-the-sun-for-ten-hours type of charity event," Lia responded.

"Oh, come on, you had fun last time, and it was for the Children's Hospital."

"Right," Lia replied, sarcastically. "I was so sore after that, I could barely work the next day."

"This time there will only be fun," Vashti assured her. "I will stop by a secondhand store before court tomorrow and get two red dresses. Then we can meet at my apartment around five-thirty to dress for the event."

"It does sound like fun and I don't work tomorrow, so you have a running partner," Lia agreed and hung up.

As she returned to her easel, Lia thought about her crazy friend. Even when roping her into back-breaking charity work, Vashti made sure they had fun. She was smart, talented, and worked extremely hard practicing law at the DA's office, yet she played just as hard if not harder than anyone else Lia knew. She envied Vashti's endless energy and love of life. For her, there seemed to be no tomorrow, only the present—which she lived to the fullest.

When Vashti hung up the phone, she felt ready for bed. For some reason she could not fathom, she had been tired lately and waking up with a backache for no apparent reason. Before giving in to her fatigue on this night, she wanted to call Brittney and tell her about the wild prophetic dream she had had about her the night before.

"Hey," Britney said when she picked up.

"You're pregnant," Vashti stated with conviction.

"What?"

"You heard me," Vashti replied. "You are pregnant, and you are going to have a girl."

"Did some little stork drop down and whisper that in your ear?" Brittney inquired.

"No, but I had one of those intense dreams in which my spirit guide appeared, so I know the essence of the dream is true."

"What did your spirit guide look like this time, and what did it say?"

"I was in a mall," Vashti continued, "where I was going to meet you for lunch. I saw you standing at the other end of the mall and started walking toward you. Then to my left I saw my spirit guide, in the form of a bent over old woman, walking beside me. She told me that you were pregnant

and going to have a baby girl. Then I woke up before ever reaching you."
Vashti didn't mention that her spirit guide had also said she would only
know the baby from afar, making Vashti wonder if she or Brittney would
be moving away.

"Well, we are trying to conceive, but not very hard lately because we
have both been so busy," Brittney said.

"Go get a test kit tonight or first thing in the morning. You'll see,"
Vashti advised.

"I can't go to bed after hearing this. I'm heading out to the pharmacy
right now," Brittney said.

When Brittney returned home, she immediately took the test. Her
husband heard a scream of joy from the bathroom, and Brittney ran into
his arms, saying, "We're having a baby." He held her for a long time. When
she pulled away, she called Vashti.

"Vashti, you were right. I'm pregnant," Brittney said excitedly.

"Love you," Vashti replied, yawning.

"Go to sleep," Brittney said. "Love you, too. Thanks to you and your
spirit guide for the good news. Your awareness is amazing," replied Brittney
before hanging up.

As tired as she was, Vashti was unable to get to sleep for hours because
her back ached relentlessly. If these backaches continued, she told herself,
she would have to see her doctor to determine what was wrong.

Early the next morning Vashti went to her favorite Goodwill store,
where she looked quickly through the red dresses and picked out two of
the most outrageous ones. After her day in court, she drove home immediately so she and Lia could spend some fun time together assessing fashion choices while dressing for the Red Dress Run.

When Lia entered Vashti's small quaint apartment and saw two taffeta
and tulle red dresses draped over the couch, she asked teasingly, "You don't
really expect me to wear one of these, do you?"

"Of course I do. Think how stunning we will look in them for all the guys watching as we run down the street, even more irresistibly brash after a few drinks."

They both laughed as they tried the dresses on. Lia had brought a red bra along that she decided she didn't need to wear under her dress.

"If you aren't going to wear your red bra, can I borrow it?" Vashti asked.

"Sure, but I don't know if it will fit you."

Vashti slipped out of her bra to try on Lia's, which was way too small.

"What size bra do you wear?" Lia asked as Vashti struggled to remove it.

"I wear a 32 E cup."

"What the heck! Bra cups go up to that size?"

"Sure they do. What size is your bra?"

"It's a 34 B cup."

They laughed again as they zipped up their dresses. Lia thought Vashti's curvy body was gorgeous. She was short but always wore high heels that made her seem of average height. She had beautiful muscular arms and legs, large breasts, and a small waist with a perfectly rounded butt, though she never intentionally dressed to accentuate her body.

With their dresses on and ready to go, they looked and felt like prom queens about to do naughty things.

"What's in there?" Lia asked, pointing to the black fanny pack Vashti was wearing.

"Tequila shooters—just to keep things interesting—and my wallet."

"I think you are one over-the-top woman."

They giggled as they walked to the starting gate. Seeing others waiting in red dresses made them feel less ridiculous. Then two handsome muscular men in red dresses joined the group, and Lia knew this would be an interesting race. She couldn't remember which charity benefited; to her it was a good excuse to run like crazy women with handsome men, stopping at bars along the way to get wasted.

As expected, they had a marvelous time that night. When Lia got home, she wrote in her journal:

The five-kilometer race took hours. Don't know if I crossed the finish line since after the first three pubs everything became a blur of hot, sticky taffeta and boozy laughter. But we certainly completed our mission of contributing to a local worthy cause and thus were champions of something greater than ourselves. In our minds, the finish line was really at the nearest Circle K, where we could eat cheap chimichangas. When we became exhausted, six of us piled into a Mini Cooper, our limbs askew and body odor blending with the smell of musky seats.

Vashti has the persuasive power to show her friends epic good times of debauchery, in the name of charity of course. From now on, I will call her the "red dress queen."

CHAPTER 7

THE DAY AFTER THE RED DRESS RUN Vashti drove to her parents' house to discuss her plans to take a month-long Spanish language immersion class in Costa Rica. She understood the language fairly well, but conversational Spanish was still difficult for her.

"*Mamacita*," Vashti shouted, walking in the back door.

"You look terrible," June replied.

"I took part in the Red Dress Run yesterday, and I think I'm still a little hung over. We had an awesome time, though. I just came to talk to you and Dad about my trip to Costa Rica."

"Conor had to go to the office to get two pleadings drafted for next week. After you mentioned the possibility of attending the class in Costa Rica, we talked about it. He was worried about your expenses, so we decided to help you financially," June said, giving Vashti a hug.

"The last time we spoke about money he made it clear that if I didn't plan to marry I should think about leaving the public sector and joining a private law practice to make a better living," Vashti recalled.

"He doesn't care if you marry or not, but he is concerned about the low salary you make at the DA's office. Plus he would like you to learn bankruptcy and tax law so you could take over his practice when the time comes."

"I know, but right now I love what I'm doing. I'll have plenty of time later for private practice." Vashti could appreciate the benefits of having a higher salary; however, helping the disadvantaged, vulnerable, and poor made the public sector of law more appealing to her.

June took Vashti in her arms and said, "Go ahead with all your plans, and we will cover any costs that you can't."

"Tell Dad thanks and that I'll keep you posted about my plans," Vashti replied. While turning to leave, she suddenly winced from the pain in her back.

"What is it?" June asked, concerned.

"I don't know. I've had this strange back pain for the last couple weeks, and I don't remember hurting myself."

"Have you made an appointment with Dr. Grand?"

"No, but I will. I promise," Vashti said reassuringly.

She arrived at the office early Monday morning to check flights to Costa Rica again before heading to court. Her docket that morning was light, so she planned to work on her trip itinerary and find out whether David had gotten her administrative leave approved. Since her back had begun bothering her, she'd had less energy for the heavy workload and long days in court she usually faced. And it was now too late to get an appointment with her doctor before leaving. If her back still hurt when she returned, she would make an appointment then, she decided.

As she walked to court, she was excited about having time off to enjoy sunny weather and walk along sandy beaches conjugating Spanish verbs in her head. Granted, she was taking a crash course that would require learning lots of material in thirty days, but it would be glorious to worry only about completing an assignment each day in such a beautiful environment. And she knew how advantageous it would be for her to learn Spanish, a language spoken by a multitude of people in Albuquerque. She looked forward to helping many of them legally if she could and was very excited to be taking her first trip alone. She had previously enjoyed traveling to many parts of the world with her parents, but now welcomed the freedom of traveling solo, following her own agenda and meeting fellow travelers.

After reaching Judge Sanchez's courtroom, Vashti took her place on the prosecutor's side and prepared the files for her cases.

"Ms. Warner, you can present your first case for the state," Judge Sanchez directed.

"The first case on the docket is Case No. 110351," Vashti replied as she stood to begin. Things moved quickly, and she concluded her last case just before noon. But as she prepared to leave, Judge Sanchez said, "Ms. Warner, please approach the bench." When she was standing directly in front of the judge, he bent down and, in a quiet voice, inquired, "Are you feeling well? You have been quite pale and moving slowly the last couple weeks, and I'm wondering if you are suffering from some illness."

Her eyes widened as she hesitantly replied, "Overall I feel okay. At least I better not be getting sick because my trip to Costa Rica is just a few days away." She was taken aback by Judge Sanchez's ability to sense that she did not feel as well as usual.

"What will I do without you in my courtroom for a whole month?" said Judge Sanchez, sighing.

"I'm sure the attorney covering for me will handle my cases well. Plus, since I'm going to spend some time on the beach in the sun, I won't be looking pale when I return," Vashti said, smiling.

"Have a good trip, and don't forget to come back," quipped the judge, returning her smile.

While heading to her office, Vashti was unsure what to make of Judge Sanchez's inquiry. None of her friends had asked her if she was sick, and though her parents had commented that she didn't seem like her old self they had never mentioned that she looked pale or moved more slowly.

Upon arriving at her office, she found David. "Vashti, I have never seen a woman run so well, totally blitzed out of her mind, in what has to be the tightest red dress on Planet Earth," he said teasingly.

"Oh, you came then. Why didn't I see you?"

"You might have been beyond seeing much. But I have some great news for you. Your leave has been approved for one month."

"That's fantastic!"

"There is something else I want to talk to you about," he continued in a serious tone.

"Is anything wrong? You don't look happy."

"Vashti, there is a good chance I won't be here when you get back from Costa Rica."

"What are you talking about?"

"I've applied for a job in the attorney general's office, and after my interview they told me I would probably be getting an offer next week."

"Why? I thought you loved our division and the work we are doing."

"I do, but it has gotten difficult working here. Vashti, I love you, and it is hard to work with you every day. In fact, it drives me crazy."

"You are one of my best friends. I have always told you that I just wanted to be friends. I love the days we spend together. Friends are the most important thing in the world. They make life worth living."

"That may be true for you. I'm not blaming you. It's just me," he said in a low voice, avoiding her gaze as he opened her door and disappeared without saying another word.

Vashti sat at her desk and threw her files on the floor. She couldn't understand why guys refused to be friends. They all wanted to go to bed with women, she figured, so if the women didn't want that kind of relationship why wasn't friendship the next best thing? She knew she should have followed David back to his office for a long heart-to-heart conversation but was confident she could talk to him later and hopefully convince him to change his mind. Right now she had to finalize her travel plans, spend hours with the attorney who would be handling her cases, and meet with her parents to discuss finances for the journey. In addition, she had to review her tortoise Bertie's feeding requirements with the neighbor who would watch him while she was gone, though her parents would be visiting him on weekends as well.

As soon as Vashti finished work, she visited her parents, who were just sitting down to dinner.

"Vashti," June said, "grab a plate and join us, I think you are going to like my new quiche recipe."

"Do you have a budget prepared for your trip?" Conor asked.

"I brought it with me," Vashti replied, handing it to him after getting a plate. "I may have to borrow more money than I originally thought."

"Lending money to family, as you know—and as I know from my bankruptcy cases—leads to all kinds of problems. So I never make loans to family, but I do give money to them as a gift," Conor replied, smiling.

She watched him review her budget while she tried her mom's quiche. "Mom, you have outdone yourself. I love it!" she said.

"I thought you would because I made it spicy this time," June replied.

Her father put down the budget and said, "You don't have a category for some spending money. I know you want to hike through the jungle, visit a volcano, and even go to Nicaragua if you have time. Those excursions will cost money."

"I know, Dad. But if I can't take the excursions that's fine. The Spanish class is what matters."

"Your mom and I have discussed what we think would be a good plan. We will cover your airline tickets, tuition for the course, and your food and lodging."

"But, Dad, that is everything."

"Not quite. You will cover the one category missing from your budget: spending money."

Vashti threw her arms around her father. "Thank you," she said. "You are the most generous people in the world. I can only hope to have as big a heart as both of you and the spirit of generosity that runs through everything you do."

"We are just happy," June replied, "that you were able to get administrative leave to take advantage of this terrific opportunity. In your office, they don't pay nearly as much as private law firms do, but they do accommodate employees in other ways."

Vashti helped her mom clear the dishes from the table then smiled at her parents from the back doorway and said, "I love you both so much. And don't worry, Mom, I will call you as soon as I land safely in paradise."

As Vashti drove to her apartment, she could hardly believe she was going away for a whole month. But David's news was bothering her, so when she got home she called Rose, one of her best friends from work.

"Are you calling to gloat about being on the cusp of a one-month holiday in Costa Rica?" Rose said, facetiously.

"You have no idea what I had to go through to make this dream a reality. The office politics almost overwhelmed me, and then I had to negotiate with my parents to cover me financially."

"I hear you. Remember when I wanted to take my kids for a surprise holiday to Disney World? That was only for a week, but because it was a last-minute trip I barely got through the red tape in time to go," Rose said, sympathetically.

"Hey, the real reason I called is I wanted to know if you heard David's news?"

"About leaving our office for the attorney general's office? I talked to him after work about a week ago, and we ended up taking Chinese food to my house for dinner. When he left, I was sick about his news. Everyone at the office loves him, and he is absolutely the best boss for our division."

"Rose, he is leaving because of me," Vashti interrupted. "He is my best male friend in the world, and I love him dearly but can't be more than his friend."

"I know, Vashti. You can't control his feelings though; he loves you and wants more. He thinks, whether you admit it or not, that you still love Jeff."

"I don't even know whether I still love Jeff."

"But a few months after you started working at the office didn't you ask one of our investigators to find Jeff?"

"Oh, that was so long ago, and I just wanted him to get me an address and find out who lived at that address, mostly to satisfy my curiosity."

"That is not how the investigator interpreted your request. He thought that you continued to love Jeff and felt terrible when he found out that Jeff was still married. The investigator thought it was insane that you were wasting your life being single because of some married guy in San Diego. He was out drinking one night with David and told him about your request without realizing he was breaking David's heart as he related the story."

"Oh, shit," Vashti responded in a weak voice.

"Maybe when you are away, walking on those beautiful, sandy beaches, you should do some soul searching about Jeff. When you get back, if you have discovered that you still love him we can put our devious heads together and think up a way to get him back."

"Thanks, but I don't think there is any way to get him back, even if that's what I wanted. When we broke up, he was devastated. He could never understand that the law is a jealous mistress, so to speak."

"Never say never. You know that when we put our heads together anything is possible."

After hanging up, Vashti sat in the dark for a long time thinking about how her past relationship with Jeff and any fantasies about reuniting with him could be affecting her present interactions with D-Chappy or any potential future relationships with other men. She had to admit that Jeff still had a hold on her heart and that no other man had made her feel such a powerful sense of destiny. When she could finally face turning on the lights, she saw it was late, so she got ready for bed, climbed in, and paged through a book on Costa Rica, hoping her time there would help her better understand her relationships.

Jeff and Karen had gone out for a lovely dinner to celebrate their completed renovation of a property they could now lease. When Karen headed for bed and Jeff didn't join her, she went to the kitchen and found him making coffee. "We're a pretty good team," she said, sliding her arm around him.

"We are," Jeff responded, distractedly.

"What are you thinking about?"

"Just something we've often talked about. I think we have poured so much of ourselves into our work that our relationship has turned into a business partnership."

"Are you saying you don't love me?"

"I love you, Karen, but I love you like a trusted and valued business partner. The magic between us seems to have disappeared."

"I know I put too much into my work, but I'm doing it for us. When we get everything we want, we can spend more time enjoying each other."

"It doesn't work that way."

"Have you found someone else?"

"No, I haven't. But it is just a matter of time until one of us does if we don't slow down and put energy into our relationship."

"Jeff, I love you. We make a great team, and I'm sure we will have lots more time to enjoy each other in the future. I think that is just how marriage works. Some couples have children, who take up most of their time; then once the children are grown the couples can focus on each other for the rest of their lives. We, on the other hand, have a real estate business."

"I don't share that view of marriage. I want to work hard, but I also want to play hard. I know it is possible to do both. You seem to work hard and then have no energy to play."

"If you are talking about sex…"

"It is more than sex. It is things like taking little adventures together. We've tried that a couple of times, but you refuse to leave work behind."

"I never thought I would have to defend myself for doing everything in my power to get ahead. You don't seem to remember that we started with almost nothing and it has been an uphill battle."

"I'm not criticizing your work ethic. I'm realizing that work is number one for you and our relationship comes after that."

"Do you want a divorce? Do you want to be business partners and forget the rest?"

"Go to bed—it's late. I'll be there soon."

Karen gave him a hug and went to bed. Jeff sat at the table sipping coffee and recalling the time soon after their arrival in California. He had started work at NCIS and liked his job. Karen had been hired by a local realtor and enjoyed her work there. The advance information she received about houses for sale below market value had led them to buy their first house, remodel it, and rent it out before purchasing more houses.

He remembered the night Karen had brought up marriage. He had suggested waiting a while to see how things went, but the fourth time she mentioned it he had agreed. They had married at a private ceremony in the mountains, after which their relationship had blossomed. Some of his cases required him to spend time away from home, which initially she hadn't seemed to mind. However, as time passed she had grown tired of managing and leasing their properties alone and welcomed his help in their joint real estate ventures, Although they were successful in their careers, the spark between them had started to flicker then went out. Now he felt trapped in a marriage that was really only a business partnership. And he had to acknowledge that, for him, their relationship had never been infused with the spontaneity, magic, and adventurous spirit he had experienced with Vashti. After reflecting on his unhappy marriage, Jeff lay down on the living room couch, where he slept until the morning sun streamed into the room.

Awakened by Karen making breakfast in the kitchen, he went in to pour himself a cup of coffee. "How can you sleep on that lumpy couch?" Karen asked.

"I stretched out and must have immediately fallen asleep. And now I need to pack for my trip to New Orleans this afternoon," Jeff replied, to avoid discussing his real reason for sleeping on the couch.

"How long do you think you will be gone?"

"It shouldn't take more than two or three days."

Karen kissed his forehead, put on her blazer for work, and said, "Call me when you get there. I have to leave now to show a house across town."

Jeff quickly packed for his trip then went to the office to interview a witness before catching his flight. In New Orleans he would be finalizing arrangements to extradite back to California a woman who had murdered a marine several years earlier. Local authorities had told him the woman was living in a crack house in a seedy part of town, but he didn't anticipate any problem with her arrest and extradition to face trial. He knew he would be called to testify at the trial, but after that he could officially close the case and feel a sense of accomplishment. It was cases like this that made his job satisfying, something he especially valued now also as a distraction from his unsatisfying marriage to Karen after such a gratifying relationship with Vashti.

CHAPTER 8

Vashti was excited when her plane flew over the lush tropical terrain of Costa Rica before landing. A representative from the school was waiting in the terminal for her. Moments later she was riding in the back of his van through the beautiful countryside and feeling like a heavy weight had been lifted off her shoulders. She rolled down the window and let the warm wind blow through the curls in her hair, savoring the exotic scents. After parking in front of the facility, the driver took her to a reception desk, where she checked in, and then escorted her to her room. He invited her to look around and gave her directions to the beach a short walk away, just beyond a stand of trees. He explained that class would begin the next day at 8:00 a.m., after which students would not be allowed to speak English.

After he left, Vashti threw herself across the bed giddy with delight. Then she quickly put on her bathing suit and, over it, a lightweight blue summer dress. Retrieving a towel from the bathroom, she went in search of the beach, all the while excited to see monkeys in the treetops. As she caught sight of the ocean, she stood silently in awe of the power it had always had over her. Being from the desert, she saw the ocean as an oasis and let the sound of the surf soothe her soul. She walked to the water's edge, unbuckled her sandals, and took a few steps in, finding it deliciously warm. Minutes later she started walking along the beach. So enthralled was she by the seabirds overhead and the shells and stones alongside her feet that she lost track of time until the sun began its descent.

Returning to her starting point, she sat cross-legged on her towel and dreamed of what it would be like to actually live near the ocean. She then began meditating. After several deep breaths, she did a mental body scan, releasing the tension in her muscles. Next she focused on her breath, emptying her mind of random thoughts, and soon felt like she was merging with the vast ocean when suddenly she felt a hand on her shoulder.

"*Hola*. I'm sorry if I startled you. I wanted to introduce myself," said a handsome man staring down at her. "My name is Andreas, and I'm from Sweden. I'm here with four friends to take the Spanish class."

Vashti stood up and replied, "*You* scared me to death."

"I'm really sorry. I didn't realize that you were sleeping, or whatever you were doing."

"Meditating," Vashti said, extending her hand to shake his. "My name is Vashti. I'm from New Mexico, and I'm here for the same class."

As they walked toward the school, Andreas spotted several friends and introduced them to Vashti. She immediately liked them all and asked if they had found the dining hall for the evening meal.

"We saw a little pub and grill just down the road that we wanted to check out," Andreas explained. "Would you like to join us?"

"Sure, but first I have to go change my clothes and get my purse," Vashti responded. They agreed to wait.

On the way to her room, Vashti called home to inform her parents that she had arrived safely.

"It is so good to hear your voice. I'm already missing you. How is everything there?" said June.

"I have come to paradise! Don't worry about a thing. I will be back with pictures and interesting tales." Vashti knew she had already fallen in love with the place, the warm and welcoming people, and the ocean that filled her soul with tranquility. She quickly dressed for dinner, grateful to have company on her first night in Costa Rica.

At the pub, the group ordered beers and fish and chips. They spoke in English the entire evening and, while coming from diverse backgrounds, were all in Costa Rica to learn to speak Spanish fluently at their jobs. As darkness fell, a group of musicians began to play and Vashti started dancing, encouraging the others to join in. Exhausted after hours of drinking beer and dancing, they returned to the school. Before finding his room, Andreas said to Vashti, "Thank you for being the life of our party. I think we are going to have an awesome experience here." She smiled as he disappeared around the corner.

The next morning they all made it to class by 8:00 a.m., though slightly bleary-eyed. Vashti's "good morning" to Andreas were the last English words she spoke in class till the program ended a month later.

The classes were long and sometimes challenging, but always interesting because the instructors were motivated and positive minded. In addition, Vashti journaled every day, recording her observations, a discipline she enjoyed because it allowed her to later relive them while reading the entries. She also found time to participate in all the adventures she had planned before coming, and to surf, which delighted her; she was good at the sport her first time out because it reminded her of skateboarding but without the danger of falling on concrete. Vashti managed to keep up with Andreas on her second day of surfing, even though he had surfed his whole life. They loved catching waves together and ended their excursions by walking along the beach practicing their new Spanish vocabulary.

On the students' day of departure, Vashti hugged her classmates goodbye as they waited for transportation to the airport. When she reached Andreas, she gave him the biggest hug of all, after which all the students from Sweden joined her in a group hug and promised to keep in touch. In that moment, Vashti realized that she had not only vastly improved her knowledge of Spanish but had made glorious new friends from around the world. So joyful was her month of sun, surf, Spanish, and new Swedish friends that it had filled Vashti with joy and temporarily washed away any lingering sense of physical or emotional pain she had felt before arriving in Costa Rica.

After her return to Albuquerque, Vashti walked into the DA's office and found Cathy filing.

"Good lord, look at your tan, girl! We've all missed you so much," Cathy said, hugging her.

"I missed all of you, too, but I was so busy that the month flew by before I knew it." She pulled out a gift from her briefcase and said to Cathy, "It took me forever to select this for you, because I wanted it to be perfect."

Cathy removed a beautiful, brightly colored blouse from the gift box, held it up to her chest, and replied, "I love it, Vashti." Then Cathy explained that the attorneys were still in court and the DA was out of town for the week. She reassured Vashti that there were more messages on her desk than she could count and that the attorney covering her cases had said they had been handled without any problems. Following Vashti into her office, she added, "There is something else I should tell you. David is gone."

"What? That's terrible," Vashti said, shocked and saddened.

"He left just a few days after you flew to Costa Rica."

"Did you at least have a going away party?"

"We tried, but he refused."

"Well, as soon as I get my legs under me, I will plan a huge fete for him. In the meantime, I'm going to call him and ask him how he dared sneak out of here while I was gone." She regretted the fact that she hadn't had time before her trip to talk to David about his ensuing departure.

"I'll get you his new direct phone number at the attorney general's office," Cathy said as she went to retrieve it.

Just then the receptionist called Vashti to inform her of the arrival of her first client, a man who spoke only Spanish. Vashti assured her she wouldn't need a translator and felt confident that she could now speak Spanish reasonably well after her classes in Costa Rica. The interview lasted two hours, during which time she had no trouble conversing in Spanish.

Afterward she called David. "D-Chappy, this is Vashti. Why did you disappear when I was gone?"

"Hi, Vashti. I told you before you left about my plans."

"But they didn't even have a party to send you off!"

"I didn't want one."

"I don't believe that."

"Hey, I know you are going to need some time to settle in, but I want to get together so you can tell me all about paradise."

"Are you happy at the attorney general's office?"

"Of course I am."

There was a long silence before Vashti finally said, "I'll call you as soon as I'm organized, and we can arrange to get together."

After she hung up, she told Cathy she wanted help planning a party for David—the biggest celebration the office had ever had. Vashti then visited with her best friends at work and told them about her trip and the party plans. She went home exhausted yet eager to spend time in the sun with Bertie, who, she estimated, had gained at least five pounds during her absence.

By sunset, Vashti was in bed and half asleep. She attributed her exhaustion to the many hours she'd spent talking to her parents about the trip—till 3:00 a.m.—on the day of her return, followed by only one day of rest before going back to work. But the next day, her back started to hurt again, so she made an appointment with Dr. Grand for the following week.

Days later Vashti called David, excited about the upcoming party but careful not to mention it. She said she wanted to meet him for a drink and an early dinner on Friday so she could tell him all about her time in Costa Rica.

On Friday, the office receptionist stood at the window facing the parking lot and alerted the staff when she spotted David parking his car. As he opened the front door, they all sang, "For He's a Jolly Good Fellow," making him smile broadly. After an hour or so of talking, Vashti urged everyone to serve themselves from tables set up with delicious dishes contributed by the staff. Once they were all seated, she handed David an exquisitely wrapped gift. He opened the box ceremoniously and marveled at its contents: a beautiful crystal whiskey set.

Then Vashti told the group that a few friends had some words of wisdom to share as he embarked on this new chapter in his life. David appeared overwhelmed with emotion as he listened to their illuminating comments and reflections on their work with him. Bowing his head, he expressed his gratitude.

After everyone had pitched in to clean up, Vashti found David waiting by the front door. "Thank you, Vashti. I didn't expect this, but I really enjoyed seeing everyone and I deeply appreciate their thoughtfulness."

"So you did want a party," she replied teasingly, while locking the door.

"Not when I left, but I loved it now," he responded, walking her toward her car.

"I sure miss you at the office. Here, let me give you a hug," Vashti said, throwing her things in the car.

"I miss you, too," he replied as they embraced. "I didn't get to hear about paradise. Let's meet again soon so you can describe it in detail."

"Deal," she said with a big smile. Then she slowly drove away, realizing how different the office was now with David gone. There were fewer expressions of camaraderie among the staff and no more shots to drink after work to decompress.

Vashti had been back at work only for a couple of months when she told Conor she wanted to leave the DA's office and work for a private firm to learn bankruptcy and tax law. A year earlier Vashti never would have considered leaving the DA's office, but since her return from Costa Rica she simply had not acclimated to the environment without David's presence. She had therefore decided to look for a job that at least paid more.

Conor, surprised by Vashti's decision, was delighted to hear that she would like to make a lot more money than government work provided.

He talked with the owner of the firm where he had practiced bankruptcy law before starting his own law firm. The owner told Conor he wanted to interview Vashti, having known her since her childhood. The interview went well, and he offered Vashti a position that indeed paid much more than her current salary. She agreed to start within the next three weeks.

Rather than submit a two-week notice, Vashti made an appointment to talk to the DA directly. Vashti explained to the DA how difficult it had been to make the decision because she had really enjoyed her work there. The DA assured her that many government attorneys left public practice to pursue lucrative private practice careers and that she was proud of their drive and determination. She accepted Vashti's resignation but expressed dismay at losing her, telling Vashti that she would always have a position there if ever she wanted to return.

After the meeting, Vashti planned a dinner out with her best friends from the office to announce her new job, hoping they would understand. When Vashti arrived at the restaurant, Rose, Lettie, Ann, and Cathy were already there. They laughed as she came flying in, late as usual.

After they enjoyed some wine and delicious entrees, Vashti said, "I should have told you earlier, but I wanted everything ironed out before sharing this news. I'm going into private practice. I have accepted a position at my dad's old firm, and I'm really happy about it. The time is right for me to be in a practice where I can totally support myself, since before long, my parents may not be able to help subsidize my existence. I'm going to miss you like hell, but I'll be less than two miles away."

"Does this have anything to do with David leaving?" Rose asked.

"Of course not," Vashti said abruptly. Softening her tone, she added, "Well, things are different with him gone. It isn't the same for any of us, right?" They all agreed.

No sooner did Vashti excuse herself to go to the restroom than Rose mumbled, "Life is so fucked up. David couldn't bear to work with her, and she can't bear to work without him. We can all see this clearly, but they don't seem to have a clue."

"I hear you," Lettie agreed.

Vashti returned to the table, having settled the tab so they could leave whenever they were ready. They strolled to their cars giddy with happiness for her yet knowing how much they would miss her.

"You better not forget us," Cathy called out.

"Never, ever!" Vashti shouted. Then she drove home in tears. Parting with people she loved had always been difficult for her.

CHAPTER 9

During Vashti's appointment with Dr. Grand, his nurse, Kat, teased her about being only ten minutes late, saying, "You must really be sick. You almost got here on time."

"Hey, of course I'm sick. I hate coming to the doctor," Vashti replied.

After taking Vashti's vital signs, Kat asked her what was bothering her.

"I have had a crazy back pain for a few weeks, about halfway down my back," Vashti explained.

"Do you have any other symptoms?"

"I seem to lack my usual energy, but that's it."

Kat said that Dr. Grand would be right in to try to figure out what was causing the pain.

Soon Dr. Grand walked into the room and said, "Tell me when the back pain started and what it feels like."

"It started about six weeks ago. It's a dull pain."

"When the pain started, had you changed your routine in the gym or hurt yourself in any way?"

"No. That is what is so weird. I had no injuries or falls. At first, it was barely noticeable and always went away quickly. Now the pain is more severe and takes a long time to go away."

Dr. Grand started tapping down her spine. When he got to her mid-back, she flinched in pain. Further down the spine his tapping caused no pain. He directed her to raise her arms and bend first to the left then to the right, as far over as possible, movements that also caused her no pain.

"The mid-back area is affected, but I can't see anything unusual. The area isn't swollen or red or hot to the touch," he observed. "You haven't been playing rugby, have you?"

"No. My days with the Atomic Sisters are behind me."

"Okay, I want to see you again in one week. During that time, keep a journal. Every day write down when you have pain, the intensity, how long it lasts, and when it returns."

"This is going to be tough because I'm starting a new job on Monday."

"Why are you leaving the DA's office? Where are you going?" asked Dr. Grand.

"I'm going to my dad's old firm to learn bankruptcy and tax law."

"I know this is what your dad wants, since he is my patient, too. Is this what *you* want?"

"Dad isn't pressuring me except to remind me I need to make more money. I want to see if this is an area I like. If I don't like it, I will move on to something else."

"Well, no matter how difficult it will be I want to see you in a week with your journal."

"I'll be here. With this kind of pain, I don't think I have any choice."

As they left the exam room, Dr. Grand held her arm and said, "If anything changes before your next appointment, call me."

"Thank you, Dr. Grand. Who knows? The pain might be completely gone by next week," Vashti said optimistically as she disappeared out the door.

Upon arriving home, Vashti began searching her closet for clothes to wear to her new job. She selected suits to be cleaned, along with several dress shirts with French cuffs to be laundered. With an armful of clothes for the dry cleaner, she made it only a few steps out the front door before turning back and collapsing on the couch in excruciating pain. With tears streaming down her face, she wondered what was wrong with her and how she could start a new job in this condition. She fell asleep and saw her spirit guide floating over her head, appearing as a young woman dressed in white and whispering only one word: "Rest."

When Vashti woke up, she was relieved to discover her back pain was barely noticeable. Slowly standing, she whispered, "Thank God."

Vashti started toward the kitchen to make tea when the phone rang. Seeing her mom's number appear and suddenly remembering her promise to call after the doctor's appointment, Vashti picked up and said hurriedly, "*Mamacita*, don't be mad! After my appointment, I came home and fell asleep."

"I'm not mad, Love. When I didn't hear from you right away, I assumed there was no bad news."

"And you were right!" Vashti said in the cheeriest voice she could muster.

"Can you make it up here for a meal this weekend before starting your new job?"

"Sorry, Mom, no can do. I need to get my clothes ready. At the DA's office, we could get by with casual attire, but this job will require more attention to dressing the part."

"You're right. However, Dad and his old boss are still good friends, so I'm sure he will take it easy on you and you will become one of his favorite new lawyers. Remember, Vashti, this is just something new to try. If you don't like it, you can move on to something else."

"I know. Tell Dad I love him. I'll talk to you later."

After hanging up, Vashti made a cup of tea and went out to the garden to feed Bertie. He ate his bok choy so fast that she laughed and said, "Bertie, you act as if I'm starving you." Bertie stared at her as she tried to imagine what he would say if he could talk.

Stroking his head, she continued, "Bertie, I think I'm sick, but I have no idea what's wrong with me. What do you think is going on in my body?" Bertie looked up toward the sky.

"So you think the answer is up there? Well, tomorrow I will lie in the grass with you and together we can look at cloud shapes, which may give us some answers."

Jeff returned from New Orleans pleased with the way everything had turned out. When he arrived home, Karen wasn't there. He chilled a bottle of their favorite wine and started dinner. Before it was ready, she arrived, gave him a hug, and was happy to hear about his success with the case. She had good news as well. She had come across a property available at a great price and suggested they look at it together and consider buying it. They enjoyed a delicious meal and talked for a couple of hours, mostly about work.

While getting ready for bed, Jeff kissed Karen on the neck and slipped her gown over her head before gently laying her down. Stepping out of his boxer shorts, he stretched out beside her. They made love the same way they had many times before. In the past, he had asked her about her fantasies and whether she wanted to try something different. She never had answered his question, telling him several times that she liked their sex life. Their love-making didn't last as long as he wanted; still, he thought she was satisfied when they rolled apart. But then, looking into his eyes, she remarked, "You never say you love me anymore when we make love, Jeff." He pulled her close and rubbed his hands through her hair as he thought about how to respond, but before he could speak she rolled over and fell asleep.

Jeff lay awake thinking about their relationship. He was acutely aware that the spark between them was gone. He still tried to make love and satisfy her, but even that seemed to be getting harder.

The next morning Karen woke up and found Jeff sitting on the chair next to the bed staring at her. Finally, he said, "Things have changed between us, Karen, and I don't know how to get the magic back. We've talked about this before, but I think we should consider getting a divorce. We can still work together in our real estate business because we both enjoy it, but our personal life isn't what I want. You must feel the same way."

Karen reached for her robe, sat at the edge of the bed next to the chair and replied, "I don't know what to think, Jeff. I don't know anyone who characterizes their marriage as nonstop magic with sparks flying. However, if you want to try to find that with someone else, I won't oppose a divorce."

They left the house for work without saying another word.

Vashti's first week at her new job had both positive and negative aspects. The offices in the private firm were smartly decorated. Her office contained a large, carved mahogany desk with a matching credenza behind it and a mahogany bookshelf containing pull-down glass covers—a real lawyer's bookcase, she thought. The people at the firm were friendly and helpful, except for one secretary who was rude to Vashti. Vashti's personal secretary quietly confided that the rude woman was having an affair with the senior partner and felt threatened seeing him be kind to Vashti and take her to lunch on her first day and several times thereafter.

Vashti visited every attorney in the firm to learn their area of expertise and the cases they were currently handling. She was assigned to work with each attorney on at least one case, starting with simple Chapter 7 incidents involving individual filings. First, however, she was to interview people who were considering hiring the firm. None of the other attorneys enjoyed such interviews because they took a lot of unbillable time, involved the tedious gathering of financial information, and necessitated selling potential clients on the law firm. Vashti wondered how she would be able to sell the firm to clients when she didn't yet know much about its services.

Even so, on her first day she completed two interviews, each resulting in a hire. Vashti concluded that rather than attempt to sell the firm, she merely had to listen carefully to how prospective clients had gotten into financial difficulty, show concern about their circumstances, and assure them they could depend on the firm to handle the matter. This came naturally to her because she wanted to help people down on their luck and believed in bankruptcy as a superb legal means for achieving a fresh start.

Yet despite her success at work the first few days, her back pain was almost constant. Come Friday, she left work early and raced to Dr. Grand's office.

"You must be having a lot of pain today since you even arrived early, Vashti," Kat said as she took Vashti's vital signs.

"I don't know how much longer I can take it," Vashti replied. Kat nodded sympathetically.

Dr. Grand asked many questions about the pain and then reviewed Vashti's journal. "It seems your pain is progressively getting more intense and lasting longer," he observed.

"Definitely," Vashti replied.

"I want to inject the area with lidocaine to see if that helps. You need to continue writing entries in your journal, particularly information about how the injections affect the pain, if the pain returns, and how long it lasts. If the pain does not subside, I will order an upright MRI." He then gave her many injections around the area, which she could hardly feel, and instructed her to return the following week on Monday, Wednesday, and Friday for more injections if necessary. In the meantime, Dr. Grand ordered X-rays of the affected area.

By the time Vashti left Dr. Grand's office, her pain had completely subsided and she was filled with hope. She thought that maybe she was suffering from something like a mysterious muscle tear.

That evening she went out with friends and had a marvelous time. She explained to Ann, from the DA's office, that she was willing to give this new job a chance, though her first impressions had not been stellar. The work, largely involving people's financial difficulties, seemed almost boring and the office politics were vicious.

That night Vashti fell asleep but woke up at 2:00 a.m. with the most excruciating pain she had ever felt. Puzzled by its intensity, she took two strong pain pills from an old prescription and finally went back to sleep. She took pain pills all weekend to keep the pain at bay. By Sunday evening, the pain was more like it had been earlier, dull and intermittent. But she wondered how she would have survived without the opiates.

The following week she interviewed several potential clients, all but one of whom hired the firm. When she was leaving on Friday afternoon for her appointment with Dr. Grand, the senior partner explained that she had gotten more clients from initial interviews than any attorney before her and wondered what secret technique she had been using. She laughed and explained that she had no tricks up her sleeve, that she just cared about the people she interviewed.

Vashti drove to Dr. Grand's office prepared to tell him that she could not go on with the pain and that the injections had only worked for a few hours before the pain returned worse than before. After Dr. Grand examined her and reviewed her journal, he was concerned enough to set up an appointment for an upright MRI the following Wednesday. He said he would call her as soon as the results came in, probably later that day. He also gave her stronger pain medication.

Once back at her apartment, Vashti took two pain pills and then sat in her lawn chair to talk to Bertie. She told him about her appointment with Dr. Grand and her frustration about not knowing what was wrong with her. But she assured him that if she didn't have something life-threatening like cancer she would eventually be well again.

Cancer was hard for her to consider since she had witnessed the last days of her friend Jen's life as she suffered from cancer in a local hospice the year before. Jen, the sister of her childhood friend Dave, had been diagnosed with colon cancer a few years earlier and, successfully treated, had gone on with her life. Jen had been the only person Dave had told about the friendship ritual that he and Vashti had performed when, hidden behind Vashti's parents' house, they had punctured their index fingers with a needle until drops of blood appeared then touched fingers and promised to be best friends until they died.

It hadn't surprised Vashti's parents that her best friend was a boy, since she was an athletic tomboy who seemed to get along with boys and enjoy their games more than those of girls. After graduating from high school, Vashti and Dave, a Mormon, had gone on to different colleges but had kept in touch. Dave had studied artistic design, and the cartoons he had drawn for Vashti over the years were now safely stored in one of her treasure boxes.

It was when Dave and Vashti were in high school that Vashti had met Jen, who had soon become her favorite party companion. At Dave's wedding, Jen told Vashti that she wished her brother would have married her. Vashti remembered laughing and telling Jen that she loved Dave but not in that way, and could never become a Mormon, as she wasn't interested in organized religion.

Shortly after the wedding Dave and his wife had moved to Utah. But Vashti still called Dave regularly. One day he mentioned that his new wife was jealous when they talked on the phone. Vashti advised him to explain that they had been best friends since childhood but never romantically involved.

When Vashti was working at the DA's office, Dave had called her one day in tears, explaining that Jen's colon cancer had returned and she was deathly ill. After work, Vashti had raced to the hospital to visit her. Seeing how pale Jen was and how much weight she seemed to have lost, Vashti was shocked at how quickly the cancer had ravaged her friend's body.

Vashti had visited Jen several times before she died. The last week of her life Vashti had stayed with Jen for longer periods so her family members could take breaks. On those nights, Vashti would talk to her parents, weeping inconsolably and angry because there was no treatment for Jen at this stage of her cancer. Jen went on to spend the last days of her life semiconscious and often moaning. Her parents were sure she was beyond comprehending any words. But this didn't stop Vashti from conversing with her in a low voice, reading her poetry, and playing songs they had danced to at parties years before.

Then one night Vashti had told Jen she would return the next day with fresh flowers in Jen's favorite color, orange. When she had bent down to kiss her, Jen had grabbed her hand, holding it until around 2:00

a.m., when Jen's grip loosened and Vashti had silently moved toward the door to go home. About two hours later Dave called to tell Vashti that Jen had died. Vashti had cried, questioning how God could be so cruel as to take a beautiful, thirty-two-year-old woman who had her whole life ahead of her. Vashti had then gone to sleep and in a dream felt a divine presence wipe a tear from her cheek, kiss her forehead, and say, "Later you will understand all."

By the time of Vashti's return the next day, Jen's body had been re-moved and Dave's family had gathered in the room. Vashti had held each one in her arms, sharing in their grief. She had then told Dave she would handle Jen's legal matters and be available for anything the family might need.

On the day of Jen's funeral, Vashti had asked her mom to go with her for support. After the service, they had talked about death for hours. They had both believed that earthly death allowed people to leave their bodies and return home, wherever that might be. Only one thing was certain: Jen's earthly journey and its lessons had ended and her suffering was over. She now belonged to something vaster, and it was up to Vashti to let her go, without ever forgetting the times they had shared.

Vashti turned her attention back to Bertie but could no longer see him. She knew he could be quite an escape artist. One time the previous sum-mer she had inadvertently left Bertie in the garden overnight, and the next morning she had found a hole under a bush in the garden; reached in, hoping to find him there; then called his name for an hour, with no success. Subsequently she had organized a search party to scour the apartment complex and the neighborhood for any sign of Bertie. As dusk had begun to fall, a tenant living at the other end of the complex knocked on her door and reported that he had just seen Bertie in his backyard eating a pink hibiscus flower off one of his bushes. Frantic, Vashti had retrieved Bertie from the neighbor's yard and, holding him close all the way home, smiled broadly as the tenants cheered. That night her dad had helped her enlarge the fenced area around Bertie's house so he would have more room to roam and she would never again have to experience such anguish. Now when Vashti got up from her lawn chair to find Bertie, she noticed him asleep under her chair, as if subtly offering her comfort during this stressful time.

Vashti went inside, took two more pain pills, and called June. "Mom—"

"I was just going to call you. We must be on the same wavelength, Love," June said, happy to hear from her daughter.

"We have always been on the same wavelength. We might as well come to grips with the fact that we will never be on different wavelengths."

"Well, I see that as a good thing."

"I agree. I wanted to tell you that I did my first Chapter 7 filing this week—for the nicest elderly gentleman."

"That's great. You're learning quickly. Are you enjoying it?"

"Not really. Bankruptcy feels boring to me, and private practice seems to be a viper's nest. Every attorney is trying to climb to the top in the senior partner's eyes. It makes me sick."

"Don't pay attention to that negative activity. Just work on the cases you are assigned and see if you enjoy them more as time goes on."

"Okay. I also called to tell you about my appointment with Dr. Grand today."

"Does he have any idea what's going on in that beautiful body of yours?"

"I don't think he does yet. He has made an appointment for me to have an upright MRI on Wednesday and said he would tell me the results that day."

"Do you want company?"

"That's not necessary. The only thing I worry about is the number of pain pills I may need to take to endure the pain."

"The pain has gotten that bad?"

"I'm afraid so, and I can't imagine what is causing it."

"Can Dad and I drive over and help with anything?"

"No, there is really nothing to do here. Dr. Grand said he wanted me to take it easy this weekend, and in the shape I'm in I can't do anything *but* take it easy."

"What are you doing tonight?"

"I'm going to be in the garden with Bertie, working on the painting I'm doing for you."

"Vashti, if you enjoy oil painting I will introduce you to a friend who would be happy to give you some lessons. She taught painting at the university for years."

"Thanks, but I don't have time now. I'm just painting a simple piece from my heart to put a smile on your face. I'll call you tomorrow."

"I can't wait to see it. Bye," June replied, amazed that Vashti was making a gift for her while in the throes of such pain and uncertainty.

June found Conor outside throwing a ball for their dog and told him, "I just talked to Vashti. Dr. Grand has scheduled her for an upright MRI next Wednesday. She said she was in tremendous pain. Seldom has she complained about pain, even when she was injured, so I'm worried."

"June, she worked all week and made it to her doctor's appointment. We are going to find out what's wrong and get it taken care of immediately. Vashti has been a healthy girl, and she is extremely fit. I can't imagine it being anything too serious."

"But what if it is something serious?" June asked, concerned.

Conor came over to her and said, reassuringly, "June, what do we tell our clients every day? We tell them not to waste their energy or time with 'what ifs.'"

Somewhat buoyed by Conor's perspective, June went inside to fix dinner while reflecting on the current state of medical practice nationally. She thought of her friend at work who became terrified upon hearing office discussions about socialized medicine, based on her belief that under a socialized program if she became deathly ill, she would have to be on a waiting list to see a doctor. Vashti was seriously ill, yet the insurance company obligated her doctor to start testing in the most conservative fashion. Once he had determined that a costly upright MRI was necessary, Vashti would be required to wait several days before having the test done. To June, there didn't seem to be much difference between patients like Vashti waiting for care in the United States and patients waiting for care under the socialized medical system in Canada.

Nor could June shake her concern about the time it was taking to diagnose Vashti's condition, which June knew must be excruciating as her daughter rarely complained about discomfort. June felt responsible for Vashti's stoic attitude. Due to her earlier profession as a nurse, she hadn't overly sympathized during Vashti's minor scrapes and bruises, but had instead encouraged her to be brave in such circumstances. Now she wondered whether Vashti's bravery about her back pain prevented her doctor from understanding the extent of her suffering and the urgency of a diagnosis. June was horrified at the possibility that Vashti's stoic attitude might cause her irreparable harm or even cost her her life.

CHAPTER 10

On the evening before her Wednesday MRI appointment, Vashti phoned her close friend Tessa, a young woman who worked as a doula and natural healer. Vashti said in a weak voice, disclosing her high level of stress, "Tessa, can you come to my place tonight?"

"Sure, Vashti, what's up? You sound terrible."

"I've been sick, and I need your help."

"How about eight o'clock?"

"Could you come now?"

"I'll be right there," Tessa assured her, concerned about how weak Vashti had sounded. She quickly gathered her natural remedies and drove to Vashti's apartment.

She found Vashti laying on the floor next to her bed. "Oh, girl, what happened?" asked Tessa sympathetically, slipping her arms under her friend's armpits and slowly lifting her up. She thought Vashti seemed exceptionally light but figured she may have been on one of her diets or working out especially hard at the gym.

Once safely in bed, Vashti replied, "Tessa, I'm so sick. I have been suffering from back pain for the last couple of months. Now it is excruciating. When I walked in here, I got the bright idea to lie on the hard floor to try alleviating the pain. However, not only did it exacerbate the pain but I couldn't get up."

"You've seen the doctor, right?"

"Yes. I went to my doctor as soon as I returned from Costa Rica. He has no idea what is wrong with me. He took an X-ray and didn't see anything. He gave me lidocaine injections, which relieved the pain for only a couple of hours. I have an upright MRI scheduled for tomorrow. Tessa, can you think of what might be wrong with me?"

"Well, if you have had no injuries it could be a pinched nerve or a problem with one of your discs, like a rupture."

"I was thinking of things like that, too, but why would a disc rupture if it wasn't injured?"

"Hey, human bodies can do strange things for no known reason. That's why we need medical providers who dig for diagnoses, utilizing all testing tools at their disposal. Unfortunately, at times they never discover the causes of symptoms. But remember, Vashti, this is an acute problem that came out of the blue. It isn't a condition that has been plaguing you for years with all sorts of mysterious symptoms. I'm confident they will find the cause."

Vashti appreciated Tessa's positive attitude and support. It made her hopeful that her doctor would soon diagnose her problem.

"What can I do for you right now? Can I massage your feet and hands with a soothing ointment?" Tessa asked.

"Tessa, have I ever refused one of your special massages? They are heavenly."

"Just lie still, I'm going to cover you with a throw, then place a washcloth with aromatherapy scents over your face and ask you to take three deep breaths before I begin the massage, starting with your feet."

Vashti became totally relaxed within minutes. She then had a clear vision of an elderly man in a long white robe holding a young girl's hand as they walked toward her. The old man had a compassionate expression on his face, and the young girl was smiling as if she knew Vashti. They stopped about ten feet from where she was standing. Then the old man opened his mouth to speak but sounded more like he was singing, intoning a song about fears blocking a connection to the universe, to the source, advising that there is nothing to fear. After hearing his lilting song and feeling Tessa's soothing massage, Vashti felt largely restored, though as soon as she raised her upper body with Tessa's help, she felt the pain still there but less severe.

"Tessa," she said, "I feel much better and completely relaxed, thanks to your massage and the beautiful song. They have lifted my spirits."

"What song?" asked Tessa.

"It was in my head, a song about the need to set fears aside because they block our sense of connection to the universe, to our source. It made me feel so good."

"That is certainly an important message, and you know I consider music a universal healing balm," Tessa commented.

"I agree," Vashti said. "And setting fears aside certainly helps relieve stress and makes you relax."

"I think you should contact our mutual friend who does Reiki treatments. I have confidence in her healing abilities as well as mine," Tessa advised.

"I've had Reiki treatments in the past, and I have confidence in them too. When Western medicine embraces Eastern medicine, patients have the benefit of both," Vashti remarked. Tessa nodded in agreement.

"Tessa, thank you from the bottom of my heart. I will call you as soon as I know what demon has taken possession of my body," Vashti added and hugged her before Tessa disappeared into the fading light.

Vashti had a bowl of soup for dinner and got ready for bed. She couldn't sleep, however, because of the pain, even though the massage had relaxed her and she had taken the maximum number of the highest dose opiate pills.

In the morning, Vashti called her law firm and said she would need the entire day off because she was feeling too sick, but promised to keep them posted after the MRI. Her parents ended up driving her to the facility for the MRI. Afterward they drove her home, where she lay on the couch while her mom made them lunch.

About two hours later Dr. Grand called Vashti. "Dr. Grand, what did the MRI show?" Vashti asked, concerned. Her pain was now so bad that she had difficulty talking.

"Vashti, the MRI showed a large mass on your spine. We don't know what kind of mass yet, but we are trying to have a radiologist biopsy it today."

"Are you saying it could be cancer?" Vashti asked, desperately holding back tears.

"Vashti, we won't know until we get a biopsy. Masses can be benign. We will call you back as soon as we get you scheduled. Is your medication keeping the pain tolerable?"

"Not at all," she replied as she hung up the phone. She told her parents what Dr. Grand had said, trying to keep her voice calm. Then she started crying. June held her while tears streamed down her face, as well. Conor sat in silence, his heart pounding. After several minutes, Vashti started regaining control and whispered in her mom's ear, "I'm scared."

June replied, "I am, too, Love. I think I'm most afraid because we don't know what we are dealing with and it is hard not to jump to the worst conclusion. But I'm filled with hope that the tumor, whether or not it's benign, can be treated so you will get well again."

After sitting in silence, trying to cope with the news, Conor eventually suggested that they all go out to the garden and check on Bertie. Once outside, Vashti tipped her head toward the sky to let the sun soothe her while Bertie sat nearby, as if sensing her distress.

Soon the phone rang again, and Dr. Grand's nurse told Vashti, "The best we could do, if you don't want to be hospitalized today, is to have the biopsy at eight o'clock tomorrow morning at a hospital on the west side of town."

"I know where that hospital is, and I'll be there," replied Vashti.

"Oh, one more thing. Dr. Grand wants you to go home with your parents tonight."

"Why?"

"Think about it. You tend to be late, and if there are any difficulties between now and then your parents can help you out." Vashti agreed, feeling like she could use her parents' support anyway while awaiting more news.

By the time they arrived at her parents' house, Vashti was exhausted and lay down in the guest room to rest. When June inquired about what she wanted for dinner, she said she wasn't hungry and would get something later, but wanted her dad to call the firm and explain what was going on with her tests.

Later that evening she found her parents in the library reading and asked, trying to sound cheerful, "Who can I beat tonight at Scrabble?" Both agreed to take her on, surprised that she felt well enough to play. As it turned out, she beat them both.

Afterward, Vashti and her mom went to the guest room to meditate before going to bed. All three had meditated together for years, but this time Conor took a pass so he could feed their two beloved greyhounds, Juma and Lilly. When Conor finished, he lay down in bed and fell quickly asleep. But he woke up in the middle of the night and, realizing June wasn't next to him, went to the guest room, where he found his wife and daughter in a flat meditation pose sound asleep. They looked too peaceful to wake, so he covered them with a blanket and switched off the salt lamps. Returning to the master bedroom, he prayed for the energy of the universe to surround Vashti with healing light.

In the morning, he expressed silent gratitude upon finding June and Vashti on the back veranda drinking tea and looking better than the day before. After breakfast all three drove to the hospital, where June and Conor waited with Vashti for the doctor. Vashti felt good enough to recall their experiences during trips together. By the time the doctor appeared, they were laughing about Conor's wreck years before in a rental car near the old city center of Seville, Spain, where he had tried to drive down a path he had mistaken for a narrow road and become stuck on an iron planter until passersby had pushed the car back far enough for him to reverse direction.

Their laughter subsided as soon as Dr. Chas Lomas walked into the room. He appeared to be about Vashti's age, and he began glancing nervously back and forth between her and her chart without saying a word. Finally, Vashti looked him in the eye and asked, "Are you drunk?" Her parents knew she was teasing, though they thought the doctor must have been shocked.

But without skipping a beat he looked back at her and replied, "No. Are you?"

She laughed and responded, "I only wish."

When first meeting people, Vashti tried to be upbeat no matter what the circumstances, figuring they had experienced their own difficulties in life and wanting to lighten their loads. However, with Dr. Lomas she had met her match in quick wit and, as a result, they liked each other from that first moment.

Dr. Lomas then explained the biopsy procedure and called in a nurse to administer a light sedative. He told Conor and June to sit in the waiting area and he would return in about an hour to explain how Vashti was doing. Conor and June were startled when Dr. Lomas reappeared about fifteen minutes later and told them the equipment had broken down and the biopsy couldn't be done. He also said that he would not be returning until the following Monday so Vashti would unfortunately have to wait until then to get the biopsy, an agonizing four-day delay.

Conor and June took Vashti home and contacted Dr. Grand, who, disappointed by the delay, directed them to bring Vashti to his office for an examination the next morning. In the meantime, he assured them, he would search for an outpatient setting in which she could have the biopsy.

The next morning, with Vashti in great pain, they went to see Dr. Grand. He asked her to get up on the table so he could examine her back.

"I will, but please no tapping this time. I don't think I could take it," she warned.

As she stood up, she started swaying and felt sure she would pass out. Dr. Grand helped stabilize her by placing his hand under her forearm. Then she realized she could not move her legs, so Dr. Grand and Conor helped her back to the chair. At that point, Dr. Grand told the nurse, "Call the hospital downtown and get Vashti a bed ASAP. I want them to do a biopsy today. Also start an IV for pain medications and call an ambulance to transport her."

Minutes later the ambulance arrived. Vashti screamed in pain as the paramedics moved her to a gurney then sped off to the hospital, with Conor and June following in their car.

Vashti had just gotten settled in her room when Dr. Lomas appeared and saw her face contorted in pain. "We are taking you downstairs for the biopsy. I'm on call today at this location so I'm glad we are able to do it today," he said.

About an hour later, Dr. Lomas came back to explain to Conor and June that the biopsy had gone well but that Vashti would have to stay in the recovery room for a while because of the amount of pain medication she had needed to remain still for it. He said he and Dr. Grand were doing everything they could to get the results that day, which might not be possible because it was Friday.

After Dr. Lomas left, June looked at Conor with tears in her eyes and remarked, "The waiting is killing me!" Conor took her in his arms, nodding in agreement. Vashti's illness seemed to shake the ground beneath them. Their mutual support of each other at this time was more important than ever before in their thirty years of marriage.

A couple of hours later Vashti was wheeled back to her room. When they lifted her into her bed, she screamed in pain yet appeared to still be heavily sedated. After June asked why anyone would have this much pain while not fully conscious, the nurse shook her head and explained that a pain specialist would be there shortly to figure out how to make Vashti's situation tolerable.

The pain specialist arrived twenty minutes later, examined Vashti, and read her chart. Then he ordered that she be hooked up to a cardiac monitor so he could increase the pain medication, and he had a pain pump brought in so that Vashti could get continual morphine by pushing the button whenever her pain became intolerable. Within the next hour, Vashti was hooked up to several machines and finally able to rest. Conor went home to take care of the dogs, and June kept vigil in a chair at Vashti's bedside.

Later that day Vashti was groggy but no longer in excruciating pain. June told her to rest and not fight the effects of the pain medication. Although Vashti could not nod in response, June was sure her daughter had heard her words.

When Conor returned to the hospital, June went home to sleep for a couple of hours. Conor was thankful that Vashti slept most of the afternoon. The few times she woke up, he gave her sips of juice. By the time June returned, the biopsy results were not yet back.

For the evening meal, Vashti told June she would try some soup, which June ordered and held for her as she took small sips. Vashti's voice was faint, and she could speak only in short sentences. To soothe her, June played some of Vashti's favorite classical music at a low volume on her cell phone. After a while, Dr. Grand called and asked Vashti if the doctor had been in to see her. When she responded with a faint no, he asked to talk to Conor. By the time Conor hung up, all the color had drained from his face, though he didn't utter a word.

Vashti looked directly in his eyes and asked, "Do I have cancer?"

He reached for her hand and said, "Yes, the tumor is malignant." Those words changed their lives forever. Conor added that Dr. Grand had the biopsy results and immediately contacted an oncologist, who would explain everything. June and Conor sat on either side of Vashti's bed and, with tears streaming down their faces, held her small hands in silence, trying to come to grips with Dr. Grand's words.

Saturday morning a doctor and a nurse came into the room. "Good morning, Vashti," Dr. Lewis began. "I had planned to visit last evening, but an emergency prevented me from coming. How are you feeling this morning?"

"I feel better than when I arrived yesterday. I hadn't slept much in many days, and a night of sleep has helped," Vashti told him.

"Good. I have reviewed your chart and the material we received from Dr. Grand. I'm the oncologist on call this weekend, and I will be the one to begin your treatment. When you arrived here, you were in kidney failure, so a catheter was inserted to record urinary output. You are stabilizing, and if you continue to improve we will be able to remove it. The reason for your excruciating pain relates to the mass on your spine, which was detected on the MRI. Because of the size of the tumor, it has fractured your spinal column and is currently close to your spinal cord. You must have a strong pain threshold because, according to the notes in your history, you were up and walking before yesterday."

"And working," Vashti interjected, faintly.

"That is amazing. I know you have been anxiously waiting for your biopsy results, so let me explain what is going on. You have been diagnosed with a disease called multiple myeloma, a cancer that develops in the plasma cells. A plasma cell is a type of white blood cell found mainly in the bone marrow. Plasma cells assist the immune system in fighting off infection by making antibodies that help kill germs. When cancer grows in these cells, it causes an excess of abnormal plasma cells, which form tumors in multiple locations throughout the bone marrow. You are probably wondering how the disease is treated and if it is curable. Multiple myeloma isn't curable, but it is treatable. We have many options for treatment, and I would like to begin as soon as possible so we can get you back to practicing law.

"There are two treatments I would like to start immediately. The first is chemotherapy. We start with a low dose of oral chemotherapy and review the results. If we need to increase the dose or change the chemotherapeutic agent, we will. The second treatment is radiation. We need to shrink the tumor so your spinal cord is protected and your spinal column can begin to heal. I don't think many radiation treatments will be necessary, which means there should be no burning of the skin or undue discomfort.

The radiologist will explain the radiation treatments to you in detail. I will order both now, and before we get them started I want to give you a pain medication. In two or three weeks, you will be feeling much better. Do you have any questions about what we've discussed?"

"What did you mean when you said this type of cancer is not curable but is treatable?" asked Vashti, wanting to know specifically what she faced.

"Unfortunately, we have no cure for multiple myeloma or many of the other blood cancers, but there are several advances on the horizon for treating these types of cancers. We will keep on top of your cancer, Vashti, utilizing every medical treatment available to us."

Since no further questions were asked, the doctor got up to leave. When the door closed, tears started streaming down Vashti's checks. June bent over and put her face close to her daughter's. Any movement caused Vashti so much pain that June took care not to jostle the mattress. "Is there anything I can do for you?" June whispered in her ear.

"Mom, I'm so scared."

"I know. I am too," June confessed, "but we are going to fight this cancer right along with you, Vashti."

After the nurse adjusted the pain pump again and took Vashti's vital signs, Vashti fell asleep. Conor and June remained in the room, taking turns only to go out for fresh air.

In the late afternoon, a nurse explained to Vashti in a low voice that the medication she brought was her first dose of chemotherapy then gave her two small green pills. Vashti was barely awake and made no comment. June, however, was unable to get one thought out of her mind: that those two innocent-looking pills were poisoning her young, beautiful daughter.

Vashti slept until early evening. When she woke up, she seemed to be feeling a little better. She told her parents to go home for the night, not wanting them to sleep in chairs next to her bed. After they left, Vashti called Brittney to tell her what was going on, even though she knew she didn't have the energy to talk long. Vashti explained to Brittney the events of the last two days. Brittney told her she was taking the next flight to Albuquerque and would see her as soon as she could. As Brittney hung up, she fell to the floor crying. When her husband found out what was wrong, he immediately booked her on the first flight to Albuquerque, which was early the next morning.

After Conor and June had walked silently out of the hospital, June dropped to her knees in a small grassy area, looked toward the heavens, and screamed, "You can't take her from me! I won't let you have her!" Conor knelt beside her, pulled June's head to his chest, and rocked her back and forth as she sobbed.

Conor whispered, "Let me take you home. You need something to eat and some rest." He lifted June to her feet and escorted her to the car.

After a few seconds, she said, acutely aware of the threat to patients dealing with this disease, "This is so bad, Conor. You don't have a medical background, but multiple myeloma is a horrible disease that will kill our daughter."

"June, I know the doctor said it was not curable, but he told Vashti it was treatable."

"That is such bullshit. It is treatable for a while, and then it is untreatable, and you die."

"You know a lot more about diseases than I do, but how long has it been since you researched multiple myeloma?"

"I don't care if it's been decades. These cancers are the worst."

"June, so much has changed since you were a nurse. Please give yourself a chance to research the current treatments," replied Conor, encouraging her to maintain some hope.

"You're right. I'm very angry at the moment and need to pull myself together and research this cancer," June replied, still not hopeful but eager to better assess any possibilities for remission.

When Brittney arrived at the hospital the next day, Vashti was too sick to speak more than a few words at a time. Brittney kept her company, holding her hand. Every time Vashti woke up Brittney assured her that the fight was on and they would beat this monster with the same courage and determination they had mustered in the past to excel at sports challenges and come away victorious. Vashti made Brittney swear to secrecy about her condition, wanting to tell people in her own way or not at all. Brittney said she knew her friend was a very private person and would kick her ass if she started talking. Friends for many years, they had never disclosed each other's confidences. At sunset, Brittney explained to June that she was flying back to Las Vegas that night because of work and would return soon. Brittney had kept a brave face during the visit, but in the taxi on the way to the airport she cried so hard she could barely breathe.

Later Vashti asked June to call Tessa and explain that she was in the hospital and Tessa could visit anytime. Vashti also asked Conor to call the law firm and tell her boss that she had been hospitalized and diagnosed with multiple myeloma.

Vashti spent three weeks in the hospital undergoing chemotherapy and radiation. She shared her diagnosis with only a few close friends, all of whom gave her positive support. Brittney called or texted every day with one goal in mind—to make her friend laugh—and often succeeded. Tessa visited and massaged her hands and feet. Dave regularly texted her from Utah. One friend massaged her scalp with aromatic oils, while another took her on walks around the nurses' station and yet another arranged fresh flowers in large vases around Vashti's dreary hospital room to lift her spirits.

None of these special friends, all sworn to secrecy about Vashti's diagnosis, shared this information except Rose, who knew how much David loved Vashti. One day at lunch she said to him, "I have some bad news to tell you. I was sworn to keep this confidential, but I think you should hear it from me rather than finding out later."

"It must be serious. You're as white as a ghost," David replied as he reached for her arm.

"Vashti is in the hospital and has been diagnosed with a blood cancer called multiple myeloma."

David's eyes filled with tears as he mumbled, "This is terrible. I can't believe it." Rose reached for his hand, but he pulled away and said abruptly, "I've gotta go."

While sitting behind his steering wheel in near shock, David called his office to say he was sick and going home for the rest of the day. He then drove to his house feeling numb, as if in a dream. As he walked in, he loosened his tie, poured himself a half glass of Jameson whiskey, and searched on his computer for "multiple myeloma." After reading several articles about how terrible this type of cancer was, he couldn't imagine Vashti having it, given her prior good health and usual zest for life. Upset, he reached for the phone to call her but had no idea what to say. Instead, he nearly finished the bottle of Jameson then fell into a fitful sleep.

The day Vashti was released from the hospital she had an appointment with a psychiatrist, Dr. Miller, arranged by the oncologist. While Vashti had improved physically during the hospitalization, no one knew how she was dealing mentally and emotionally with a diagnosis of cancer that more than likely would be terminal, as she had hardly spoken about it. When June asked Vashti whether she thought her visit to the psychiatrist would be helpful, Vashti told her she didn't think so because she had to come to grips with things in her own way and at her own pace. As it turned out, the visit didn't even last the full hour and Vashti never returned to see Dr. Miller again. Vashti didn't discuss the session with June except to say that she had told Dr. Miller her soul was shattered and that, while looking out the psychiatrist's window and seeing the beautiful autumn leaves, she had wondered why, in their natural progression toward imminent death, they displayed such vibrant colors as vivid, exquisite gold.

CHAPTER 11

After Vashti's release from the hospital, where she had completed her radiation treatments, she stayed at her parents' house and received out-patient chemotherapy. Her oncologist also proposed the possibility of a bone marrow transplant. If Vashti decided to have one, she explained, it would be at a cancer center out of state. Her oncologist was hopeful about her prospects for a good outcome from the procedure. Each time Vashti saw the oncologist she asked her about potential treatment outcomes and life expectancy. Vashti's oncologist was always straightforward, positive, and caring, saying essentially that so many new chemo drugs could be used in her case it would be impossible to accurately predict her life expectancy.

Vashti knew the prognosis predictions from information she had found on the internet. She had learned that more men than women had this type of cancer, and the average age of diagnosis was sixty-five. Being so young, she thought her prognosis would be better, but no doctor had been able to confirm the accuracy of her assumption. Of course, she wanted to know if she would die, but even more importantly she wanted to know what her life would be like until then. She could not imagine life without being able to run, ride her bike, play sports, and practice law. And she feared suffering, and living a horrible existence, much more than she did dying. Besides, Vashti's oncologist had discouraged her from discussing end-of-life issues at this point because the transplant could put her into remission. Vashti had confidence in this view and in her ability to fight her cancer.

Vashti now spent most of her time with June. They meditated together every morning and night, and, when Vashti could, they took walks through the neighborhood. Vashti exercised as much as possible to gain strength in case she decided to have the transplant. Her pain was tolerable, and she seemed to get stronger each day. Emotionally, she felt hope and fear in equal measure. She knew that while the transplant might put her into remission there was also the chance of complications and even death. She had the option as well of staying on chemotherapy and, without risking the transplant, waiting to see how the disease progressed. Vashti talked with her parents for hours about complications she might experience from the transplant, what she could expect as a result, and the potential advantage of simply staying on chemotherapy and hoping for improvement—an approach she considered inferior because if the chemotherapy stopped being effective she would have to face a transplant in poorer health, with increased risks. To get more information before making a final decision, Vashti decided to visit the Mayo Clinic in Phoenix, Arizona, and MD Anderson Cancer Center in Houston, Texas.

Dr. Lomas, who had developed a friendship with Vashti outside the hospital, was supportive of her choices. When Vashti was well enough to go to a restaurant for dinner, the first person she went with was Dr. Lomas. They were kindred spirits who even under such difficult circumstances had a wonderful time together. Conor and June often talked about how much alike Dr. Lomas and Vashti were. They both worked hard in their professions and were committed to playing just as hard. They liked many of the same activities, including travel, active adventures, music, and comedy. But the most striking resemblance between the two was their tendency to look on the bright side of life, so while spending time together they lived life to the fullest.

When Vashti and her parents arrived at the Mayo Clinic, they didn't know what to expect other than the appointment with an oncologist to explore the transplant procedure. As the oncologist entered the examination room, he said, "Good morning. I'm Dr. Arman."

"Good morning. I'm Vashti, and these are my parents, Conor and June Warner," she replied.

"How much do you know about multiple myeloma, Vashti?" Dr. Arman asked.

"Well, not a great deal. I was only recently diagnosed with this cancer."

"Then I'll start with a brief summary of multiple myeloma before we discuss the transplant. Are you a realist?"

"Yes, I consider myself a realist."

He stared at Vashti for a minute before continuing. "Multiple myeloma is an incurable cancer. I would be surprised if your life expectancy is more than three years."

Conor and June watched Vashti's face collapse, with tears rolling down her cheeks and her lips trembling, as her entire life crumbled in front of their eyes. June wondered how Dr. Arman dared to play God in predicting Vashti's life expectancy but was too stunned at his insensitivity to utter a word. Conor was thinking about taking Dr. Arman's realism and stuffing it up his ass.

Upon recovering somewhat from the shock, which had made her feel an odd cold sensation course down her spine, Vashti asked, "Three years from today or from when I was diagnosed?"

Hearing his daughter's question, Conor felt more agony than ever before, realizing that she was asking if she had already lost two of the thirty-six precious months of life expectancy that Dr. Arman had estimated.

"Unfortunately, three years from when you were diagnosed," Dr. Arman replied. "Now, on this chart I have diagrammed plasma cells to illustrate a simplified progression of the disease." He spent a few minutes talking about the disease, but outraged by Dr. Arman's brutal manner, Vashti and her parents didn't register a word he said. After briefly addressing the bone marrow transplant, Dr. Arman inquired whether they had any questions then headed toward the door. When no one responded, he left. Never had any of them been treated so insensitively.

After what seemed like an eternity, the door opened again, and the nurse stated, "Dr. Arman has completed your appointment. You are free to take a tour of the facility any time between the hours of nine and four."

Vashti stood up and said, "I have several questions for Dr. Arman. He left before I could ask them."

"I'm sorry. If you would like to write your questions here, I will be sure he receives them," the nurse replied, handing her a sheet of paper. "You can do this in the waiting area and leave the paper with the receptionist."

The three retreated to the waiting area, where June sat next to Vashti, put her arm around her, and declared, "Dr. Arman is a monster. He is not God, and he has no idea when you are going to die."

Vashti looked at her mom with the saddest eyes imaginable and whispered, "I know, Mom, but the prognosis isn't good all the same."

June and Conor sat in silence as Vashti reached for the notebook she'd brought and composed five pages of questions. When she finished, she asked the receptionist to call Dr. Arman's nurse so she could deliver the questions to her. The nurse looked shocked at the number of questions, whereupon Vashti simply turned and walked back to her parents.

"Do you want to take a tour of the facility?" Conor inquired.

"I don't think I will be coming back here. In fact, I don't think I will see this place again in my whole life—or at least not in the next three years," Vashti replied.

They wasted no time in speeding off in their rental car to a restaurant. On the way, Vashti noticed a cotton field and asked her dad to stop the car. She got out, handed her mom her cell phone, and said, "When I raise my arm, take a picture of me."

June, clueless about Vashti's reason for such a request, watched her trek into the cotton field, bend down and grab a ball of white cotton, and raise her arm, her dark skin contrasting sharply with the cotton. June snapped a couple of photos as requested.

As they picked at their food in the restaurant, Vashti sent off a text then said to her parents, "What I can't understand is if I'm going to be dead in three years or less, why I should go through something like a bone marrow transplant?"

"I don't understand it either, Vashti. All the doctors we have spoken with told us that multiple myeloma isn't curable but is treatable. None attempted to predict your life expectancy except Dr. Arman. If the prognosis is as grim as Dr. Arman said, why does the Mayo Clinic bother to do transplants on multiple myeloma patients and why do insurers pay?" June replied.

Suddenly Vashti began laughing then she handed June her cell phone and told her to read the text. "Chas, I'm done at the Mayo Clinic, and we ran into a problem. If my insurance covers only part of the cost of the procedure, I would have to commit to working here (see picture) until the balance is paid off," June recited. Directly below the text was one of the photos of Vashti in the cotton field and Chas's response, which June also read aloud: "I thought slavery was outlawed, but maybe not in Arizona?" Conor and June were amazed that Vashti could express humor in the midst of this horrible experience.

Next they drove to the mall, where they planned to shop before their flight departed. They were in Neiman Marcus when Vashti's phone rang.

"Hi, Dr. Arman,"Conor and June heard her say. They led her to a bench where she could sit, then waited for about forty-five minutes while Dr. Arman did all the talking.

"I have no other questions, Dr. Arman. Thank you for calling," Vashti finally said.

After setting down her phone, she told her parents, "He explained more about the procedure and why it was worth a try. He also backtracked on his three-year life expectancy prediction."

"And he's right. A prediction like that certainly doesn't help patients who are considering risking their lives in the hope of gaining a remission." June said as she hugged Vashti, relieved that Dr. Arman had left more room for hope.

"I'll try to forget his prediction, Mom, but I will still have to think hard about having the transplant."

"Vashti, as soon as we get home I'll arrange a trip to MD Anderson Cancer Center for a second opinion about the procedure and the possibility of a prolonged remission from this cancer."

"Thanks, Mom. Let's get out of here and go to the airport," Vashti said, eager to put the bad experience with Dr. Arman behind her.

CHAPTER 12

VASHTI FELT DREAD AS THE PLANE LANDED IN HOUSTON, not knowing if she could take another experience like the one she had endured in Phoenix. The worst part was that she had to decide if she wanted the transplant, not a choice all doctors advised patients to have.

At MD Anderson Cancer Center, the transplant physician introduced himself and, since his last name was difficult to pronounce, told Vashti she could call him Dr. M. He then said, "It is a pleasure to meet you and welcome you to MD Anderson. I have received your medical record from the University of New Mexico. The transplant we propose doing is called an autologous bone marrow transplant, a procedure where we collect your blood-forming stem cells then use them for the transplant. After we collect your cells, you are treated with high doses of chemotherapy, which kills the cancer cells but also kills many of the blood-producing cells left in your bone marrow. Afterward the collected stem cells are put back into your bloodstream, allowing the bone marrow to produce new blood cells. What we are hoping for after the procedure is remission."

"With all of that said, will I be dead in three years or less?" Vashti asked.

"Vashti, no one can answer that question. Where did you get the three-year time period you are referencing?"

Vashti described her visit to the Mayo Clinic, the negative attitude of the oncologist, and her concern about agreeing to have the procedure if it didn't alter the course of the disease.

"Vashti, I don't share the opinion of the doctor at the Mayo Clinic. I would not suggest the procedure if I didn't think a remission was possible. In fact, there are lymphoma patients who have survived beyond the ten-year mark following an allogenic transplant procedure. No one can make accurate predictions because it depends on the type of blood cancer we are dealing with and how the patient responds after the transplant. If the autologous transplant is not successful, there is another type of transplant to consider, called an allogenic transplant, where a live donor is used. Later today an oncologist will explain the many types of chemotherapy with which you can be treated, and new drugs are always being approved."

"Thank you, Dr. M. I now feel much better about perhaps having the procedure," Vashti confided. Dr. M had at least left room for the possibility of a successful remission and thus did not extinguish the hope she had needed to make a realistic decision, she thought.

When Vashti saw the oncologist about an hour after her appointment with Dr. M, he was extremely knowledgeable about the different chemotherapy drugs used to treat multiple myeloma and had a positive outlook. By the time Vashti and her parents boarded an early evening flight back to Albuquerque, she was in a positive mood though not yet willing to commit to the transplant as she first wanted to discuss it with her local oncologist. But she remarked that if she decided to have the procedure she would definitely have it at MD Anderson. Before seeing her oncologist, Vashti asked many of her closest friends what they would do in her situation, and they all said they would have the transplant in hopes of a remission. When Vashti finally discussed the procedure and possible complications with her local oncologist, the doctor was positive about its prospects. At the end of the appointment, Vashti asked her to schedule the transplant at MD Anderson.

While waiting for the transplant to be scheduled, June and Conor had many conversations about how best to start transferring Vashti's inheritance to her so she could enjoy using it now, in case the transplant did not result in the desired remission. It was their faith that helped them focus on Vashti's future without knowing what it held. June wondered how people survived tragedy in life without believing in the Creator's energy of love, which, she felt, had the power to sustain individuals during any hell on this earth as it now sustained their hope for Vashti's remission.

The first thing June and Conor did about Vashti's inheritance was buy her a beautiful house in the North Valley of Albuquerque, in an older residential area close to the Rio Grande, with large stately oak trees. By the time they moved her things from her downtown apartment to the new house, Vashti was feeling well enough to stay there until the date of the transplant in Houston. Her excitement as she first stepped inside her own house filled their hearts with joy. Over the following days, Vashti added personal touches to the furnishings and décor, and exercised and meditated there each day to increase her physical and mental strength while waiting for her transplant. She relished time alone for grounding herself and soul searching when she didn't have visitors, such as her parents, Dr. Lomas, and other close friends who came to admire her house and offer support.

One day when June visited she found Vashti in the sitting room looking at old photographs. "You seem to have saved every picture you have taken over the years," June remarked.

Pointing at one photograph, Vashti replied, "This guy was a complete nerd in high school. One night I went to a school dance with some friends and noticed him leaning against a wall with a sad expression, so I asked him to dance. He was so shy that at first I thought he would say no, in which case I would have physically pulled him to the dance floor. But he surprised me and walked right out there. He wasn't a bad dancer, but I could tell he was nervous. When the song ended, he started to bolt, but I grabbed his arm and asked if he wanted to keep dancing. We danced to three or four more songs, then his nervousness disappeared. By the time we walked off the floor, he was smiling. I talked with him for a few minutes as we each caught our breath. I told him he was good a dancer and that he should never waste his time holding up the wall. We laughed, and then I went back to my friends.

"A few years ago he tracked me down at the DA's office when he was back in Albuquerque visiting his parents. He had gone on to medical school at Harvard and was doing some awesome research in Boston. He thanked me for being his friend, for always greeting him when we passed in the hallways after the night we had danced together. He told me it had given him confidence and brought him out of his shell, able to overcome his shyness and loneliness. He had grown up to be quite handsome and witty. I was thrilled to hear that he was happy, married, and successful."

"This story doesn't surprise me, Sweetheart," June replied. "You've always reached out to those who feel alone or left out. At restaurants you would often spot an elderly man or woman eating alone and go talk to them, sometimes inviting them to join us at our table."

"I know, Mom. I couldn't stand to see them sad and eating alone."

June picked up the small, nearly smooth heart-shaped rock propped next to Vashti on the couch. "Where did you get this?" she asked. "When I pick you up for chemo, you always have it in your hands."

"Gabe, one of my best friends from college, gave it to me on his wedding day. He said he had carried it in his pocket for most of his life and that it had brought him good luck—he had met the girl of his dreams and married her. He told me he wanted me to have the good luck now. Gabe was one of the most wonderful people I've ever met. He was deep and spiritual, and we had the longest talks about energy forces, gods, faith, and various world beliefs. I was so happy for him when he got married, and since he had brought a gift for me to his own wedding, I will always treasure it."

June, moved by the story, wrapped her arm around Vashti. Then wanting to offer support, she asked her, "Do you feel anxious waiting for your transplant date?"

"I'm less anxious having this time in my new house to emotionally and spiritually get it together. I thought I would have one of those special dreams in which my spirit guide gives me some direction, but I have slept so soundly here that I haven't. I think my spirit guide is taking a break to be ready for bigger things down the road," Vashti said apprehensively, laughing at her own comment.

"Well, Brittney will be here shortly, and I'm sure she will have some advice and encouragement to share," June remarked.

"I know she will," Vashti said. "She always makes me feel like nothing is impossible. We planned a sleepover because we've missed them while doing grown-up things, though I don't know if I'll be much fun." June left Vashti buried in pictures and memories, waiting for Brittney to arrive.

Soon the doorbell rang. "Brittney!" Vashti exclaimed, giving her friend a gentle hug. "You even have the same little sleepover bag you always used. Come in, girl."

"Vashti, I'm so happy to see you looking much healthier."

"Let me show you the changes I have made to the house since you were here last. The front bedroom is a study now. I brought in my books and bookcases, and Dad moved the desk close to the window. Then there's the guest bedroom. You'll be the first person to use it, so promise me you'll give me your honest opinion about how comfortable it is and any further changes you would recommend."

"It is beautiful. I love the way you decorated the room in gray. Let me check out the bed," Brittney said as she threw her body over it. "Oh, this is heavenly."

"Get up, lazy girl, I want to show you the rest of my house. They viewed the main bath with its huge tub then the sitting room."

"Oh my god, you've got thousands of photographs out. What were you doing?"

"I was looking at pictures from back when life was wonderful."

Brittney put her arm around her best friend and said reassuringly, "Life will be wonderful again. You've just got to get well to enjoy this beautiful house."

"At least I'm enjoying it now. Come look at my bedroom. Dad got the idea for creating a cool reading area from one of my mom's home decorating magazines. He bent a heavy curtain rod to make a half circle matching the dimensions of the window. Then he ordered these exquisite, flowing drapes; hung them; and placed my favorite reading chair beneath the window. When I read, I can have the drapes open or closed. When they are closed, I can bask in the sun streaming through the window, enjoying my own little sunroom."

"How awesome. Also I really like how your bedroom turned out," Brittney answered, spinning around for a panoramic view of it.

"I'm happy with it. Now let's order a pizza and open a bottle of wine."

"I'm in, but I thought you weren't allowed to have alcohol."

"I'm not. However, I have three bottles of French wine that were given to me as gifts, and I'm dying to taste them. I'm going to at least have a small glass of each one."

Vashti turned on the gas fireplace in the living room as Brittney ordered pizza. Then they opened the first bottle of wine and found it delightful, with Vashti sipping slowly from her glass and Brittney generously imbibing. After the pizza was delivered, they sat together on the couch eating it and talking about some of the crazier things they had done together, laughing so hard they could barely breathe. Then Brittney turned on some music, and they danced around the room talking about the guys they had considered "the one."

"Vashti, what was the name of that wine connoisseur you dated who could tell the year of a wine just by tasting it?"

"That was John. I was never disappointed with his wine selections. I tried to become more knowledgeable about vintages, but I could never outdo him."

Brittney laughed as she flung herself onto the couch but suddenly began to sob uncontrollably. She looked at Vashti beside her and said, "I don't want to lose you."

Vashti put her arm around her friend and, with tears rolling down her cheeks, replied, "You're not going to lose me, Britt, even if I die. I believe we aren't dead after we die. Physically we are a mass of energy, and energy can't be destroyed. Do you remember physics class and the first law of thermo-dynamics? We are divine spirits who are on earth in a physical form that is like a temporary suit of clothes. The physical body gets old and dies, but the divine spirit lives on for eternity."

"Vashti, I can't eat pizza with the divine spirit part of you."

"Heh, it felt to me like you just did," Vashti replied.

"Stop it. How can you see humor in such a potentially serious scenario?"

"Because I feel it's important to be as alive as possible each moment, living life to the fullest. And seeing humor and joy in painful situations allows us to maintain a broader perspective on the totality of life. I'm putting on some Josephine Baker to dance to," Vashti said.

They danced around the room singing to the soulful music. When the record ended, they savored the last bottle of wine.

Now feeling more relaxed, Brittney talked to Vashti about what she had been doing in her photography studio in Las Vegas. During a lull in the conversation, Brittney asked, "Are you scared to die even though you believe the spirit lives on afterward?"

"Of course I'm scared to die. Everyone is scared to die because it involves a journey into the unknown. We fear things we don't know anything about, even here on earth. But the thing is, when we die we don't go into the unknown but back to where we came from before we were born, to our divine spirit's home. This earth life is just a short gig. We all are destined to die, and some even welcome their time to go home."

"You are so young. You aren't telling me you want to go home, are you?"

"I would love to live many more years because there is so much I want to do, but apparently that isn't my destiny, Brittney. When I first found out I had terminal cancer, I was in shock. I couldn't believe that the lab slip had my name on it. Then I went through a period of red-hot anger, wondering what I had done to deserve such a terrible disease. I was mad at everyone and particularly at God, shouting to the heavens, "Why was I even created if I am to die so young?" Slowly, my anger shifted into some strange bargaining, thinking that if God would only cure me of this disease and let me live I would become a nun or refuse to commit another sin. Only much later did I come to accept my destiny."

"You've walked a difficult road."

"It's been difficult, but I've never been alone."

"Of course not. You have a million friends, and your parents are awesome."

"No, I mean even when I am alone I'm not alone. There is Christ energy all around me. It's this amazing love that connects me to everything and everyone. When I was at my sickest, that is what I remembered. To relieve the pain caused by the tumor on my spine, they hooked me up to a monitor and gave me the maximum amount of pain medication without causing a respiratory arrest. Even with that much morphine I was in excruciating pain, but what got me through it was the Christ energy surrounding me. That experience made me realize that death is not something I had to fear."

"You have taken this shit storm and made sense of it."

"I don't know about that, but this loving energy is giving me the will to fight the cancer with everything I've got. If I can't beat it, I'm going to go down kicking and screaming, and my spirit will survive."

"I don't doubt that for a minute."

"We better go to sleep. You have an early flight in the morning, and Mom's coming to take me to another appointment."

They embraced warmly before retiring to their beds. From across the room Brittney whispered, "Love you, Vashti."

"Love you, too, Brittney. Forever."

CHAPTER 13

Vashti had to wait almost a month to be given a date for her bone marrow transplant at MD Anderson. During that time, her local oncologist had been increasing her dose of chemotherapy so she'd have the fewest cancer cells possible in her blood by then. The increased doses, though, had made Vashti sick and weak. She had also lost 11 pounds and now weighed 117.

When June arrived to take her to her last appointment before the transplant, she found Vashti sitting on the edge of her bed dressed and looking in her full-length mirror. "Mom, this cancer is going to take everything from me. It will take my hair, the warm glow of my skin, the curves of my body, and my profession. I won't be me anymore," Vashti stated ruefully.

June sat beside Vashti and replied, "I want to tell you a story. I had a close friend in college who was diagnosed with cancer. I talked to her for hours as she went through treatment. She had long, beautiful hair just like you. She cried for days as clumps of her hair began falling out. One evening while I was sitting with her, her elderly grandmother came to visit. She told her grandmother something like what you just told me. Her grandmother, after a moment of silence, explained that with many physical attributes stripped away my friend might discover who she really was, adding, 'Finding out who we are is what our life journey is all about.'"

Vashti, moved by this view of life's meaning, realized that she had in fact uncovered new parts of herself since her diagnosis. Squeezing June's hand, she said, "Thank you, Mom. I love you."

At her appointment, Vashti was pleased to hear the oncologist, upon examining her, express confidence about the transplant. "*Mamacita*," she said as they pulled out of the parking lot, "let's go to Saggio's for their fantastic cannoli. I think I could eat that."

"Great. I haven't had one in a long time," June replied, glad that Vashti felt up to such a treat.

When they arrived, they picked a table by a window with the sun streaming in. June selected two cannoli and ordered two teas, then noticed Vashti staring out the window. "A penny for your thoughts," June said.

"Oh, *Mamacita*, you'll need to cough up more than that," Vashti replied, teasing. "I was just thinking about places around the world that I have visited with you and Dad. We met such interesting people, ate delicious foods we had never heard of, and had exciting adventures. You insisted we see the main attractions, which I enjoyed though not nearly as much as wandering off the beaten path with no destination in mind."

"I remember," June said, "that you and Dad sometimes stole the itinerary I had meticulously prepared and instead of following it we just wandered around. What I loved most about our trips was that we always returned with parts of those faraway places, giving us a new perspective."

"Yes, much of what I learned about other people and places on those trips deepened my ability to empathize with individuals of different cultural backgrounds at the DA's office. It is partly because of those trips that my short life has been so full. The only major thing I haven't done is get married."

"I didn't know marriage was high on your list of priorities."

"If I had left for California with Jeff and finished law school there, I would have married him for sure," Vashti stated emphatically, still feeling some regret about having missed that opportunity.

"Really? In the many years since, has there been anyone else you would have married?" asked June.

"Only one person, D-Chappy," Vashti confessed.

"Dad and I knew David was one of your best friends at the DA's office, but we thought you were only friends."

"What better person to marry than a good friend?" Vashti observed.

Before work, Jeff sat at his computer and, realizing he hadn't been on Vashti's Facebook page in a long time, logged in. He gathered that she hadn't been out raising hell with her friends recently since there was no mention of parties or sports events. But a lot of people had been thinking about her lately, which seemed odd. Then he came to a post that read, "I know this will cure you." Why did she need to be cured? he wondered.

When he arrived at his office, he tried Vashti's parents' old number but got no answer. He then scanned an outdated telephone book in search of anyone who might have an update on Vashti. He came across the name Marcus, a friend of Vashti's she had called Brother Marcus because she thought of him as the brother she never had, Jeff dialed Marcus's number, hoping it was still current. "Hello, this is Jeff Kaufman. I'm looking for a woman named Vashti Warner. She and Marcus have been good friends since high school," he explained.

A female voice replied, "I'm his girlfriend. Marcus took his boys on a camping trip, but he'll be back in a couple days."

"I really need to get hold of him. Is there a number where I can reach him?"

"Sorry. When he takes the boys camping, all cell phones are left at home. I will give him the message as soon as he gets back, and I'll have him call you."

Disappointed at having to wait for two days, Jeff tried to convince himself that Vashti could only have a minor illness of some sort. Yet he couldn't shake the feeling that something was very wrong. After work, his best friend, Paul, called. "What's up?" Jeff asked.

"I could use a cold one. What about you?"

"Hell, yes. I can meet you at our favorite bar in about forty-five minutes."

"Perfect. See you there."

Jeff hung up, relieved that his friend had picked this night to go out for a couple of drinks. He called Karen to let her know he was on his way home but would first be stopping for a drink with Paul.

When he walked into the bar, Paul was already seated at a table. He ordered a drink for himself and one for Paul.

"You look wired," Paul said. "Tough day downtown?"

"Not really. I'm just worried. You remember me talking about Vashti?"

"Of course. She's the standard by which all other chicks are measured."

"I check her timeline on Facebook occasionally to see what she's doing."

"Occasionally? You Facebook-stalk her, man."

"Well, she's not a big Facebook user, so I end up reading what her friends post. One alarming comment referred to having something done to cure her."

"Of what?"

"I have no idea. There are also a lot of posts from friends telling her they are thinking about her. Almost all our mutual friends have since left Albuquerque except for a guy I called today, and his girlfriend told me he had taken his sons on a camping trip for two days. There is no way to get hold of him, and it's driving me crazy. I have a terrible feeling that something is seriously wrong."

"You still love her. Don't you?"

"Yes. When we were together, it felt like I had always loved her. Maybe I loved her in another lifetime or something. When we broke up, I thought I would be able to forget her. I started seeing Karen, and that made things better. But the truth is I never stopped loving Vashti."

"What about Karen?"

"I love her in a different way. When we first got married, I really tried to make it work. It seemed good for a couple of years, and then I quit trying so hard. We make great business partners but not good life partners. Though I've talked to her several times about getting a divorce, we just keep going on with everyday life."

After talking to Paul, Jeff felt better. Even so, he hoped that when he got home Karen would be busy and he would be able to crawl into bed and pull the covers over his head.

On Vashti's last night in Albuquerque before leaving for MD Anderson Cancer Center, Lia came to visit. They sat in front of the fire in the sitting room and enjoyed a bowl of the delicious homemade soup she had brought.

"Is there anything I can help with before your trip tomorrow?" Lia asked.

"Not really. I know exactly what I'm going to take and just have to pack my bags."

"I'm going to miss you. There is no one else I can go out and have so much fun with."

"I have really missed doing crazy things together, and I count the days until chemo no longer rules my life."

"Do you feel good about this transplant, Vashti?"

"I wouldn't call it feeling good, but I'm ready for it and hope like hell it puts me into remission."

Lia wrapped her arms gently around Vashti, who felt like skin and bones, and answered, "I'm not going to say good-bye, because it sounds too final. You will be in my thoughts every day, and I know your spirit guide will watch over you."

"Thank you, sweet Lia."

After Lia had gone, Vashti lit a smudge stick and carried it slowly through the house in an act of purification and communion with the spirit realm. Next she lit vanilla-scented candles in her sitting room, still strewn with old photographs; sat on her meditation cushions; and meditated, releasing tension in her body and quieting her mind. Then she prayed, "Father, my parents are getting old and sometimes forgetful. I worry about them, and I know how much they need me. As I go through this transplant, give them strength to face whatever the outcome may be. I know my spirit guide and angel will be with me, but my parents need divine guidance as well. I feel the Christ energy of love completely surrounding me tonight, eliminating all fear and bringing me deep peace."

As Vashti sat in silence with the photographs, she looked briefly at old friends' faces. How grateful she felt to have been blessed with many wonderful people in her life who had given her cherished memories.

While slipping into her nightgown, she heard June call out, "Have you gotten ready for bed, Honey?"

"I'm in my nightie and about to set the dreaded alarm clock."

"Is there anything Dad and I can do for you before we go to bed?" June asked, wanting to show her receptivity should Vashti feel like talking about the upcoming procedure.

"No. I'm going to say good night to Bertie then call it a day. See you in the morning. Love you," Vashti replied, wanting to remain in her state of gratitude for the people in her life rather than thinking about her upcoming ordeal. However, she did want to set Bertie at ease before leaving.

When Vashti stepped into her garden, Bertie was already in his house for the night. She poked her head inside and said, "Bertie, I have to go to the hospital to have a serious procedure, a bone marrow transplant. It will take me away from you for a long time, but I will be back. You know I could never leave you unless I had to. I love you over the moon, Bertie." Satisfied that Bertie had somehow gotten the message, Vashti went back inside and fell asleep.

In the morning, she packed two large suitcases for her two months in Houston. When Conor rang the doorbell, Vashti was ready to go. As his vehicle pulled away, she stared out the window at her house with tears in her eyes, wondering if she would ever be able to live there again.

"Sweetheart, I know you are going to miss your beautiful house," June said compassionately from the passenger seat.

"It's not that, Mom. It's that I may never see it again."

"We'll be back, Love," her mom said reassuringly.

When Conor pulled up to the airport, he unloaded the bags and said, "I wish I was going with you, but now that I have my own practice I'm stuck with no one to cover for me." Then he hugged Vashti and said encouragingly, "They don't know the strength of the girl heading their way. Vashti, you are braver than all of us put together. Remember, you are surrounded by our love and the love of the gods. I will think of you every day, and I will be right here waiting to pick you up when it's over."

As he released Vashti, she saw tears in his eyes—something she had never seen before. "I'll be back, Dad. Try not to worry. I love you more than you will ever know," said Vashti, trying to comfort him rather than focusing on her own challenges. Then mother and daughter walked toward the terminal doors, aware that Vashti was now on the most important journey of her life.

CHAPTER 14

As Vashti and June arrived in Houston to begin preliminary appointments before Vashti's transplant, she was painfully aware that another month of Dr. Arman's thirty-six-month life expectancy prediction for her had passed while simply arranging for the transplant. They picked up a rental car and drove to the apartment they had rented, which had been equipped for transplant patients and sterilized with special cleaning products. They were impressed with the two-bedroom, two-bath unit and its lovely surroundings, especially its exquisite landscaping and its gorgeous pool encircled by teak chairs of all shapes and sizes.

Vashti headed to the pool and sat down. "Are you tired?" June asked her.

"No. But I want to savor this beautiful view. I wish I were here for a vacation and able to enjoy the amenities," Vashti replied wistfully.

"Well, you will be in the transplant unit for two or three weeks. After that you will be out of the unit for four to six weeks of tests. You might feel well enough those last few days to enjoy the place more."

"Fingers crossed, Mom," replied Vashti, trying to keep her hopes up.

After resting, they decided to buy groceries to stock the kitchen. In the apartment parking lot, they caught the attention of a young Chinese man. "Excuse me," June said. "Would you happen to know where the closest grocery store is? I'm June Warner, and this is my daughter, Vashti. We are moving in today so she can begin treatment at MD Anderson."

"I'm Paul Wong. I brought my sister here from China for cancer treatment. If you are looking for a general grocery store, there is one three blocks north of here. If you are looking for a health food store, there are some about six blocks south of here."

"Thank you very much," June said.

"What apartment are you staying in?" Paul asked Vashti.

"Our apartment is on the ground floor, number 33," Vashti replied.

"Can I visit later today for a few minutes?" Paul asked.

"Sure," Vashti said, sliding into the passenger seat of the rental car.

They found the grocery store easily, and June picked out some staples. As Vashti's appetite had been poor since she had started the higher dose chemo, they selected ingredients for a variety of mild soups.

When they returned to the apartment, June set Vashti up in a recliner in front of the TV and covered her with her favorite blanket. Soon after, Paul arrived carrying a large bouquet of flowers. "I thought these blooms might cheer Vashti up," he said as he slipped his shoes off and stepped inside.

"They are magnificent. Vashti is watching TV in the living room," June replied, leading Paul down the hallway.

"Hi, Vashti. I thought these flowers might lift your spirits. Also I wanted to welcome you to MD Anderson," Paul said.

"Thank you, Paul. It is a lovely bouquet. Sit down, and I will tell you why I'm here, and you can tell me about your sister."

Meanwhile, June called Conor and updated him about their living arrangements and Vashti's condition. He was pleased that everything had gone well and explained that Juma, their white greyhound, missed her and had to be bribed with beef jerky to climb onto Conor's lap to be consoled.

June found Conor's description of their dog comforting. As she hung up, she heard the front door close, followed by the delightful sound of Vashti's laugher, which she hadn't heard in a long time. When June went to see what was so funny, Vashti said, "Oh, *Mamacita*, I couldn't help laughing. Paul meant well, but he thought I was around his age, nineteen. When I told him I was over thirty, he was shocked and couldn't get out of here fast enough. I almost told him he could take the flowers back." Laughter erupted between them as they sat shaking their heads. Then Vashti continued in a more serious tone, "Mom, tomorrow we are going to MD Anderson to look around, but I also want to visit the Houston American

Cancer Society to pick up some brochures about multiple myeloma and other blood cancers. I think it is in the downtown area."

"With GPS we'll find it," June assured her.

The next morning they drove to MD Anderson, a couple blocks away. They found the office of doctor M, the head of Vashti's transplant team, whose positivity and caring attitude Vashti liked and whose transplant plan she trusted. The floor above his office was the check-in point for transplant patients, and because the staff were close in age to Vashti, she easily warmed up to them. They, in turn, accustomed to having multiple myeloma patients much older than Vashti and often depressed about battling blood cancer, were delighted to meet a young patient with a sense of humor who looked on the bright side, figuring there were quite a few treatment options that could be tried. Tucked away on the top two floors of the building—to protect the weak immune systems of transplant patients from as many in-fection risks as possible—was the transplant area. Here Vashti was told that when admitted to her transplant room she would only be allowed to bring a few personal items, which would be sanitized and remain in the room until her discharge. And all people entering her room would be required to wash their hands and put on a gown, masks, and gloves.

After touring the MD Anderson facility, Vashti and June found the Houston American Cancer Society. A kind lady at the front desk invited them to take whatever booklets they wanted. Vashti selected one about an organization that used the hair of cancer patients to make wigs for other cancer patients. She also took all the booklets available on multiple myeloma, telling the lady, "Most of these have older men, often black, on their covers. Only two show older women. I have multiple myeloma but don't see a booklet with a young female face on the cover. Please request that your board of directors provide at least one multiple myeloma booklet with a young person's face on the cover."

"Yes, I will do that. What is your name, and how can I contact you?"

"My name is Vashti Warner, and my temporary Houston address is 333

Broadway Avenue. I can be reached at 505-821-4233. I would appreciate a response to my request."

"I will get back to you after the board's next meeting two days from now."

When they left, June told Vashti she was proud of her for advocating for others with multiple myeloma despite the trauma of her own recent diagnosis, saying, "It doesn't make people your age want the booklet when there are no young faces on the covers. I'm glad you brought it to their attention."

The next morning they returned to the clinic for the first of Vashti's two days of testing before her confinement on the transplant floor. The requisition slip from the lab alone was longer than Vashti was tall, requiring her to hold it up to see all the tests scheduled for the day. June's heart ached when she realized how many vials of blood would be taken from her daughter's small arm. Vashti, however, smiled throughout the procedure as she counted the vials each time her blood was drawn. At one point, she couldn't resist asking when she would be getting a transfusion to replace some of the lost blood. The technician laughed and told her that despite the many vials, the actual amount of blood taken was much less than one would think.

Mother and daughter then went to a respiratory clinic, where Vashti had several lung function tests. The first one involved blowing into a tube connected to a strange-looking machine, and the second required sucking up as much air as she could from a tube connected to another machine. The person administering the tests was patient while Vashti took several breaks to overcome dizziness and exhaustion.

Following the battery of respiratory tests, the two retired to the cafeteria. There Vashti sipped tea to regain some strength before leaving.

"Mom, let's pick up tacos for dinner. I have been craving tacos all day," Vashti suggested on their way back to the apartment.

"Are you sure they won't upset your stomach?"

"I don't care. I will enjoy eating them, and then I'll just throw them up," Vashti explained, resigned to this new perspective on eating desired foods.

"I'm game for whatever you are craving," June said, and, within moments, had pulled up to the window of a Mexican restaurant and placed an order to go. When they reached the apartment, June set the table for their taco fiesta. As it turned out, Vashti managed to eat two tacos without getting sick. In fact, she seemed to have more strength, and her pain was tolerable.

After dinner, June called Conor to report the day's activities then lay in bed unable to sleep. She prayed, asking God to be with her daughter throughout the bone marrow transplant. She ended her prayers by questioning why such a horrible thing was happening to her kind, loving daughter, angry at God for what seemed like the unfairness of life on earth. Nevertheless, she knew she had to stay strong to give Vashti as much support as possible.

June had just dozed off when a scream pierced the quiet night. She raced to Vashti's room and found her sitting on the edge of the bed breathing rapidly.

"Vashti, what happened?" she asked.

"I had a terrible dream. Please lie beside me for a few minutes."

"What was your dream about?"

"I was in a clinic or hospital, and they were taking me to surgery on a gurney. They told me they were going to remove my heart because it was slowing down. I started shouting for you, but you weren't with me. I tried to jump off the gurney, but they injected a drug into my vein that paralyzed me, including my vocal cords, so I couldn't scream or get away. My spirit guide was there, in the form of a large white bird making cawing sounds that seemed to be telling me not to worry. But the other people present didn't seem to see the bird, much less hear it."

"Honey, that sounds terrifying, despite the reassurances of your spirit guide. Roll onto your side and let me rub your back to help you sleep, We have two big days of tests ahead in preparation for the transplant." While rubbing Vashti's back, June hummed lullabies she used to sing while rocking her to sleep as a baby. Within minutes, Vashti was sound asleep.

June, a longtime fan of dream interpretation, recalled that in dreams a bird, especially a white bird, often symbolized a wish for transcendence. She reflected on the many white birds she had seen in her dreams over the years, representing her wish for transcendence. And she could understand Vashti wanting to transcend the procedure ahead,which was both as life-threatening as the slowing heart in her dream and as beyond Vashti's control, as if she were paralyzed like in the dream. June only hoped the bird's advice—not to worry—was prophetic of a promising outcome and not simply reflecting the spiritual attitude that extends beyond life on this earth.

CHAPTER 15

THE NEXT MORNING WHILE MOTHER AND DAUGHTER were driving to MD Anderson, Dave called Vashti from Utah. Her face lit up when she heard his voice. He wanted to know how the tests were going and the date of her "incarceration," which made Vashti laugh. She explained that while many of her past behaviors could have led to her incarceration she hoped she had outgrown such conduct—or maybe she hadn't, she added. She then told Dave she had two days of freedom left before confinement for the transplant.

"I'm asking for the date because I thought I would get to work on a cartoon or some other illustration for the wall of your new room," Dave said. "Are your spirits holding up?"

"I'm doing the best I can. I'm hoping for a remission after having the transplant."

"I love you, and I'm sending you waves of healing energy. Bye for now." Vashti felt better after talking with Dave. He always made her laugh and look on the bright side of things. And soon she would be receiving a work of art from him to help brighten her hospital room.

After arriving at MD Anderson, June and Vashti attended a class for transplant patients and their caregivers, which provided essentially the same information that had been sent to them weeks before. They next went to Dr. M's office to find out about Vashti's test results. "Good morning," Dr. M said as he entered the exam room. "How are things going so far?"

"Tests, tests, and more tests. I just want to have the transplant and go home," Vashti replied.

"We must be certain about many things before jumping to the transplant itself," explained Dr. M.

"I know. However, patience has never been my strongest attribute," admitted Vashti.

"I understand. You look strong and ready for the procedure. So I have decided to admit you to the transplant ward tomorrow morning, and we will start collecting stem cells tomorrow afternoon. You'll need to have a spinal tap when you leave here, and you are scheduled for a bone marrow biopsy after lunch. You will then have more blood work and an MRI. The last thing you will need to do today is go to the outpatient clinic, where they will administer a medication necessary before we start harvesting your cells," Dr. M said.

"When you do cell collecting, is it a one-time procedure?" June asked.

"Normally we can get the cells we need in one collection, but occasionally we have had to do it more than once. The medication Vashti receives this afternoon will stimulate her bone marrow to produce cells, which should help us get what we need."

"Dr. M, does everybody lose their hair when they have a bone marrow transplant?" Vashti asked.

"The chemotherapy used for transplants differs from the chemotherapy you've received up to this point. Your past chemotherapy did not cause hair loss, but I am not aware of any transplant patient who hasn't had hair loss," Dr. M stated.

Vashti's mood darkened. She had the most beautiful hair and couldn't imagine losing it. But, having read the criteria for donating hair, she at least knew what to do when the inevitable happened. For people with curls, the hair had to be recently washed, straightened as much as possible, banded at both ends, placed in a sealed bag, and mailed. June, as if reading the thoughts going through Vashti's mind, knew that when this happened it would be a terrible day for Vashti, but she hoped that donating her hair would give Vashti a gratifying sense of helping others.

They next went to the clinic for the spinal tap. The area around Vashti's spine was numbed via several injections, each causing her to grimace, yet she did not make a sound. Once the area was numbed, the withdrawal of spinal fluid caused her no discomfort.

While at the cafeteria for lunch, Vashti doubted she could eat any-thing, but June ordered two ice cream cones, making Vashti smile faintly. She ate some of the ice cream then asked June to take her to a lounge for patients, where they were escorted to recliners in a darkened room to help them rest between tests. June sat on a recliner next to Vashti's and read a book until it was time to wake Vashti for the most painful test she could imagine—the bone marrow biopsy.

The nurse motioned June to remain in the waiting area, but Vashti made it clear that she needed her mom at her side for the procedure. In the exam room, the area around one of Vashti's hips was injected with a numbing agent, causing her face to lose most of its color. June's eyes widened when she saw the size of the needle prepared for collecting the bone marrow. She had a fleeting thought of grabbing it from the nurse but instead asked Vashti to squeeze her hand hard while they did the biopsy. The nurse in-jected the needle deep into Vashti's hip bone, causing her face to contort with pain. As the nurse pulled back on the syringe to aspirate the bone mar-row, Vashti screamed in agony and squeezed June's hand so hard that it turned purple. When the nurse finally said she had enough bone marrow for the test, Vashti released June's hand and lay completely still on the exam table, colorless and covered in sweat.

"Help me up, Mom," she whispered.

"Okay, grab my arms. If the pain is too much to bear, let me know and we can stop for a minute," June instructed. June slowly raised Vashti to her feet, carefully pulled her sweatpants up, then sent for a wheelchair.

As June was helping Vashti into the wheelchair, the nurse returned and announced, "You did very well during this difficult procedure. The site will stay numb for a couple of hours. You might experience some dis-comfort in your hip after that. It looks like you already have plenty of pain medication. Don't hesitate to take it if you need it."

"Thank you," Vashti whispered, and June wheeled her off for the MRI.

As a nurse wheeled Vashti in for the procedure, June collapsed in a chair in the waiting area, feeling helpless in the face of Vashti's painful medical tests. She e-mailed Conor about the horrors of the day. She wished he were there to help so she could take breaks to recover her strength, but knew someone had to be making money to pay the bills, and she felt somehow they would get through this.

When Vashti was wheeled back to the waiting area, she appeared lifeless. The nurse explained that they had given Vashti more pain medication to get through the MRI and that she would be very drowsy. Hospital regulations required that she be transported in a wheelchair for the remainder of the day as she was in no shape to even attempt standing.

June bent down in front of Vashti and explained, "Sweetheart, I'm going to take you to the outpatient clinic for that medication Dr. M explained would cause your bone marrow to produce cells. I will inquire whether they can also draw your blood there. If they can, I will then take you home to rest. You have done very well with these tests."

Jeff was at his office desk in San Diego when his cell phone vibrated. For two days he had been waiting for information about Vashti and hadn't slept much.

"Hello," Jeff said.

"This is Marcus. I have a message to call you."

"Thank you for getting back to me. I don't know if you remember me…"

"Of course I remember you, Jeff. Vashti remembers you too, man."

"That's why I'm calling. I read on her Facebook page about having something done to cure her. Alarmed, I tried to find someone who could tell me what was going on and came across your number in one of my old phone directories."

"The news isn't good. I would like to tell you what I know, but you would be better off hearing it from Vashti."

"Marcus, what the hell is wrong?" Jeff asked.

"Vashti is extremely sick. She has gone to MD Anderson to be treated."

"Oh God, she must have cancer if she went to MD Anderson. When did she go there?"

"A few days ago. I think her mom took her."

"I'm going to call MD Anderson as soon as we hang up. I need to talk to her. I need to hear her voice. Thank you, man."

Jeff hung up and immediately called MD Anderson, but was told no patient named Vashti Warner had been admitted to the hospital. They suggested checking back the next day. Jeff threw his cell phone across his office, shouting, "Dammit to hell!" Jeff was scared to think what must be happening to Vashti if she was at MD Anderson.

Thinking some fresh air would help calm him, he grabbed his jacket, told the secretary he'd be back later, walked to a nearby park, sat on a bench, and tried to focus his racing mind. Within minutes he was lost in memories of when he had taken Vashti home with him to Boston to meet his family, one of the best times of his life. They had both been so happy and imagined they would always be together. Vashti had lived in nearby Cambridge as a baby, and her mom had taken her all over the city by subway, including to Paul Revere's grave. But visiting Boston with Jeff had been a new adventure for her.

He had taken her to many of the places he had enjoyed while growing up. They had stopped at Fenway Park, where he had taken her picture and told her about the exciting games he had attended there. They had also gone to the Northside for the best Italian food outside of Italy, though while visiting Italy with her parents years before, she had had the real thing. She and Jeff had ordered two bottles of wine, and by the time they left the restaurant they were flying high but had walked arm in arm around the neighborhood until sobering up enough to drive home. They had also visited the ocean, for which Vashti had a special affinity. She loved being around water, one of the only things she missed living in the desert.

On their last day in Boston they had driven to Cambridge and found the two-story condominium where she had lived as a baby. It was in a group of condominiums for married Harvard students, called Holden Green, close to Harvard Square and Savenor's Market. Vashti had recalled June telling her that one day she had taken Vashti in her baby carriage to Savenor's, where Julia Child shopped and Julia happened to be in front of them in the checkout line. She had looked into the carriage and remarked that Vashti was a beautiful baby. While wheeling her back to Holden Green, June had explained to Vashti, who at the time was too young to understand, that she had just met one of the best cooks in the world. June had then described to Vashti her attempt to make a soufflé from a recipe in Julia Child's cookbook that had turned out dreadfully.

During their trip to Boston, Vashti had even enjoyed meeting Jeff's parents and brothers despite their idiosyncrasies. She told Jeff that she thought every family was dysfunctional in some way.

Jeff had asked her about the adage that it takes a village to raise a child. She had expressed her view that a village would be an ideal place to raise a family and that she had grown up differently from Jeff, who had siblings and relatives nearby. At the time of Vashti's birth, she had only one aunt and a grandfather, both of whom lived in Montana, so she had rarely seen them. Then her grandfather had died while she was young. When her mom had married Conor, his parents were deceased. Conor had a sister who lived in North Dakota, but with Vashti moving to the Southwest at age five, she hadn't gotten to know her either. June, sensing that young Vashti missed having grandparents, had enrolled her in a grandparents' reading program affiliated with the university Home Economics Department, where a variety of grandparents read fascinating stories to her every morning. Vashti had adored the program and was even photographed for the cover of its annual report sitting in the lap of a radiant old lady with snow white hair named Elizabeth, listening to her read a story. That cover had been the first photograph of herself Vashti had shown Jeff, and he had found it reflective of her natural ability to connect with people, making him love her even more.

CHAPTER 16

WHEN JUNE STARTED THE CAR TO TAKE VASHTI back to the apartment after her exhausting tests, Vashti looked at her and said, "Let's go for a ride, Mom. We can slowly drive through that neighborhood with large brick houses north of MD Anderson."

June, shocked at Vashti's sudden burst of energy after her exhausting day, replied, "That is the best idea I've heard all day. Would you like me to first stop and get something delicious for dinner tonight?"

"I couldn't possibly eat. I just want to roll my window down and breathe the fresh air," Vashti replied.

June drove leisurely through the neighborhood Vashti had in mind, noticing how many of the huge, classy brick houses had ivy growing on the walls. Suddenly she realized Vashti was fast asleep. Not until they arrived back at their apartment did Vashti wake up and, with June's help, make it inside. June took the tennis shoes and socks off Vashti's feet and tenderly held them in her hands, wondering how Vashti sprinted so fast on such small feet. "I know you are looking at how small my feet are," Vashti remarked, "but you have small feet, too, and you told me your mother had even smaller feet. I think you said she wore a size five shoe and still had to pad her shoes to keep them on."

"You're right. I guess small feet run in the family," June concluded.

June retrieved a clean nightie from the closet for Vashti, helped her into bed, then asked, "How is the pain?"

"My hip is starting to hurt, but that's all."

"Should I bring you a pain pill?"

"I don't think I need one. Just lie down by me and talk to me or read me something interesting."

"Well, I started a new book, which is good. I'll read you a bit and see if you like it." June had only read two pages when she saw that Vashti was asleep. She turned off the lights and quietly went into her bedroom to call Conor.

"According to your e-mail, you two beautiful women had one hell of a day," Conor said.

"I barely made it through all the tests; imagine what Vashti must have felt like. Yet she got through them like a champion. I'm so proud of her." As soon as the words left her mouth, June started to cry.

"I can't imagine how difficult it must have been. Don't forget, though, Vashti is strong in mind, body, and soul. Remember how we thought she could move heaven and earth ever since she was a little girl?"

"You're right. It just kills me to witness her enduring so much pain without being able to relieve her of it."

"You can only stand with her every step of the way and shower her with as much love as you possibly can. Love is the strongest force in the universe. It will get you both through this hell."

"Thanks, Babe. I needed to hear those words because this process is so arduous."

"Did you tell me that Vashti gets admitted tomorrow?"

"Yes. We have to be there early for that," June explained.

"Then you should take a warm bath and get to sleep," advised Conor.

"You're right. That sounds like a great idea."

"Call me when Vashti has her room. I love you, June. Both Vashti and I are lucky to have you on our team."

"Love you, too."

June hung up and drew a bath. She soaked for a while then slipped into her nightie. Suddenly she heard a scream from Vashti's room and dashed in to find Vashti on her back in bed, writhing in pain.

"The pain in my hip woke me up. Then slowly a pain started deep in my bones—all my bones. It is now getting unbearable, Mom," Vashti exclaimed.

June gave Vashti two pain pills and lay down beside her as Vashti moved her head back and forth, moaning. More than an hour later, with Vashti still writhing in pain, June called the MD Anderson Emergency Clinic and described the situation to the nurse. The nurse replied, "I believe her pain is from the strong medication she received to stimulate her bone marrow to produce stem cells. In the process, the bones can become very painful. Just keep giving her pain medication as often as it is prescribed."

"I am, and she is still in agony."

"I'm afraid it's all that can be done at this point. As soon as the bone marrow drug starts wearing off, her pain will quickly lessen and her bones will feel more normal."

"Why isn't this medication administered in the hospital, where she can be given pain medication through an IV?"

"Administering it on an outpatient basis keeps the costs down. However, if you feel the need to bring her in, go directly to the emergency room."

June hung up the phone and lay beside Vashti, hoping that her next dose of pain medication would offer relief. After Vashti took the next pills and her moaning softened, June began counting the minutes until the next dose. Finally, June relaxed, knowing her alarm would wake her in time to give Vashti more pills at the start of the new day.

The next morning June slowly raised Vashti to a sitting position and gave her the pain medication.

"Mom, my bones are less painful this morning. They hurt, but I can tolerate it," Vashti reported.

"Wonderful. I will help you get dressed and then take you to sit in the recliner while I get ready."

June helped her into sweatpants and an oversized shirt and walked her to the bathroom so she could wash her face and brush her teeth. Next she assisted her to the recliner and made her a cup of tea. Then June showered and dressed in jeans and a sweatshirt, put blush on her cheeks, brushed her teeth, and pulled her long hair into a ponytail. June told Vashti not to worry about packing a bag because she would come pick up clean clothes for her after she was admitted.

On their way to the hospital, Vashti held her head out the car window. "I better enjoy this sun and fresh air while I can. Even the parking garage is shrouded in darkness," Vashti said.

While wheeling her into the hospital, June received a text to take Vashti to the outpatient clinic first for another injection of the drug that stimulated bone marrow. June mumbled under her breath, "Shit."

She wheeled a sleeping Vashti to the outpatient clinic.

"Honey, you have to have one more injection of that medication," June explained.

"I can't take the pain again, Mom."

"This time you will be in your room with an IV and monitor, and they can give you enough medication to help you tolerate the pain," June said reassuringly.

"Easy for you to say," Vashti responded as the nurse wheeled her away.

When they returned, the nurse advised June to take Vashti up to the transplant floor. There they were met by another nurse, who was escorting them to Vashti's room when her cell phone rang.

"This is Vashti. Oh yes, I remember. Of course I would be willing to have my picture taken. But I'm to be admitted for my transplant today. Maybe they could postpone my admission for a couple hours."

Covering the phone, Vashti said to the nurse, "This is a lady from the American Cancer Society downtown. She has asked me to come have my picture taken for a brochure on multiple myeloma."

"I'm sorry, Vashti, but that is out of the question. We are hoping to harvest your cells this afternoon, and there are too many things to do first."

Vashti replied to the caller, "I'm sorry to say that my admission must take place right now, so I won't be able to come. But I appreciate both your bringing my concern to the board and the American Cancer Society's agreement to act on it. Hopefully you will meet another young person with multiple myeloma and print their photo on the cover of the new brochure so that young people with this illness will be better able to identify with others similarly challenged and not feel alone with their disease." Vashti was glad to have contributed to this development even if her photo could not be on the cover.

The admission procedure went smoothly. The nurse, patient and kind, understood how difficult it would be for an active young person to be cloistered from the outside world for a month. In her room, Vashti could wear her own clothes, but everyone else who entered had to first slip on a gown, mask, foot coverings, and gloves, as did Vashti whenever she left the room.

Vashti and June were impressed with the size of the room, which had a lot of space around the bed for medical equipment, a large bathroom, a couch that opened to a single bed under a window, and next to the couch two reclining chairs. Vashti and June had already decided that June would go back to the apartment for about six hours every night to sleep soundly. They had to balance June's need for rest with Vashti's need for support.

For the next twelve hours, Vashti was assigned to a very friendly and helpful nurse who quickly got an IV inserted so that pain medication could be administered as necessary. A lab tech came in several times to take blood for testing, and then Vashti fell asleep. Watching her sleep, June felt relieved knowing her daughter was now in the hands of experts. Even though she had spent over a decade as an emergency room nurse, June had never cared for a transplant patient and had little experience with cancer patients.

Before long, Vashti's nurse returned and said, "Unfortunately you will not have cells collected today. The lab tests showed that we will have to wait and administer more medication before the procedure."

"Not more of that wicked stuff," Vashti remarked, wincing. "Do you think we will be able to do the collection tomorrow?"

"It depends on how your body responds and the rate at which your bone marrow produces cells. Meanwhile, it is time for dinner, and I will show you how to order your meals. You can order food anytime of the day or night. The food here is excellent. We even have a deli."

The nurse showed Vashti the numbers to call and the menu, which could be viewed on her big screen TV. Vashti looked the menu over and told the nurse she didn't think she could keep anything down. The nurse encouraged her to try some soup and a meal replacement drink. Vashti reluctantly agreed, and June went to get a sandwich at the deli so they could eat together. Vashti was only able to eat half her bowl of soup and part of the meal replacement drink before feeling nauseated and lying back to rest.

CHAPTER 17

After her attempt to eat dinner with June, Vashti dozed off and was sleeping soundly when her room telephone rang. "Hello," Vashti whispered. Her eyes opened wide and she tried to sit up, prompting June to elevate the bed a bit. The next word out of Vashti's mouth was *Jeff*.

Hearing Jeff's name, June backed out of Vashti's room and sat in a chair near the nurse's station. She wondered why Jeff was calling and how he had found out that Vashti was at MD Anderson for treatment. She watched the nurse enter Vashti's room; hang a new IV bag; and emerge, smiling strangely, to say that Vashti had agreed to turn her light on after finishing her call. Hours later, when Vashti's light came on, June stepped inside. She was amazed to find Vashti sitting on the edge of her bed, her cheeks flushed with color and a radiant smile that June hadn't seen in a long time.

"Mom, can you go to the airport in the morning and pick up Jeff?" Vashti asked, excitedly.

"Su–re," June stuttered. "He is coming here in the morning?"

"Yes. His plane arrives at eleven, and he said he can meet you outside the baggage claim area."

"Okay. I'll be here early tomorrow morning and drive from here to the airport," June assured her.

"We talked about so many things. He cried, and then I cried. He told me that he was arranging a flight while we were talking, and he took the first one he could get. Mom, my heart is pounding. I'm so happy."

June sat in shock listening to Vashti explain how Jeff had found her after so many years and how much he still loved her. This news confused June, because she figured that Jeff, probably still married, must have known how gravely ill Vashti was. She worried how a reunion between Jeff and Vashti, after all these years of leading separate lives, would affect Vashti physically and emotionally during such a precarious time.

The next morning when June arrived at the hospital, Vashti was trying to eat a poached egg and toast.

"I'm glad you ordered something to eat. I don't know what you weigh now, but you look skinny," June observed.

"The nurse said I weighed 108 when I was admitted. She hoped I would eat as much as possible before they start the high-dose chemo for the transplant. All the medication has made my stomach upset, Mom, but today I vowed to try to eat for more strength. I can't wait to see Jeff. While talking to him last night, it seemed like we had never broken up or been apart."

"Do you think it is a good idea for him to visit so close to the time of your transplant?" June asked cautiously, not wanting to detract from Vashti's excitement.

"Mom, he told me he needed to hold me in his arms, kiss my lips, and hear my voice."

"Does he know how sick you are?"

"Yes. I told him everything about my cancer journey, and when he heard how much pain I have endured he cried."

"Vashti, is he still married?" asked June, concerned about her daughter getting involved in a situation that could further deplete her energy at a time when she needed all her strength.

Appreciating June's concern, Vashti replied, "He and Karen are married, but they haven't been happy for years. They have been buying houses in San Diego, fixing them up, and leasing them. They have a great business relationship in their real estate ventures, but soon after marrying they drifted apart. Still, they are friends and like working in the housing market. They have talked about divorce but never done anything about getting one."

"Remember how soon he married after the two of you broke up? I was worried about him because he didn't take time to heal following his long-term relationship with you," June confided,

"Mom, men are from Mars, women are from Venus. They are different from women."

"I worry about you getting excited like this when you have so little energy and your transplant is so soon," June confessed.

"Don't worry about it. He is just coming to see me. It will make me happy to see him again."

"I know it will," replied June, aware of Vashti's anticipation of such a reunion despite her own concern about the potential for disappointment if it did not go well.

"I asked the nurse what Jeff would have to do before coming here. She said that after flying in to Houston he should stop at the apartment to shower and change into clean clothes as a precaution," Vashti added.

"Okay. I will drive him to the apartment before bringing him here," June assured her.

Just then the nurse darted in to say that due to the lab results, they would not be harvesting cells that day, and that the next day's results might be better. She told Vashti to walk the entire wing of the floor three times that day. She asked Vashti to keep track of her walks because at the end of the week she could get a bandanna in a color that reflected the total number of rounds she had completed.

Vashti said to June, "I think we should walk the wing right now."

June helped Vashti into a gown, mask, foot coverings, and gloves and walked one lap around the transplant unit with her. Vashti wanted to do another round, but June advised her to take it easy the first time out. So they sat on the couch in the rays of sunlight shining through Vashti's hospital window. After a few moments, she said, "Remember when I was a little girl and first heard about heaven after asking where we go when we die? We agreed that whichever one of us died first would let the one left behind know, through some sign, that they were okay and everything in heaven was glorious. And then we stayed up late into the night imagining ways to communicate this information back to earth."

"That's what we agreed," June replied, marveling at the peace of mind such a message could instill in the one still alive.

"Well, the agreement is still on, Mom. For months I have been focusing on my mortality. I can tell you it is a revelation. Each individual soul, in the words of poet William Butler Yeats, "is fastened to a dying animal." It is hard to let go of all the things we cling to in life. We think they are precious possessions, but deep in our consciousness we know they really don't matter and are only fleeting illusions. I have been attempting to release my grip on such things during my meditations, and I think I'm making progress."

"You are wise beyond your years. I'm sure this cancer diagnosis has brought thoughts of your mortality to the surface, yet you have always been at peace talking about life and death, as if somehow aware that death of your earthly body simply transitions you to new life," June reassured her daughter. Still, June was sad that Vashti felt the need to focus on her mortality at such a young age and wondered how, in this vulnerable state, she might be impacted by Jeff's visit.

When June arrived at the baggage claim area, she quickly spotted Jeff, opened the trunk for his bag, and welcomed the hug he gave her. They engaged in conversation immediately. As they pulled away from the airport, June asked about his family in Boston and if he still enjoyed his work at NCIS. He assured her that overall his life was going well—he loved his job and his parents still drank a little too much but remained in good health. Then Jeff asked June how she and Conor were holding up during this difficult time. June explained that because Conor now had his own law firm it was difficult for him to be in Houston since he couldn't be out of communication with his clients for extended periods of time.

When June drove to the apartment, she asked Jeff if Vashti had told him what he needed to do.

"Vashti texted me that it would probably be best if I showered and put on clean clothes," Jeff replied.

"Good. I will take you to her bedroom and the adjacent bathroom, then I'll rest while you get ready."

Later, when they reached Vashti's door at the hospital, June helped Jeff put on a gown, mask, foot coverings, and gloves then she did the same. After June opened the door, Jeff rushed to Vashti's side and wrapped her in his arms, whispering her name. Vashti buried her face in his chest, and they embraced for several minutes. June was filled with joy for Vashti, thinking that the long embrace must have felt marvelous to her even with a battered body.

As they separated, June cleared her throat and said, "I think I will go down for a cup of coffee and check back with you in a bit."

After leaving the room, she called Conor and told him that Vashti and Jeff seemed to have picked up where they had left off years earlier and that it was as if there were nothing in the world but the two of them.

"I am so happy for Vashti. How wonderful it must have been for her to be held in the arms of the man she has always loved," Conor replied.

"The Christ energy of the universe works in the most amazing ways," said June. "But Jeff told me he had to return to San Diego tomorrow, so he wouldn't have much time with Vashti. I will take him back to the airport to catch his flight home."

"There is nothing else you can do. They will probably just want to talk. Call me when you get back to the apartment tonight," Conor said.

When June returned to the hospital room, she saw Jeff and Vashti sitting on the couch under the window, with Jeff's arm around her and Vashti leaning into his shoulder. To avert any awkwardness, June said to Vashti, "I wonder if you'd like to take a walk around the unit. You could log in one more lap by taking Jeff to the sunny lounge we found on the other side of the unit, the one with two sets of windows."

"That's a brilliant idea, Mom."

Down the hall they went with arms linked, a sight that brought tears to June's eyes. She had never imagined seeing them together like this again in any situation, let alone at a hospital with Vashti so ill. Vashti seemed like a new person, as if her hope had been restored by Jeff's presence.

When they returned, Vashti reported, "Mom, we went to the glass-paneled lounge and sat in the sun. It felt heavenly."

"Good. I'll go run some errands now. I'll come back to take Jeff to the apartment for some sleep and bring him back when he's awake in the morning," June said.

"My plane leaves midmorning, and I would prefer to stay here until the very last minute," Jeff insisted.

Vashti added persuasively, "We don't want to miss a minute of the time we have together. We have so much to catch up on, and Jeff can sleep on the couch. Besides, you need a break, Mom."

Seeing their determination to remain together, June replied, as she left the room, "I'll see you in the morning then."

At first, June sat in the chair outside Vashti's door, reluctant to leave her with anyone else. But then she recalled Vashti's remarks about her meditation focus to loosen her grip and realized she too had to let go of her fears and be more accepting of things as they were. On her way to the apartment, she vowed that she would ask for guidance in doing that.

CHAPTER 18

WHEN JUNE RETURNED TO THE TRANSPLANT FLOOR the next morning, the nurse was outside Vashti's room smiling broadly. Opening the door, June saw Vashti and Jeff asleep, with Vashti lying on her right side in a fetal position and Jeff, also in a fetal position, lying next to her, making it hard to tell where her body ended and his began. As she took in one of the most beautiful scenes she had ever witnessed, tears came to her eyes and she backed slowly out of the room.

The nurse said, "The doctor has already been here. He saw what you just saw, and he didn't want to wake them. He felt it was more important that his patient get rest. Vashti suffers from insomnia, which is a real problem because patients need sleep to recover from major procedures. The doctor will return later, and, based on today's blood work, we will begin collecting cells this afternoon."

"That's good news. The sooner we do the collection, the sooner we can do the transplant," June observed.

"You're right. At noon today we have to begin the high-dose chemo so we kill as many cancer cells as possible before the collection."

"Is this the chemo that will cause Vashti's hair to fall out?"

"It is. However, it might not happen right away. Some of our patients have not lost their hair until day two or even three after the chemo, depending on their reaction," explained the nurse.

Later June heard Vashti and Jeff stirring in Vashti's room and went back in.

"Good morning, Mom. We just woke up and realized it was almost time for Jeff to leave for the airport," Vashti pointed out.

"Good morning, you two. I was here earlier but saw you sleeping and didn't want to wake you. The nurse told me that the doctor was here, too, and also wanted to let you sleep."

"I haven't slept that well in years," Vashti said.

"That is good news because your lab work is back, and they are going to do cell collection later this afternoon."

"That's great. I want to get it over with so I can have the transplant."

"I agree," June said. "The sooner we have it done, the sooner we can get you to outpatient status. I brought all of Jeff's things with me this morning. I'll wait in the sitting area, and Jeff can meet me there."

June read while she waited. When she next looked at her watch, it was only one hour until Jeff's flight was scheduled to depart. She tapped on Vashti's door. Moments later Jeff came walking toward June arm in arm with Vashti. As they approached the elevator, Jeff slowly released her from his embrace, and, as he and June stepped inside, Vashti blew him kisses until the door closed. When the elevator started descending, tears flowed from Jeff's eyes. It broke June's heart to see his agony at having to leave Vashti.

June and Jeff raced to the airport. "I'll see you this weekend." he said, jumping out with his bag and disappearing inside the terminal. June wondered about the implications of Jeff's parting words. She wasn't sure she could take more stress, though she knew that Jeff had made Vashti happy during this visit.

By the time June got back to Vashti's room, the nurses had already started giving her the high-dose chemotherapy. June silently prayed that they would have the strength to get through this next stage of treatment.

Vashti smiled and said, "I'm sorry Jeff and I waited so long, Mom, but we couldn't say good-bye. I remember when you were finishing your last year of law school and Dad was loading his things in the car before leaving for a job interview in the Southwest. It was the first time you two had ever been apart. I was riding my little bike around his car, shouting, "Don't go!" to make him feel as guilty as possible. As I recall, he left over two hours past the time he intended to leave." They both laughed at the memory. June looked at Vashti in awe, wondering how this sick girl could make people laugh and how she could shift attention away from Jeff's tardiness with such an adroit display of diversion tactics.

"I understand. So many years have passed that I'm sure you and Jeff had a lot to catch up on and only a few hours in which to do it," June said compassionately.

"We picked up right where we left off twelve years ago, Mom. We both realized that our love for each other never ended."

"Well, your love never ended, Vashti, but Jeff did get married," June noted, as if her daughter's romantic encounter had blinded her to the reality of the situation.

"Oh, Mom, that doesn't mean anything. His heart was broken, and he ran into Karen's arms. He later discovered that he had made a mistake, and he is ready to rectify it now. They have already talked about divorce."

"So, let's say he gets a divorce. Then what? Vashti, you are fighting for your life. We all hope and pray we can get this cancer in remission and you will have time to revel in life. But..."

"I know what you were going to say, Mom. What if it doesn't work, and I die," Vashti interrupted as tears flowed down her cheeks.

June lay on Vashti's bed beside her and confessed, "I don't want to make you sad, but I'm having trouble getting my head around this whole thing."

"Mom, love is an energy force that can't be denied. It is the energy force that sustains life. It is the energy force that created the world. It is truly the breath of God that holds this whole universe together. Would I want many years to love Jeff? Of course I would. If I only had a few days to love Jeff, would I take those days? In a heartbeat. Love can't be measured by the days you have left to live or by the amount of money you have in your pocket. We are placed on earth to love others as the Creator endlessly loves us," Vashti explained.

"You are a phenomenal human being, Vashti. If the world were filled with humans like you, it would be a deeply loving, peaceful place," June remarked. "It is not only Jeff you love but everyone in your life, even people you have never met. Your compassion was evident when you were a young child, and it has only grown more intense. Remember when you took your first philosophy class at the university and we stayed up extremely late talking about an idea you were writing about in a paper due the next morning?"

"Yes, and Dad found us asleep the next morning by my computer about an hour before the class was to start," Vashti recalled. "I was trying to write about the idea that if we are intentionally a burden to others it is like a particularly grave sin. Our existence requires that we help our brothers and sisters without expecting anything in return. We don't know what their life journeys have been like or how they have suffered. If they are down, we must help them up. Why? Because everything and everyone is divine, and because we are all connected. If one of us is lost, we are all lost, in a sense."

They lay together in silence as June reflected on her daughter's admirable desire to help people both personally and professionally. Then suddenly nausea from the chemo swept over Vashti, and she vomited up everything she had eaten that day. After an hour of dry heaving, she fell asleep, whereupon June didn't move a muscle for fear of waking her from this reprieve.

After another hour, the staff came to take Vashti to the lab for cell collection. She heard their voices in her sleep and said, "Let's go. I'm ready." June followed as they wheeled Vashti to a small room in the lab, containing a chair, a bed, and a glass wall behind which people were seated before large medical machines and computers. Vashti climbed onto the bed, and a nurse placed two heated white blankets over her, making her look like a mummy, while advising her to lie still and talk as little as possible. Within minutes, Vashti asked June to get more blankets because she was freezing. June, who by contrast had been sweating in the small room, returned quickly with hot blankets, placed them over her daughter, and pulled the cooled blankets away. Every couple minutes Vashti was signaling for more hot blankets, which helped until she began shivering again. By the end of the cell collection, there was a pile of blankets at the foot of the bed almost as high as the bed itself.

Finally, the nurse informed Vashti that the collection was over and they would transport her back to the transplant floor as soon as she warmed up. Vashti gave June a high five and said, "We did it, Mom." Once back in her room, Vashti was again freezing, and the nurse assured her that she would get increasingly warmer as her body temperature returned to normal.

As soon as the nurse left the room, Vashti whispered from under the quilt on her bed, "Mom, could you hand me my cell phone?" June held it out to her, then Vashti pulled the quilt over her head, called Jeff, and told him, "The cell collection is over. When I feel better tonight, I will call you and tell you all about it. I love you, Jeff." Moments later she lowered the quilt, smiled at June, and fell asleep. June rested her head on Vashti's bed and dozed off as well.

Later a nurse dashed in to say she had discussed the results of the cell collection with Dr. M and he had given orders to schedule Vashti for another cell collection in the morning. He also boosted the dosage of medication she was receiving to increase cell production in her bone marrow.

"Will I need to have more of that high-dose chemo?" Vashti asked.

"The doctor didn't order more at this point," the nurse replied.

"Good, because it makes me so sick I can't keep anything down."

"Tell me when you are ready to eat, since I need to strictly monitor your input and output. The measuring device for the output monitoring is in the commode, so that is no problem," the nurse advised.

"Do you know what time in the morning I will be taken for the next cell collection?" asked Vashti.

"I think they start picking patients up around nine o'clock."

"If I feel better in the morning, I want to order breakfast—hot cereal and a pot of hot tea—because if I hold that down maybe I won't get so cold during the procedure."

"You can try that. However, when blood is pumped out of the body, the body temperature drops dramatically. Fortunately, when the procedure is over, patients quickly warm back up," the nurse commented.

"Your strength is boundless, Sweetheart. I hope I would be as brave if I ever go through a cell collection," June said supportively.

"Mom, tonight I want you to leave early and get a good sleep. I'd like to call Jeff, and the conversation may be long," Vashti explained.

"Hey, are you throwing me out of here?" June asked, amused.

"Never, but there's no need to waste your time here while I'm on the phone."

"Okay. You have twisted my arm," June said. "I'll tell Conor how strong you were during the cell collection and that you have to do the damn thing over again. I love you. I'll be back early in the morning and ready for anything."

CHAPTER 19

Following Vashti's afternoon call to Jeff, he left his office like a man on a mission, determined to tell Karen that he wanted to start divorce proceedings as soon as possible. He felt like the brief time he had spent with Vashti had awakened him from a long sleep devoid of love. And he berated himself for foolishly marrying so soon after he and Vashti had broken up. Had he instead taken time to sort out his feelings, surely he would have realized that his heart belonged to Vashti alone.

"It's time for us to go forward with divorce proceedings," Jeff told Karen when he arrived home. "We are wasting our lives staying in this marriage any longer."

"What's happened?" replied Karen.

"Nothing. I feel like I've woken up after sleepwalking for years."

"Are you calling our marriage a waste?"

"No. It just lacks the love I need—the love you must need, too."

"Something has changed you overnight. Speaking of which, where were you last night?"

"In Houston, Karen."

"What were you doing in Houston? I believe you forgot to mention anything about it before you left."

"I was visiting a sick friend."

"You expect me to believe that? What sick friend?"

"Vashti."

"Oh my God. I knew it! You have hooked up with her again, and I have been in the dark."

"Karen, I haven't hooked up with any other woman since we married, and I think you know it."

"Well, what were you doing in Houston with Vashti?"

"I went to visit her at MD Anderson. She has a terrible incurable blood cancer, and she is there to have a bone marrow transplant in hopes of re-mission."

"So, what does that have to do with us getting a divorce?"

"Karen, I love Vashti. To be honest, I never stopped loving her. I started seeing you right after she and I broke up. You told me you felt terrible about my having to go through a breakup but since the relationship was over there was no problem with us hooking up. The problem was that it wasn't over. I'm sorry I wasn't honest about that with you, but I'm not sure I was aware of it myself."

"Are you telling me that you want a divorce to get back together with Vashti, who happens to be dying of cancer?"

"Yes."

"Why would you ever get back together with a woman who is dying? Have you completely lost your mind?"

"I love her. I want to spend every moment possible with her. I don't care if it's one day, one week, one month, or one year."

"You are crazy. Do whatever you want. I don't care," Karen bellowed, locking herself in the bedroom.

Jeff stepped outside and gazed at the stars. He didn't want to hurt Karen, but he knew their marriage had actually ended long before. In a strange way, he wished Karen had found the man of her dreams and left the marriage rather than the other way around. At that moment, bathed in starlight, he was sure of only one thing: he loved Vashti more than life itself. Never before had he experienced love's power to so completely transform ordinary moments into transcendent ones.

The next morning, June arrived at the hospital while Vashti was still sleeping, so the nurse suggested ordering her some breakfast. She explained that Vashti had not eaten since the high-dose chemotherapy but had only sipped a small amount of water and a couple ounces of a meal replacement beverage. The nurse informed June that Vashti's weight was still dropping, now down to 102 pounds, and the doctor wanted her to gain some weight if possible. The nurse suggested that if they all encouraged Vashti to eat small amounts they might help reverse the weight loss.

June ordered a poached egg and toast for Vashti. Soon after, Vashti opened her eyes and, grimacing with pain, whispered, "Mom, the bone pain last night was intolerable, and is still bad."

"It should be decreasing with every passing hour as you get that drug out of your system," June observed.

"I heard you order breakfast for me, but there is no way I will be able to eat," Vashti insisted.

"That's okay. If you can't eat by the time it is delivered, we will send it back and order something later."

"I called Jeff last night, but I could only talk a few minutes because of the pain. Would you call him and tell him we are waiting to go down for the next cell collection, and I will call him when it is over?" Vashti asked.

June found Vashti's cell phone under her bed covers and dialed his number. She explained how Vashti had been in great pain during the night because of the medication that increased cell production in the bone marrow and that one of them would call him when the cell collection was over. Then she sat by Vashti, holding her hand.

"When I meditate, Mom, I can tolerate the pain. I'm so glad we have been meditating for many years. Remember teaching me how to meditate when I was young and how much I hated it?"

"Yes. Getting you to sit still for three minutes was nearly impossible. Then a brilliant idea occurred to me. I told you that if you agreed to meditate for three minutes you could skip your nap."

"That got me on board. At the time, I thought the only thing worse than meditation was taking a nap."

"You were a ball of energy from the moment of your birth. I realized that something like meditation would calm you down and serve you well throughout your life."

"It worked. I would never be able to handle this pain without it. You have to transcend the pain to maintain your sanity," Vashti confided.

The second collection went better than the first. Vashti trembled throughout the procedure, but June's quick retrieval of hot blankets made it tolerable. When Vashti was back in her room and warmed up, June went to the cafeteria for a salad and tea, at which point Vashti called Jeff.

"You sound exhausted," she said after hearing his voice.

"I didn't get much sleep last night. I talked to Karen about divorcing, and she got pretty mad. Eventually she went to bed and locked the bedroom door. So I ended up on the couch. Today I'm going to call Paul and ask if I could stay with him for a few days. I can find my own place after this week-end. I just want to focus on getting back to Houston."

"I can't wait to see you, Cookie."

"I didn't think I would ever hear you say that nickname again. It melts my heart."

"I have had the second cell collection. I'm praying they will have enough cells, and I can get a transplant date."

"I'm praying right along with you. I wish I could be there to help you."

"Your love has given me more strength and determination. Your love is the most important thing in the world to me."

"And your love will see me through the things I have to do out here," Jeff replied. "I'm going to call a divorce lawyer today and see if I can get an appointment for Karen and me."

"I know there are no child custody issues, but how will you divide the property?" Vashti inquired.

"When we acquired our first house, we agreed that if we separated or divorced we would split the property fairly between us."

"Remember, that agreement was made when you were in a different position. You may face some opposition now."

"That's why I am going to see if we can agree on a settlement before hiring a lawyer. I think Karen will be reasonable about it. She knows a fight would only enrich a divorce lawyer."

"Hey, be careful with that kind of talk. You are now involved with a family of three lawyers."

"How can you joke after what you have been through today?"

"If I can't laugh about it, then I would have no choice but to cry about it."

"Vashti, I am counting the hours till I can hold you in my arms again."

"Thank God we will be together in just a couple days," Vashti said as she hung up, feeling like their mutual love had become a powerful incentive to fight for her cause and maintain a broader perspective on life.

June came back with Italian ices for them both, and Vashti enjoyed hers, though she had trouble identifying its strawberry flavor. "Jeff talked to Karen as soon as he got back to San Diego. He mentioned his visit to Houston to see me, news that she did not take well," Vashti confided. "He is determined to get the divorce proceedings started as soon as possible."

"It may take him time to get his life ironed out, but you need time as well to get this transplant behind you and recover from it," June stated.

"I know, but I want us to be together as soon as possible."

"That's understandable, but sometimes life prevents things from moving at lightning speed."

"Remember my second philosophy paper, about the premise that life is unfair?"

"I remember that paper and what a struggle it was to fully develop the assertion. Thinking life should be fair is just another human illusion," June observed.

Moments later a nurse appeared at the door to tell them the results were back from the cell collection and that Dr. M had ordered another cell collection for the afternoon.

"I thought it was customary to get the cells in one procedure," Vashti stated.

"That is true but not always the case. We will get what we need eventually, so don't worry. Just try to get some rest before the next round," the nurse advised, closing the door.

"What were we just talking about, Mom?"

"The unfairness of life, I believe."

"How appropriate," observed Vashti.

"We can ask Dr. M why you've had to have so many stem cell collections. He probably has a physiological explanation that will make perfect sense," June said.

"Who cares? Having to go through this three times is dreadful, Mom. Where is your anger about the bad luck we are having collecting these cells?" Vashti asked.

"It takes every ounce of my self-control to keep it in check," June acknowledged.

"If I go into remission, I am going to write a book to prepare others in this situation for what they may face, giving a worst-case scenario—a Vashti scenario—so nothing they encounter will cause them to give up," Vashti revealed.

"That is a fantastic idea which could help a lot of people. I admit we have had a setback collecting cells, but everything else has gone smoothly, so it seems an exaggeration to claim this is a bad-Vashti scenario."

"Mom, why do you insist on taking the fun out of everything?"

"Just keeping a fellow lawyer on her toes."

"I need someone to commiserate with me. When is Dad coming to take your place?"

"That was a low blow. Conor won't be here for several days and will stay for only two while I attend a hearing in Albuquerque. We will have the cells by then, so he will be of no help."

"Then I will have to find someone else to listen to my woes and pity me," Vashti said, with a smirk. There is nothing Vashti enjoyed more than verbally sparring with her mom, even to the point where one of them would leave the room in a snit. After things cooled down a bit, Conor would mediate and everything would return to normal until the next exchange. That was the tenor of life in the Warner household, and Vashti loved it.

The nurse returned and injected Vashti with more medication, after which she went to sleep. Only when the transport team arrived to take her for her third cell collection did she wake up. June sent out a prayer to the universe asking for this to be Vashti's last cell collection. Vashti herself was confident it would be because, as she explained to June, it was the third collection and therefore sure to be a charm. Also she was wearing her Larry Bird jersey, number 33, convinced that her lucky number, three, had magical powers.

By the time they reached the lab, Vashti had become philosophical. She revealed, "Mom, since my diagnosis I have experienced more love and suffering than at any other time in my life. I believe that great love, which heals, and great suffering, which wounds, are both paths to human transformation because they are strong enough to still the pretentious ego. Remember the day I was looking into my mirror bemoaning how this cancer would take my hair, my figure, and the glow of my skin? You shared the story of your friend and her grandmother's observations about discovering one's true self when the body's physical characteristics are lost. What she said is so true, Mom. I look in the mirror and see that cancer has taken so much of me physically, yet something remains: my true self. And that self is beautiful because through suffering I have been transformed. During my meditations, I fall into the arms of the Divine One and I am restored. The depth of this transformation allows me to function from my highest self despite my illness. Even in my unenviable position, love and compassion pour out of me to others. Nothing in the world can feel better than that."

"Vashti, I am so proud of your faith, your heart, your mind, your compassion, and your deep understanding. Listening to you restores me and gently directs me back to the path I have chosen to walk. Thank you," June said, grateful for Vashti's perspective and ability to understand love's power.

As June spoke these words, a nurse came in with the first set of warm blankets, ready to begin the collection. When the procedure was over, she explained that the transport team would be there shortly to take Vashti back to the transplant floor, where warming up would be much easier because Vashti could cover herself with heavy quilts.

"I don't mean to be rude, but I'm praying that I will never have to see you down here again," Vashti replied.

The nurse laughed and said, winking, "Between you and me, Vashti, I don't think you will have to see me down here again."

Vashti's lucky number seemed to have worked since the nurse went on to say that the doctor had collected enough cells and was ready to schedule the transplant. Vashti and June celebrated with another round of Italian ice whose flavor Vashti couldn't taste. The nurse explained that the high-dose chemo had affected her taste buds and that most patients recover their sense of taste, though others, for unknown reasons, do not.

Vashti thanked her for the explanation and told her mom to go get some sleep. She promised that after calling Jeff with the good news she, too, would get some sleep. Then Vashti raised her hand to high five her mom, and together they shouted, "We did it!" Vashti then looked at June wistfully and asked, "If I don't live to write the book, sharing my experience to help others, will you write it?"

June looked into her eyes before responding, "I could never do it justice like you could. You are living it. I could write in detail about everything I have watched you go through, but reading it might be so grim that no reader would opt for this treatment. Also since it would be about multiple myeloma it may not pertain to people with other types of blood cancers."

Vashti stated confidently, "The book would be about treatment for multiple myeloma, but some lymphoma patients have bone marrow transplants, too. More importantly, it would be a book about living life to the fullest, the power of love to heal, overcoming fear of death and the unknown, and transformation to new life—all challenges for everyone. And I don't think that telling the story truthfully will lead readers to reject the transplant option if you portray the grisly parts with humor; in fact, doing so can help readers, especially those who are patients, realize that keeping their sense of humor will help them get through the most dreadful experiences. So will you promise to write it if I can't?"

Seeing how important it was to Vashti to leave such a legacy, June whispered, "I promise."

CHAPTER 20

The next morning Vashti woke June from a deep sleep by calling with an urgent message, saying, "Mom, could you come to the hospital right away?"

June's heart was pounding so hard she had to take a deep breath. "What's wrong, Vashti?" she asked.

"During a dream, my spirit guide visited me in the shape of a woman with long, thick hair flowing out behind her as she ran in the wind. Then she suddenly stopped, and her hair started falling out. The sight of this startled me awake. I turned my head, and saw a clump of my hair on my pillow."

"Don't say another word, Love. I'm on my way," June reassured her.

June quickly dressed and pulled her hair back in a tight bun because she didn't want Vashti to feel bad seeing her long hair. She found Vashti lying perfectly still on her bed. "Sweetheart, the first thing we have to do is wash your hair. Stand in the shower, and I will help you carefully wash and condition it."

Vashti stood under the warm water as June shampooed and conditioned her hair. Next she patted Vashti's hair dry and, after Vashti got dressed, attempted to untangle the snarls without pulling out more hair, using one hand to hold strands of hair about an inch from Vashti's scalp and the other to gently comb through them. Then, with the hair dryer set on low, June dried Vashti's hair in sections.

After turning the hair dryer off, she steeled herself to help Vashti cut her hair. "Love, I think we can gently pull your hair back in a ponytail and secure it with bands on both ends." June suggested. She gathered the hair in a ponytail and retrieved the scissors.

Vashti reached out for them and said, "I'll cut it off myself, Mom," wanting to face this challenge bravely. Vashti looked in the mirror and, with tears streaming down her face, snipped off her long ponytail.

June laid the ponytail on the bed and pulled the ends as tightly as possible while binding them. She placed the ponytail in the special bag and mailer, then sealed the package and asked Vashti, "Do you want me to mail this out at the post office on the main floor?"

"Yes," Vashti replied confidently, determined to have something good come from the misfortune of her chemotherapy. As she stepped out of the room, June heard Vashti sobbing and felt her own eyes well up with tears.

After depositing her daughter's beautiful curls in the mailbox, she returned to Vashti's room and found her sitting on the couch by the window now flooded with sunlight. Vashti said, "You know, I've been focusing in my meditations on loosening my grip on worldly things. I think I will focus now on acceptance, because when I can accept situations as they are I'll have freedom to live more fully in each moment. To be fully in the present is a wonderful way to live."

"This is something I have worked on for years. A person might think it would be easy to live in the present moment because they know it is all they have—that yesterday is gone and tomorrow is not promised," June observed. "But it is very difficult to do."

"Some moments are filled with so much suffering that it is hard to stay present, but I'm going to try to be present in each moment of suffering as well as each moment of joy," Vashti vowed.

Seconds later her phone rang. "Hi, Jeff," she said. June prepared to leave, but Vashti motioned her to stay. "Mom and I just cut my ponytail off and mailed it away. Now I have only patches of hair and bald spots. Could you bring your clippers and shave off the hair that's left?" Vashti asked. "Then all of my hair can grow back at the same time. I don't have my transplant date yet, but I have my fingers crossed that it will be soon.

Call me tonight and let me know when your flight gets into Houston. Mom will pick you up. I can't wait to see you. Love you, Cookie."

No sooner had Vashti hung up the phone than food service arrived with an order of soup she had requested. After taking some sips, she told June, "Jeff will shave my head when he comes. If you remember, when I first met him he was in the air force and shaved his own head every week."

"Shaving is probably the best way to go. You won't be troubled with clumps of hair falling out, and your hair will grow back evenly," June said, approvingly.

"I can't imagine what I will look like with a shaved head, but I guess I'm about to find out."

"I have never seen you bald either. You were born with a full head of dark hair. It wasn't very thick, though, and whenever I set you in the sink and scooped water over your hair, I would marvel at the perfect shape of your head."

As the sun was setting, the nurse came in with medications and good news, saying, "We have a transplant date, Vashti. You are scheduled for next Tuesday, so we will be doing another round of high-dose chemo on Monday. After the transplant, we'll be able to schedule a discharge date, at which point you'll become an outpatient."

"That makes me happy. My boyfriend Jeff is coming for the weekend, so I can enjoy his visit before the transplant."

"The timing sounds perfect," the nurse commented before leaving.

June watched, lost in thought, as Vashti half finished her soup then reached for the memoir lying beside her—*Everybody's Got Something* by Robin Roberts—which June had passed along to her, having found the author, a cancer survivor, to be much like Vashti: tenderhearted, caring, and kind. From an early age Vashti, always empathizing with others, had repeatedly told June about her friends' woes.

June recalled when Vashti had first become a DA and worked on cases with a young public defender she liked. She had loved going on dates with him, then one weekend, while riding his motorcycle to a lake, he had been hit by a car, leaving him with a severed leg. Vashti had been heartbroken. With no money saved, she had asked June to pay for flowers to be delivered to his hospital room. June had overheard her explaining to the florist that the flowers had to be the brightest ones in the shop, to lift her friend's spirits as he had just lost his right leg, then describing in detail how she wanted the arrangement to look. Vashti had also visited him several times in the hospital. Upon his release, the young man had moved to California to be with his parents during his long rehabilitation period. Months later he had written Vashti a thank-you card saying the flowers had made him happy and she had been his only visitor in the hospital. Hearing this, Vashti had spent weeks mortified that no one else from either the DA's or the PD's office had gone to see him.

Aware of the emotional toll Vashti's empathy could take on her well-being, June had tried over the years to impress upon her the importance of recognizing that ups and downs, including tragedies like accidents and injuries, are part of living. Now June wished that her daughter not only embraced this understanding but could apply it to her own circumstances. She hoped that Vashti would at least welcome that the core message of the memoir she was reading—that "everybody's got something"— was a fact of life and that the way people grapple with challenges reflected their strength of character.

June tucked Vashti in bed, kissed her good night, and said, to help set her at ease about the upcoming procedure, "Sweetheart, when I return tomorrow morning Jeff will be with me."

Vashti replied, "I can hardly wait to rest in his arms. Besides, he will make the experience of shaving my head fun."

After June left, Vashti called Jeff. "Cookie, what are you doing?"

"I was just sitting here hoping you would call. I'm all packed for my early flight, but I'm so excited to see you I don't know if I will be able to sleep."

"I feel the same way."

"How do you feel about having your transplant on Tuesday?"

"Partly scared, partly relieved, and hopeful."

"We will get your strength shored up this weekend, and then you'll be ready for anything."

"Jeff, you packed your clippers, right?"

"Packed and ready for use."

"How do you know that you will love me when I'm bald?"

"Because I would love you any way you are. But as soon as you end this type of chemo your hair will start growing back. You have thick, beautiful hair, and my guess is it will grow back more quickly than you can imagine. So don't worry about shaving your head. The secret to looking good with a shaved head is how your head is shaped, and yours is perfectly shaped."

"You don't know that for sure."

"I do know that for sure. Remember how I used to run my fingers through your hair? I recall the day I told you that your head was perfectly shaped. I didn't feel a single bump or indentation."

"I know shaving my head is the right thing to do. It can't be worse than cutting my ponytail off. I knew if I controlled the scissors I could wait until I was ready to meet that challenge directly. And when I helped Mom stretch and bind each end, and pack it for mailing off, I felt I was doing something good to offset my bad experience. Only then did I look in the mirror, have a good cry, and try to accept being bald."

"I wish I had been there to help you through it, but you and your mother are two of the strongest women I know. If anyone could get through something like that, it would be you two. When I get there tomorrow, I want you to tell me what happens during a bone marrow transplant so I'll know what you have experienced."

"I'm aware of the general procedure and the result they are hoping for, but I don't yet know the specifics of how it is done," Vashti stated.

"But you did tell me that you will have that high-dose chemotherapy before the transplant."

"Yes. They are trying to wipe out as many cancer cells as possible before putting my washed, treated cells back into me. I've had chemo before, when they did cell collection, and survived, so I hope it won't be worse than that."

"You are so brave, Vashti. After all you have been through since being diagnosed with multiple myeloma, you haven't once complained to me."

"Complaining about the pain and agony actually makes me feel worse. Instead, I try to deal with things as they come. When pain gets unbearable, I meditate and try to rise above it," Vashti explained.

"I remember how you had me practicing meditation. I still practice, but not regularly. I meditate when I'm really stressed out, and it helps considerably. But I never meditate just because it is a good thing to do."

"I think it has to be a daily practice, because we all need to escape our monkey minds, those jumping thoughts that influence our behavior. Meditation is like a healing balm. After an over-the-top session, you can not only calm your monkey mind but actually enter another dimension, a different level of consciousness."

"It must take a lot of practice to get to that point."

"I never had experiences like that until I had been meditating for many years, though it may be different for some people. I never compare myself to others; I just keep my practice going day by day. Over the years, I have noticed many positive changes in my life as a result of meditation. It is now easier for me to be present in each moment and to feel pure wonder at the craziest things, like seeing a beautiful wildflower while hiking or a strange-looking bird in a tree. All these experiences give me pleasure."

"I want to get back to the practice. I want to meditate with you this weekend if you don't mind."

"Of course I won't mind. Anyone meditating brings me joy because I know they will receive many benefits in their life."

"I better let you go to sleep or your mom will have some words for me in the morning."

"I am getting tired. Love you over the moon, Cookie."

"Love you, Vashti, forever and a day."

CHAPTER 21

THE NEXT DAY WHEN JEFF AND JUNE entered Vashti's room, the loving energy between him and Vashti was palpable, as if time stood still and they were in a world of their own. When June told them she would give them time alone and come back later, Vashti remarked, "That's a good idea, but not until Jeff shaves my head. I want you two to be the first people to see my new hairstyle, the bald-do."

Vashti sat in a chair, then Jeff draped a towel over her shoulders, plugged in his clippers, and started shaving her head, going slowly to avoid nicking her. When he was finished, he looked at his work and remarked, "Great cut and the most perfectly shaped head I have ever seen."

Vashti stepped into the bathroom and minutes later emerged strutting in one of her sexiest garments, as if on a runway. She was wearing deep red lipstick and giving a running commentary on hairstylists featuring a minimalist cut and makeup trending toward bold colors "with a pop," at which point she puckered up her lips for a kiss.

Jeff picked her up in his arms, carried her to the couch, set her in a ray of sunlight, and proclaimed, "I love you more than you will ever know."

June cleared her throat and said, "I think I will leave now." Free for the day, she decided to shop at the mall and relax at a nearby park. While June was in the park, a former prosecutor from the DA's office, Gwen, called to find out how Vashti was holding up. June explained that Vashti was scheduled for the transplant on Tuesday and had been remarkably strong and courageous throughout a series of procedures that could only be described as pure hell.

Gwen remarked that this didn't surprise her. She then told June about an event that occurred when Vashti had first come to work at the DA's office. One afternoon Gwen had been leaving court when she noticed a woman running down the street in heavy traffic after a confused little white dog, determined to bring the dog to safety. Cars were swerving and tires screeching, and finally the woman was able to get the dog into her arms and run toward the sidewalk. People cheered, and the woman smiled while waving at them. Gwen had been shocked to discover that the woman had run through traffic in spiked heels and was now headed toward the DA's office. When Gwen had arrived and asked the secretary the identity of the woman who had just come in with the little dog, the secretary had explained that it was Vashti, the new assistant DA. Gwen had e-mailed Vashti, "Great rescue!" About an hour later, Vashti had appeared in her doorway and recounted her hilarious version of the rescue story. That was the day Gwen had met Vashti, and she had loved her ever since.

When the call ended, June sat with tears in her eyes imagining the entire scenario. Then she recalled a similar incident that had occurred about a week after Vashti got her first car, at age sixteen. She had taken it to a drive-through car wash on the corner of a busy intersection. When it came her turn to roll down her window and insert money for the wash, she had heard the screech of a terrified bird and spotted a pigeon with its foot caught in the metal arm that rotated back and forth spraying water. Putting her car in park, she had gone into the establishment and asked for assistance or at least a ladder to help get the bird untangled, explaining that if she drove through the car wash the bird's leg would surely break. The owner, busy with customers, had shouted at a young assistant to get a ladder from the basement. Vashti, meanwhile, had called June and asked her to bring a box and a screwdriver as quickly as possible. By the time Vashti had returned to her car, a rough-looking man about three cars back was shouting for her to get the hell out of the way. No sooner had she looked him in the eyes and given him the finger than the assistant had appeared with the ladder and, simultaneously, June had pulled up with one of Conor's shoe boxes and a screwdriver. Climbing the ladder and noticing the pigeon had one toe caught in the device, Vashti had managed to pry the spray mechanism clear of the bird's toe, and the terrified pigeon had flown to freedom. Then Vashti had driven to the back of the line to await her turn once again for the car wash, thanking as many people as she could for the patience they had exercised. Reflecting on this incident, June was amazed at her daughter's natural empathy and caring actions for animals as well as people.

During June's absence from the transplant floor, Jeff and Vashti walked a couple laps around the unit and off to a small lounge they had started calling their secret meeting place, one of the few public areas on the floor with sunlight and peaceful silence. There Jeff tucked Vashti under his arm and asked her questions about the transplant procedure. She explained that it was done in her room and that the washed cells would be put back into her body through an IV line. The procedure wouldn't cure her of the cancer but could result in a remission, leading to a longer life expectancy.

"Vashti, you said it was possible to die from having a transplant. Are you scared that you might die?" Jeff asked.

"Sure. I think everyone is scared to die. But I believe that in death life doesn't end but simply changes form. When we die, we go home to our foundation in love, to the energy of the universe."

"I envy your beliefs and your trust in this energy. When you talk about it, you seem to be remembering the place you came from and will be returning to."

"When I meditate, I feel a union with God. I release all that is and rest in the loving Presence. I'm in need of nothing there because I'm complete."

"You are amazing, Vashti," Jeff said, deeply moved by her views on life and death.

Then Vashti changed the subject, saying, "Let's not waste time talking about dying. I want to talk to you about your wife and getting a divorce. I don't want you to get a divorce because of me. If we got back together, you would likely have to go through losing me. That could be the worst agony on earth to endure."

"Vashti, I love you more than life itself. I have loved you since the moment I met you so many years ago." Jeff paused and rested his face in his hands then added, "The biggest mistake I have made in my life was walking away from our relationship. I was young and crazy. All I could think of was having you with me and making love to you. Now I know I want to spend the rest of my life with you, however long that may be. If I get hit by a bus three months from now, you would be devastated. If this cancer kills you three months from now, I would be devastated. But it wouldn't change how I felt. Am I willing to suffer that plight? Damn right I am. We must base our decision not on the amount of time we will have together but on the quality of our time together. I believe this transplant, the aggressive treatment you are receiving, the strength of our love, and the mercy of God will give us some time. Will it be enough? Never, because even a lifetime of your love would not be enough for me. But I'm willing to take whatever time we're given."

Vashti buried her face in his chest, and soon they fell peacefully asleep. Only when the nurse came to give Vashti her medication did they wake up and return to Vashti's room, where the nurse suggested they order something to eat.

"I'm hungry," Jeff said. "How about you, Vashti?"

"I'll try to eat, but I get nauseated and can't taste anything."

"Why can't you taste?" Jeff asked.

The nurse answered for Vashti. "The high-dose chemo affects patients' taste buds. Some quickly regain their sense of taste; others never do."

"Vashti will be one who regains it. She loves to eat yummy food," Jeff asserted, in a tone of hopefulness.

"I have been nauseated so much of the time here that eating is difficult, and I think it would be even if I could taste the food," Vashti commented.

"Well, let's look at the menu together and see if we can find something that sounds good to you," Jeff suggested. He jokingly tried to talk Vashti into sampling one of everything on the menu and determining which items, if any, she could taste. Then he became serious and ordered a sandwich and salad for himself, as well as a bowl of soup, a meal replacement drink, a banana, and a hot fudge sundae for Vashti.

While waiting for the food, they caught up on some details of their lives. Jeff told Vashti about the people he worked with, saying that they also socialized outside of work, often going on hikes or to baseball games, concerts, or parties. He said he knew Vashti would enjoy these people and that they would love her. Vashti told Jeff she didn't really like the private practice she had recently joined to learn bankruptcy law and that when she could return to work she would either go back to the DA's office or look for an interesting position in the public sector. She had determined that life was too short to be spending so much time on tasks that didn't interest her, even if the pay was better and that working in the public sector provided more opportunities to help people in need of support—one of her aims in life.

When the food was delivered, Jeff laid it out across the bed as if they were having a picnic. Then he held spoonfuls of soup up to Vashti's mouth, and with his encouragement she nearly finished the entire bowl. She also drank half of the meal replacement beverage, had two bites of the banana, and swallowed two spoonfuls of hot fudge sundae. Jeff remarked, "We screwed up. We should have started with the hot fudge sundae so you could have enjoyed more of it."

After they finished eating, Jeff took Vashti for a couple more laps around the unit. Then they napped until June called. Vashti answered and quickly told her, "You don't have to come back tonight. Jeff and I are going to watch a movie." Jeff ordered popcorn and two Cokes before they settled in to watch the film.

June returned to the apartment and called Conor. "Hi, Honey. Is this a good time to talk?" she asked.

"It is a perfect time. I've walked and fed our wonderful greyhounds, and I am sitting on the couch with them reading the paper. What are you doing?"

"I'm calling you from bed. I picked up Jeff from the airport and haven't been back to visit Vashti since."

"That sounds like just what the doctor ordered."

"I didn't realize how much I needed a break. I went to the mall to look for a new outfit for Vashti to wear when she's released. Then I went to a splendid park and sat on a bench in the sun reading. I feel like a new woman."

"Speaking of Jeff, how are things going?"

"I can only assume very well. When I didn't hear from them for a long time, I called. They had been doing laps around the unit, having a picnic, and were getting ready to watch a movie. Vashti said to tell you that she sends you hugs and kisses."

"I think that's great. You are getting a break, and Vashti is happy in the arms of the love of her life."

"Do you think he is aware of how sick Vashti is? I can't understand why he would do this knowing that if they get back together he could end up losing her sooner rather than later," June said.

"I doubt Vashti would hide the gravity of her situation from him. She is very direct and truthful," Conor replied. "Maybe he is doing this because he loves her so much that he wants to experience whatever time they have together. This transplant could put Vashti into remission, and no one knows how long such a remission would last. I hope like hell it lasts a long time. Don't worry, June. Let unfold whatever is unfolding. They are no longer kids. It is up to them to decide what to do. They are so in love. In fact, I don't think they ever quit loving each other."

"That is probably true. I'm happy for them, Conor. Their love is strong, a once-in-a-lifetime kind of love. I pray that they have time together to enjoy it," June stated.

"We are all praying that will come to pass."

"I love you, Conor. You're my hero, my Rock of Gibraltar, the yang to

my yin. I can't imagine having to get through something like this without you."

"I feel the same way, June. We are blessed to have each other. And
Vashti and I know that you are the captain of the Warner Team. I don't know
what we would do without you at the helm."

"I will call you late tomorrow night once I've taken Jeff to the airport."

After hanging up, June prayed and meditated, desperately needing the
peace she knew it would bring. Then she slept until her phone rang.

"Hello," June said in a sleepy voice.

"Good morning, Mom. I wanted to let you know that we have had
breakfast and are getting ready to take some laps around the unit. Jeff
wants to help me get the coveted purple bandanna—the prize awarded
for the most laps. Dad uses bandannas as handkerchiefs, so I want to take
home every color for him."

"He will be impressed when he finds out what you had to do to get
them," June assured her.

"You don't need to come to the hospital until tonight, about an hour
before Jeff's flight, to give him a lift. He and I have so much to talk about.
We have both tried to get the word out to our friends to become bone
marrow donors. Later we're going to compare lists to see how many donors
we have recruited."

"That's wonderful, Vashti."

"See you tonight. I will call you if we need anything."

That evening when June arrived at the hospital to give Jeff a ride to
the airport, she found him in one of the recliners holding Vashti in his
arms. He kissed her one last time and told her he would arrange a long
weekend with her as soon as she was released from the hospital. If her discharge ended up being more than two weeks away, he would come back
while she was still there.

Jeff was in a good mood as June drove him to the airport. "I had a great weekend here with Vashti," he said. "Thank you for helping us have this time together."

"Thank you, Jeff, for making her so happy." June pulled up to the departure area, and Jeff hugged her as he said tearfully, "I love Vashti with all my heart."

CHAPTER 22

WHEN THEY STARTED THE PRE-TRANSPLANT CHEMO the day before the procedure, June was reading *Everybody's Got Something* to her daughter. Vashti's expression was pained because she knew how she would soon feel, despite the anti-nausea medication she had received. But rather than expressing her anguish she said, "Everybody's got something, Mom." June suggested they meditate together, which helped a bit. Late that afternoon Dr. Lomas called Vashti to see how she was doing. He told her that he had sent her a gift, a wireless speaker for her music. She was thrilled, and they planned to celebrate as soon as she returned home.

In the early evening, Vashti sent June for a good sleep so she'd be rested in the morning. After talking to Jeff, Vashti knelt by her bed and implored the energy of the universe to aid her body in killing any remaining myeloma cells so that the transplanted cells would lift her into remission. Then she meditated and felt the Divine Presence envelop her in an embrace of deep peace.

When June arrived early the next morning, Vashti was meditating, so she quietly joined her. Soon the nurse told them that the transplant team was ready to begin. The procedure was similar to receiving several blood transfusions. Vashti lay in her bed as they infused the contents of several small bags of cells, which the relay team outside the room had brought in one at a time after the cells had been heated and tested. When the transplant was over, Vashti slept between dry heaves, which, to June, who was holding her hand, seemed particularly violent. The nurses told her that all they could do now was wait until Vashti's bone marrow started producing white blood cells. Meanwhile, they would be drawing blood regularly to determine the white cell count.

Hours later Vashti sat up and, in a soft voice, asked June to tell Conor and Jeff it was over. June first phoned Conor and handed Vashti the phone.

"Dad, the transplant is over. I'm doing okay," Vashti whispered, returning the phone to her mom.

"Hi, Babe," June said. "Vashti is doing remarkably well considering everything she has been through the last couple days. She is nauseated from the chemo, but she can rest between bouts of intense vomiting. We're waiting for her bone marrow to start producing white blood cells. I will call you later. I love you."

June then called Jeff. Vashti was too weak to hold the phone, so June put it on speaker.

"Jeff, the transplant is over," Vashti whispered.

"Thank God. How are you doing?"

"I'm really nauseated and weak from the chemo."

"I'm sending you all the love in my heart and all the energy in my body. You have been pushed to the bottom, but now you are on the way back up. I know you can do it."

"I love you, Cookie. I'll call you later."

As night approached, Vashti dozed off and slept fitfully, her episodes of nausea gradually diminishing. June finally fell asleep on the couch.

A ray of morning sunlight woke June at 6:10 a.m., at which point she evacuated the couch and returned to the chair beside Vashti's bed. An hour later Dr. M arrived and gently touched Vashti's arm, waking her.

"How are you feeling this morning, Vashti?" he asked.

"I'm terribly nauseated."

"The chemo has caused that, but as it is absorbed by your body you will start feeling much better. We need to wait until your bone marrow starts producing cells again then see how long it takes to get your cell counts within a normal range. At that time we'll start testing your blood for multiple myeloma cells and hopefully find none, or very few."

"When can I be discharged?" Vashti asked.

"As soon as you are stable. I would guess in a couple of weeks if things go well," Dr. M said. His comment brought a smile to Vashti's face.

When Dr. M left, June told Vashti that she would help her walk if she was up to it. Vashti agreed, but she was so weak she had to take frequent breaks. By the end of the day, she was able to eat Jell-O and an Italian ice. Later in the evening Vashti sent June to the apartment to sleep, promising she, too, would sleep after calling Jeff.

The next morning June didn't get to the hospital until 8:30 a.m. Vashti was awake and had eaten an egg and half a small bowl of applesauce. She told June, "I didn't get much sleep last night. The nurses kept coming in, and even though they used flashlights they woke me up. There are no white cells yet, but they will hopefully show up today. The nurse said once my bone marrow starts producing cells the counts can come up quickly. Keep your fingers crossed."

During the day, Vashti and June read, walked, and meditated, but by the time June was ready to leave for the night Vashti's bone marrow had still not produced white blood cells. It took several more days for her bone marrow to become active and for her cell counts to rise. Meanwhile, she tried to ride an exercise bike in the hall two or three times a day. One morning a doctor seeing her on the bike asked where she was headed so fast. She told him she was riding to Galveston to walk along the shore of the Gulf of Mexico. He chuckled and told her that unfortunately she was riding in the wrong direction and had better turn the bike around.

Finally, the morning came when a nurse gave Vashti the news she had been waiting to hear—that she was to be discharged the following day and become an outpatient. As an outpatient, she would need to remain within a thirty-mile radius of the hospital and come to the hospital every day for testing and appointments. Vashti called Jeff with the news, and he said he would leave after work on Friday and could be with her until Tuesday morning, lifting Vashti's spirits.

Before leaving the hospital, Vashti saw Dr. M, who was encouraged by her progress. He told her some cancer cells had been detected in her blood work and that he would put her on a light chemo medication, which should solve the problem. Hearing that cancer cells were back after all she had endured to rid her body of them broke her heart. "I had hoped there would be no cancer cells in my blood after the transplant. What will happen if the light chemo medication doesn't work?" she replied.

"I think it will work, but if necessary, we will use a stronger chemotherapy agent to get the result we want," Dr. M replied.

When June and Vashti pulled out of the parking garage on Thursday, they laughed and sang at the top of their lungs. The first thing Vashti wanted to do was go to the park. Once there, they headed toward a very smooth rock that came up to Vashti's waist and was shaped like a laid-back letter *L*. A moment later Vashti was curled up in it, her head tipped toward the sun and her eyes closed. Never had June seen anyone with a more ecstatic expression on their face resting in the sunlight, and she thanked the universe for allowing Vashti such peace and communion with nature.

Once back at the apartment, Vashti wanted to lie down and call Jeff. She promised her mom she would try to eat something for dinner later. About two hours later June picked up tacos from the Mexican restaurant, and when she returned with the food Vashti, with a dreamy look on her face, said that Jeff would be there the next night and she would be waiting to see him in a real bedroom. She asked June what she would be doing then. June looked at her strangely and asked, "What should I be doing?"

"Well, *Mamacita*, you wouldn't have to be here with us," Vashti suggested, coyly.

"In that case I will make myself scarce. I will go to a late movie and then sit by the pool. If I fall asleep out there, I will stay out there."

"Perfect," Vashti replied, with a huge smile, "but you don't have to spend the whole night away, just part of it."

"Vashti, I know I don't need to remind you that your immune system is compromised. Every possible precaution would be necessary," June advised.

"*Mamacita*, don't worry. I know what I have to do," Vashti assured her. She then ate two tacos, which made June happy.

The next morning, June took Vashti to her appointments and lab tests, then to the airport to pick up Jeff. Vashti and Jeff talked animatedly and laughed all the way back to the apartment, where June collected her things and, heading to the pool, told Vashti she wouldn't be back until late.

After June left, Jeff slowly approached Vashti, kissed her softly on the forehead, then her nose, the side of her neck, and her lips. Her kisses tasted like the sweet vanilla he remembered from the past and had longed to taste again for what seemed like an eternity. As their kissing became increasingly passionate, Jeff picked Vashti up, slowly carried her over the threshold to her bedroom, and set her on the bed. He lay beside her and, with his index finger, traced every inch of her face, saying, "You are so beautiful. I love your eyebrows and your big brown eyes. I love your cheekbones and your nose. I love your full soft lips. I love your small neck and your collar bones." He traced around her left breast and her right breast and kissed the space between them. He continued down her stomach and kissed her belly button. Moving toward the lower end of the bed, he held each of her feet in his hands and slowly kissed her up her left leg and her right leg. Then he lifted Vashti's body on top of his and they made love gently, because of Vashti's physical condition, yet passionately. Their climax seemed to last forever. Afterward, Vashti lay on her side with Jeff cuddled up behind her.

"I love you and making love to you. If the world ended at this very moment, I would leave it the happiest man on earth," he said.

"I have missed you so much. I dreamt of us making love like this, as before. And now you've made my dream come true," Vashti replied.

"Let me make it come true again."

"Hey, slow down. I want to savor every moment. Making love with you, Jeff, was always my wildest passion. How did I ever let you go?"

"I'm never going away again. I can't live without you in my life."

Vashti smiled slightly and said, "Well, then how did you live the last twelve years without me?"

"I wasn't really living, but I didn't realize it." Propping himself up on his elbow, he added, "Do you want me to get you something to eat or drink?"

"I would love that. Mom left stuff in the refrigerator. There is a tray behind the toaster. Surprise me."

Jeff went to the kitchen and returned with a tray full of treats—cucumber slices, crackers and hummus, red grapes, celery, and glasses filled with ice and bottled water. They then fed each other, the love between them enveloping them so powerfully that they never wanted it to end.

Finally, Jeff cleared away the tray and helped Vashti get comfortable under the covers. Crawling in beside her, he said, "Be mine, forever and ever."

Vashti looked at him in silence, placed her hands on each side of his face, and said, "Yes." Then tears started to fall from her eyes.

Jeff kissed each one away and whispered, "Please don't cry."

"I'm just so joyful. I have never been happier in my life." They fell asleep in a loving embrace.

Once June had returned to the apartment and prepared for bed, she reflected on the long day. She had placed a call to Conor from the pool, asking him what he thought about the detection of cancer cells in Vashti's blood. Conor had thought that since Dr. M wasn't very worried it must be a situation the doctors could deal with in some fashion. June agreed, and, while she wished there were no cancer cells present, she thought they should be grateful for the progress they had made. Having felt the Divine Presence with them throughout the transplant procedure and silently thanked the Divine One for getting Vashti this far, June prayed that the strongest force in the universe—love—would surround her daughter and kill any cancer cells in her blood. She then thanked the universe for leading Jeff back to Vashti so she could experience the extraordinary love they shared at this pivotal time in her life and receive more support for healing.

CHAPTER 23

EARLY THE NEXT MORNING JEFF AND VASHTI woke up and made love again. Then they lay in each other's arms as he told her about the magic of living by the Pacific Ocean. He promised that when she moved to San Diego she would be ecstatic; after all, walking along the shore almost every night had helped restore his soul and set things in perspective. "I've got to tell you about the green flash," he added, excitedly. "As the sun sinks into the Pacific, its last light is said to sometimes flash green—a rare phenomenon caused by light refracting in the atmosphere. It's believed that once you see a green flash you'll never go wrong in matters of the heart. I've lived in San Diego for over ten years but never seen it."

"I think you'll see it when I am there with you," Vashti assured him.

"I think so, too," Jeff agreed.

Tapping softly on Vashti's door, June announced, "We have to be at the hospital in an hour."

"We are getting up now, Mom," Vashti assured her.

June made coffee and prepared a plate of fresh fruit, along with croissants and two flavors of yogurt. Then she watched in wonder as the sleepyheads joined her, their faces glowing—something she had never seen before. They ate lightly, only fruit, and then drove to the hospital. There the doctor, again pleased with Vashti's progress, told her that if things kept going well she would probably be released to go home to Albuquerque in two to three weeks. This news made Jeff and Vashti so happy that they shared a long hug.

After the appointment, Vashti and Jeff dropped June off at the apartment and planned their day. Vashti told Jeff she wanted to drive to Galveston to see the Gulf of Mexico. He replied that he thought Galveston was much farther than the thirty-mile distance she was allowed to travel; but at her insistence Jeff drove toward Galveston, with the radio on, windows rolled down, and his arm around her, more uplifted than he had been in years. Vashti couldn't believe how much better she felt when she was with him.

On the outskirts of Galveston, they took a road to a resort on the Gulf, where they removed their shoes and walked in the white sand. Further down the beach they found a bar and grill built on stilts over the water, where Jeff ordered a beer for himself, a lemonade for Vashti, and a sandwich to share. Sitting at a table over the water, they peered through the floor slats, enjoying the marine life that was visible below them. After eating, they spread a quilt from the car on the sand, lay down, and talked.

"Vashti, there's some surprise good news I've been waiting for the perfect moment to reveal. I rented a beautiful place for us to live on the beach by the ocean, knowing you would fall in love with it. I can see you strolling along the beach with the surf surging over your feet, like today."

"Jeff, that makes me so happy. I can't wait to have you carry me over the threshold of our new home," Vashti said, thrilled at the prospect of living near the ocean. "I'm sure it will be the best place I've ever lived—with both the ocean and you."

"I also wanted to tell you that Karen and I have visited a divorce attorney and made a plan to divide the property, so I think we will be ready to file when I return to San Diego."

"It would be wonderful to be together in San Diego. But how do you feel about everything?" asked Vashti.

"I feel relieved and hopeful. I can't wait to be with you."

"How has Karen been during the process?"

"Some days she seems reasonable, and other days she seems angry that you and I are so in love and together again. I encouraged her to see other guys. She needs to start living her life like I hope to be doing with you soon in our beach house. I can see us walking along the beach at sunset and suddenly seeing the green flash. Then we live happily ever after," said Jeff.

Looking at his watch, he realized they had better start back to Houston so June wouldn't have the police looking for them. They laughed as they returned to the car and, before slipping into their shoes, whisked the sand off their feet to avoid getting busted for driving as far as the Gulf.

It was dusk when they reached the apartment. Happy to see them, June called out, "Can I take you both out for a bucket of crab legs?"

"That sounds awesome, Mom. I will lie down and rest for a few minutes first."

When they arrived at the restaurant, Vashti looked tired but ordered a bucket of crab legs and ate half, which amazed June and Jeff. He thought she was able to accomplish this feat because it required eating slowly due to having to crack each leg, but they both agreed that Vashti cracked crab legs faster than anyone else they knew. She had come to love crab legs while in grade school and had perfected her cracking technique over the many years since. She had tried to teach her mom how to crack them efficiently, but June never mastered the technique.

As they dined, June asked them what they had done that day.

Vashti hesitated a moment then confessed, "We drove to a beach near Galveston."

"Galveston. That's at least fifty miles from Houston," June replied, shocked that they had apparently disregarded the medical restrictions.

"That can't be right, Mom. We were there in no time," Vashti exclaimed abruptly, wanting June to think about their adventure instead. "We had a fabulous afternoon walking along the beach; eating lunch in a little restaurant on stilts above the water, where fish were swimming; and resting on a blanket in the sand."

"Being at the ocean together was heavenly," Jeff interjected. "And I told Vashti about a place on the Pacific Ocean in San Diego that I rented just before coming here, which I'm sure she will love."

Hoping they had escaped June's displeasure about the Houston trip,

Vashti continued, emphasizing her food consumption, "We shared the best sandwich, and I ordered lemonade and Jeff had a beer."

But June scolded, "You're both aware that Vashti cannot be more than thirty miles away from MD Anderson. They created that requirement for a reason. Some patients have probably lost their lives being too far from a specialized center that could handle their emergencies. I won't say anything else but this: the restriction could be a matter of life and death—Vashti's life and death."

After several minutes of silence, while Vashti and Jeff absorbed the importance of June's admonition without regretting their magical afternoon at the ocean, Jeff changed the subject. "I thought I would take both of you to a museum tomorrow," he said, "depending on how Vashti is feeling."

Vashti was acutely aware that Jeff had probably conjured up this museum idea to change the subject, but since there were museums she eventually wanted to visit, she replied, "Jeff, are you thinking of the Houston Museum of Fine Arts or the Museum of Natural History?"

"I would be inclined toward the Museum of Fine Arts," Jeff answered.

"I am up for either one," June replied. "Vashti would have to take it slow because her energy runs out quickly, so she should be the one to decide on the museum." Now anticipating their forthcoming visit to a museum June never again mentioned the trip to Galveston.

The next morning when they arrived at the hospital for Vashti's tests, she sat beside a young man who didn't look well, and asked, "Did you just have your transplant?"

He turned toward her with a pained expression and replied, "Yes."

"I had mine not long ago, and I know just how you're feeling."

His mother, who looked tense and irritated, replied, "The doctor said my son is supposed to walk each day, but he wouldn't get up this morning to do it."

Vashti placed her hand on the mother's hand and responded, "I know about those instructions, and my mom was the same way with me. However, they are merely guidelines, and following them depends on the energy level of each individual patient." Vashti then turned to the young man and said encouragingly, "Your strength will come back. It takes a while, but you'll be up and running again before you know it. Some things they do here are over the top, but you just have to roll with it." Then as they called Vashti's name, she stood, held up her lab requisition slip, and shouted, "Like this. It's taller than me!"

Vashti disappeared into the lab, and June noticed a smile on the face of the young man. She was again amazed at her daughter's ability to make people happy in even the worst of circumstances.

When Vashti return to the waiting room after her tests, she announced, "I'd really like to go to the Rothko Museum and Chapel because Rothko is said to have created his art specifically for meditative purposes." Once inside the museum, they meditated, absorbing the energy of the large paintings. During their drive back to the apartment, Vashti commented, "This was the most mind-blowing, energizing, unorthodox, and flat-out coolest place I have ever experienced art." She added that if time permitted she wanted to return.

Later that day she and Vashti drove to the park and sat on the special rock Vashti had discovered. "Jeff, next time we are together I should be home," Vashti mused. "I can't wait to show you my new house. It's in the North Valley, surrounded by large cottonwood trees. The backyard is paradise. There is a covered veranda with a brick floor, which comes off the master bedroom. There is lush green grass except for Bertie's living area, which has a nice sand bed."

"It sounds like you love the place and have fixed it up just the way you want. I know I will like it, and I can't wait to see Bertie."

"I'm ready to go home. I never want to return to Houston."

"Won't you have to come back for checkups?"

"Well yes, but then I'll just be in Houston a day or two each time. I can handle that, yet not a minute more."

"I don't blame you. You have come so far in this journey and done so well. I don't know if I could have handled it like you."

"Don't give me that. You have proven that with determination you can get through anything. Remember when your toenail was infected and you learned the army wouldn't take you if you tried to enlist with an infected toenail, so you pulled it out? I never could have done *that* to myself."

"It hurt like hell, but in a few days it healed up and away I went, eager to leave home."

The two could not stop talking. June, seeing them conversing by the pool hours later, came out and offered to make them dinner, but they wanted only a plate of cheese and fruit to eat outside. June, feeling celebrational, took them a tray with four types of cheese, three kinds of crackers, two varieties of hummus, veggies with two dips, and a bowl of sliced fruit with chocolate dipping sauce, along with nuts, wine, beer, and lemonade.

June was thrilled that her daughter could experience this kind of love in her lifetime, unlike so many other people. She felt she had also enjoyed this kind of relationship with Conor over the last thirty-five years, although many of her best friends were getting divorced. She wondered how couples could spend over thirty years building a relationship and then just call it quits. She thanked the universe for the love flowing freely between her and Conor and between Jeff and Vashti.

The next day she and Vashti drove Jeff to the airport. There the lovebirds kissed and hugged repeatedly till Jeff entered the terminal. It broke June's heart to see Vashti watch him disappear out of sight, but young love was beautiful to observe, she thought.

When Vashti climbed back in the car, she was silent for a few minutes then said, "Let's go to Dairy Queen and get a hot fudge sundae."

June laughed and said, "I'm in."

The rest of their days in Houston passed quickly. The last time they saw Dr. M he said he would send orders to Vashti's local oncologist and, though they had been unable to eliminate the cancer cells entirely, Vashti's current chemo treatment was keeping the cell count low, indicating favorable prospects.

"So I guess I never went into remission. I really was hoping for so much more, Dr. M,"Vashti admitted,

He agreed, saying, "We didn't get the remission we hoped for, but I'm still optimistic because the cancer cells are quite low using a tolerable amount of chemo." He then talked to her about other treatment options, such as a live donor transplant if that became necessary. Despite the disappointing news, as she and June boarded their flight to Albuquerque, Vashti felt good, excited to go home, converse with Bertie, and eagerly await Jeff's next visit.

CHAPTER 24

Vashti beamed with joy as she stepped into her house. The first person she called was Gabby, who said she would visit as soon as she got off work at the university, where she was employed part-time to supplement her scholarship.

After talking to Gabby, Vashti snuggled into her favorite recliner and fell asleep. Moments later she was visited by her spirit guide, who said, "Remember to loosen your grip. Release your attachment to earthly things. They are only dust and will disappear."

Vashti replied, "It seems you are determined to ruin my homecoming, which is downright mean." Her spirit guide laughed deeply then disappeared, obviously not inclined to take her earthly demands seriously. Vashti heard pounding on her front door and thought the spirit guide might be returning to comment on her annoyed response. The pounding, she discovered, was Gabby at the door.

"Vashti, I'm so glad you're back!" exclaimed Gabby, with an armful of fresh flowers.

Vashti hugged her and replied, "Gabby, you are growing into the most beautiful woman in the world, and I, stuck on a transplant floor in Houston, am missing your transition." They giggled with joy at the chance to be together once more.

Gabby said, "Tell me where your vases are, and I will create a big bouquet for you."

"Come in the kitchen, and if you can reach the vases in my upper cabinet we will create an arrangement together."

When their lovely arrangement was complete, Gabby said, "I know you always have fruit and veggies in your refrigerator, so let me make smoothies for us."

"I don't know if I will be able to keep anything down, but I will try," Vashti replied.

"Vashti, you must try. You are so skinny that I hardly recognized you when you opened the door."

"You have twisted my arm. You are the bartender today, so create whatever flavor tastes best to you. When the smoothies are ready, we can enjoy them in lawn chairs on the veranda," Vashti replied, hoping Gabby's encouragement would help her drink one.

"I am so glad you survived the ordeal in Houston and are now back with us looking even better than Halle Berry but very skinny. Tell me what happened," Gabby urged, handing her friend a drink on the veranda.

"The procedure wasn't bad, but all the preparatory testing was another story. I made it through everything with Mom's assistance."

"Are you in remission?"

"That's not the best part of my tale. Soon after the transplant they started seeing myeloma cells, so I had to begin chemo again, and for now it seems to be holding that cell count down. I'm taking a low-dose chemo that doesn't have too many side effects, so I feel good; but if this dose quits being effective they will have to increase it."

"And if they increase the dose what happens?'

"My quality of life may go way down."

"I'm not liking any of this. Isn't there something else they can do?"

"I could consider an allogeneic transplant from a live donor."

"But you haven't yet recovered from the first transplant."

"Don't worry, Gabby. I don't have to make these decisions now. I'm just taking one day at a time and enjoying everything about being alive."

Seeing that Vashti had taken only a few sips of her drink, Gabby asked, "Didn't you like the smoothie?"

"I loved it, but I have stomach issues. Let's put it in the refrigerator, and I will sip it throughout the day." They enjoyed the rest of their time together, and as Gabby left she told Vashti, "I'm going to pray for you every day."

After Gabby's departure, Vashti went back out on the veranda to reflect on her recent experiences. Despite the disappointing transplant results, she remained hopeful and, at the moment, felt blessed to be marveling at the grass gleaming below in the bright sunlight. She had never before noticed how vibrantly green and plush the grass was, as if the Creator had fashioned it to be a spectacle with which no carpet engineered by humans could ever compete. The thought inspired her to remove her shoes and delight in feeling the grass under her feet, aware of how her appreciation of mundane moments had been intensified due to her illness.

A week later Jeff arrived, having taken seven days of annual leave to come to Albuquerque. By that time, Vashti felt recovered from the transplant, her hair was growing back quickly, and friends had boosted her morale by telling her she looked like Halle Berry in spite of her weight loss. Their first night together Vashti and Jeff made love and lay in each other's arms for hours. When the sun came up the next morning, Jeff suggested a fun excursion that would not be overly taxing. "Good morning, love of my life. Would you like to go see the Very Large Array, about a two-hour drive from here?"

"What a fantastic idea. I have always wanted to see that radio telescope facility. I have heard it is really impressive."

"It is. We can go at your pace and stay only as long as you want."

When they arrived, they were amazed at the magnitude of radio dishes that, working together, formed one giant radio telescope measuring about twenty-two miles across, After touring the facility at a gentle pace, the two went to the visitor center to see an award-winning documentary narrated by Jodie Foster, which they enjoyed immensely. Once back outside, Jeff spread a blanket on a secluded patch of lawn beneath a tree and, reaching into his backpack for a picnic lunch he had packed, laid out an inviting meal. Vashti stretched out on her back and commented, "The sky seems intensely blue in New Mexico. I'm trying to determine if I never really looked at it before or if I am now better able to appreciate its vivid color. I have been working on releasing my attachments. As a result, I seem to have gained the freedom to be awed by creation."

Jeff kissed Vashti gently on the lips. Then he lay on his back beside her and replied, "It does appear to be a deep shade of blue, I probably have not just gazed at the sky since I was a child. You've reminded me of what that was like—to see with a sense of wonder."

Once back in Albuquerque, Vashti napped while Jeff prepared dinner. As they ate on the couch, in front of the fire, he asked, "Can you taste anything yet?"

"Not really, but I'm imagining that it is delicious because you made it for me."

"I'm in awe of the woman you are. You can't taste food yet you make a delightful dinner companion. Rather than complain about things, you accept them as they are and enjoy what you can. That takes my breath away. I've never known anyone like you." Vashti smiled, resting her head on his chest. They fell asleep on the couch, and only much later did Jeff carry her to bed.

The next day they stayed at Vashti's house, spending some of their time imagining what color to paint the master bedroom. In the afternoon, they set Bertie free and lay in the grass beside him, laughing as he chomped on the blades with gusto.

"At this rate, Vashti, you could cancel your yard service and let Bertie keep the grass clipped," Jeff quipped.

"Actually, if Bertie is left out here unattended, he eats the grass until it is so short that he pulls out its roots, leaving bald spots that make the yard look terrible. So we would have to monitor his zealous chomping."

The next morning Vashti asked Jeff if he wanted to drive south on the interstate to a secret spot she had discovered along the river. "I like to go to this peaceful place to meditate and enjoy the silence," she explained.

"That sounds wonderful," he replied. "I'd feel honored if you would share your secret spot."

When they arrived, the setting was so serene that Jeff loved it immediately. As they lay on a blanket to relax, he told Vashti, "One of the reasons every minute we have together is special to me is that I have missed you for over twelve years." She rolled onto her side, and he snuggled up behind her. Before long, they were sound asleep, only to wake up as the sun was setting.

Vashti observed, "I have never before taken a nap here, and I loved it."

Jeff replied, "I just experienced the deepest sleep of my life lying beside you in this peaceful spot by the river, a nap I will remember forever."

The next evening, they came up with a new experience to share. They invited June and Conor to dinner, deciding to cook a goose from Vashti's freezer.

"Do you think we'll be able to cook this goose since neither of us has roasted one before?" Jeff asked, unsure if their culinary skills would produce the desired results for company.

"Don't worry. I've got a great recipe. We just need to follow the directions," Vashti assured him. Although she had no idea how this dish would turn out, she knew they would have fun preparing it, which was more important, she thought. And indeed they did, while making an outrageous mess.

June and Conor thought dinner was surprisingly delicious and were impressed by Vashti's cooking skills. She told them, "I watched a cooking show where they roasted a goose, and it looked so good when they pulled it out of the oven that the next day I bought this goose to try the recipe. That was months before my treatments, and finally I've done it. Better late than never."

During their drive home, June and Conor discussed how glad they were to see Vashti focusing on new experiences. And they marveled at how inspiring it was to be with two people whose love seemed to magically affect those who interacted with them.

Back at Vashti's house, she and Jeff fed Bertie, sat and talked to him as if he were taking part in the conversation, then let him out of his sand area to enjoy the grass. Bertie stayed close to Vashti, rarely taking his eyes off her. Jeff had no idea a tortoise could be so attached to a human, but Bertie made it obvious that he was aware of Vashti's affection for him. Soon they put Bertie safely back then curled up in bed and talked until Vashti fell asleep. As he looked tenderly at her, Jeff silently prayed he would have many years by her side.

On the last night of Jeff's visit, Vashti took him to a Japanese restaurant for dinner, one she thought he might remember. As they walked inside, he said, "This is where we had dinner when we started seeing each other years ago." Vashti's heart filled with appreciation in response to Jeff's recognition of this place so rich with happy memories.

Once back at Vashti's house, they took a long walk around her neighborhood beside the Rio Grande, talking about their past together and more so about their present happiness and the future they hoped to share. Vashti expressed her excitement about moving to San Diego and her certainty the follow-up medical needs could be handled in a city that size. Later, aware that these would be their last hours together for the foreseeable future, they made ecstatic love, wishing the night would never end.

The next morning Vashti drove Jeff to the airport. She wasn't feeling well, and assumed it was due to sadness over his departure.

"Vashti, I wish you could come with me now. It's hard being without you," he said.

"I would love to leave with you, but you know I can't go just yet. I may need to have more treatment, though I pray to God that won't be necessary."

"I know. I will come back to see you as soon as I can, even if it means taking some unpaid administrative leave. I have money saved, so it wouldn't be financially impossible."

"I love you, Jeff, and that's forever. I had the best time this week. I will never forget the happiness I felt with you here."

"It won't be long before we can be together forever, however long that might be. We will live each moment to the fullest, stretching time in a way." They held each other for several minutes before Jeff turned and slowly approached the security point. Vashti drove home uplifted by the thought that they would not be separated for long.

Conor and June, worried about how Jeff's departure would affect Vashti, had put on their gardening clothes and were busy pulling weeds around her lilac bushes when she returned from the airport. Seeing them made her feel less sad.

Three days later Vashti woke up feeling extremely sick. June made her an appointment with her local oncologist. During their visit, the doctor explained that the recent lab results indicated an increase in Vashti's myeloma cell count and a stronger dose of chemotherapy was therefore needed. On the new dose, Vashti experienced nausea and energy depletion. She mentioned the change to Jeff, assuring him she would adjust to it and everything would work out.

However, after her first few weeks on this treatment her cancer cell count unexpectedly increased again. Her local oncologist called her doctors at MD Anderson to discuss the change. Dr. M suggested a different chemo drug and a conversation with Vashti about possibly having an allogeneic bone marrow transplant, using cells from a live donor. He said he would expect a much better response to this type of transplant than she'd had to the autologous bone marrow transplant using her own cells, and thus a greater chance for remission. Vashti's local oncologist spoke to her at length about having the allogeneic bone marrow transplant, but Vashti didn't know if she could survive another transplant procedure, especially one much more complex than the first and requiring a longer stay in Houston.

While considering this option, Vashti consulted numerous people, including Dr. Lomas. She also discussed it with Jeff, who then researched allogeneic transplants and became alarmed by the many potential problems and the high death rates associated with this procedure. June and Conor were scared when they realized that chemo, administered in a dose Vashti could tolerate, could not stop her cancer cells from increasing. But they had no advice to give Vashti about possible alternatives. Vashti's best friends said they would try the allogeneic transplant because the other option—increasing the chemo to the point where it would reduce Vashti's quality of life—would be intolerable.

After much soul-searching, Vashti decided to go back to MD Anderson and discuss the allogeneic transplant procedure with Dr. M. There she went through a battery of tests. Then Dr. M explained in detail what an allogeneic transplant involved. He told her that the immune systems of healthy people killed cancer cells daily but because her immune system could not do this she had developed multiple myeloma. About six months after a transplant from a live donor, he added, her new immune system could be fully active, killing cancer cells daily—a remission capable of lasting a long time.

He also informed her that during those first six months they would have to keep her new immune system suppressed or it would kill her, so they would bring it up slowly to a fully functioning level. The first one hundred days after the transplant would be the most critical because this was when the most serious complications could occur, including rejection, which almost always led to death and which was impossible to assess in advance. As an added precaution, she most likely would have to take anti-rejection medication for the rest of her life. Dr. M then answered Vashti's many questions, and she said that at the end of the week she would let him know how she wanted to proceed.

When Vashti and June landed in Albuquerque, Jeff was there with Conor to greet them. Thrilled to see him, Vashti ran into his arms. With tears running down his cheeks, he refused to let her go for several minutes.

Conor dropped the two of them off at Vashti's house before driving home with June. On the way June explained what Dr. M had reported, and said, "Vashti now needs to decide about having an allogeneic transplant with high risks. If it works perfectly, she could enjoy a remission lasting a long time, maybe the rest of her life. But if it doesn't work she could experience complications due to rejection, with death likely to follow. How could anyone make such a decision? God help her."

Conor replied, "We are the Warner Team, and we have what it takes to get through anything. We will pray for the best outcome, and the universe will give us guidance. We may even receive divine guidance from trees, as any good Druid believes, and we'll take it without question." June had often told Conor that, based on his experiences in the cottonwood grove by the farm, surely he would have been a Druid had he lived in ancient Celtic culture.

As Vashti and Jeff sat by the fire at her house, they considered every potential outcome of her difficult decision. Eventually, Jeff carried her to bed, saying, "Let me hold you in my arms all night so you can rest peacefully, without further worry. Tomorrow we can talk about your dilemma." Vashti buried her face in his chest and fell into a deep sleep.

When the morning sun caused her to stir, she was still in Jeff's embrace. He awakened too, pulling her close, wishing time would halt so they could remain this way. Vashti told him she felt much better after her sound sleep, which pleased him because she would need strength and a clear head to decide about having another transplant. She kissed him and asked what he would do if asked to make this decision. He looked into her eyes and said that if he had to do it now, he would schedule the allogeneic transplant.

Vashti said that she would make the same decision, explaining, "The allogeneic transplant is the only option I have for going into remission and enjoying the rest of my life with you. The chemo makes me so sick I want to die. I don't want to live like an invalid, too sick to do anything meaningful. To me, that is far worse than death. Plus, chemo is so uncertain. They try this dose and that, and then a larger one. Nor do I want to be a burden to others. Mom and Dad would do anything for me, even give up their professions to become my full-time caregivers if necessary, which would break my heart. They have worked so hard to give me a fulfilling life that I'd rather die than deprive them of a rewarding retirement. I want their golden years to be some of their best whether I'm with them or not. And if I die as a result of having the allogeneic transplant, I will have at least done it to fight for my life. Better to go down fighting than linger on in misery."

"Vashti you are the most intelligent, bravest individual I've ever met. I have never known a person so capable of understanding their own mortality and expressing their appreciation for what they were given in life. You have greatly changed my view of fear, death, and valuing life," Jeff said, holding her close.

Vashti replied in a steady voice, "Jeff, I have never been a religious person, but over the last several years I have developed a spiritual foundation that gives me the strength to face my mortality. I believe with my heart and soul that the energy of the universe, the Christ energy of love, is all that matters, and the rest is just illusion masterminded by our egos. The Christ energy of love never fails us or leaves us. It is with us before birth, throughout life, and in death, leading us home to new life." They lay in silence, certain that right now everything was as perfect as it would ever be during their time on earth.

After a while, Jeff leaned on his elbow and said, "Vashti, can I at least buy you a new Larry Bird jersey, number 33, for the big day?"

"Have you lost your mind? The jersey I have is the lucky one. It's faded and threadbare, but it will get me over the finish line. Remember the story I once told you about the poker tournament many years ago? My friend won a purse of several thousand dollars there while I was standing behind him in my number 33 jersey."

Jeff replied, "And you think that your jersey caused his win that day? You, my love, are the one who has lost your mind."

At this, they both laughed.

CHAPTER 25

VASHTI'S ALLOGENEIC TRANSPLANT WAS SCHEDULED for early September. She had to go to Houston the last week of August for preliminary tests and classes. One of the classes she had to take with June was on caring for her port, a tube that would go into the large vein to her heart through her chest. The port and the area around it had to be cleaned daily, which involved creating a sterile field.

Meanwhile, Dr. M and the transplant team found a perfect donor for Vashti, a young man from Germany. This was exciting news because young males were supposedly the best donors.

Vashti and June had fun imagining what life could be like after the transplant, knowing that if a donor's blood type was different from the patient's, the patient would have the donor's blood type after the procedure. They envisioned several different crimes they could commit, such as robbing a jewelry store like Tiffany's then purposely leaving some blood, which would be traced to the man in Germany, who would have an airtight alibi because he wasn't in the United States when the robbery occurred. But as it turned out the German donor had the same blood type as Vashti.

The day before the transplant Vashti told Dr. M, she wanted the donor's name.

"What would you do if you had his name?" asked Dr. M.

"Well, if things go perfectly I would buy him a great gift, like a house. Or I would marry him so he could become a United States citizen," Vashti replied.

Dr. M laughed and said, "In case you haven't noticed, Germany isn't a third-world country. He may not want United States citizenship, but he'd probably really appreciate a house. Seriously, though, every country has its own requirements about releasing donor names. In the United States, donor names can be released after one year, but I'm not sure about Germany. Our transplant coordinator can give you that information."

Later that day Vashti was pleasantly surprised when the young depressed man she had met in the blood lab came to see her. He had been in Houston for an appointment and, on a hunch, had asked if Vashti was a patient there.

"How nice of you to track me down," she told him.

"I guess this means your first transplant didn't work. I'm sorry," he replied.

"It worked somewhat, but I still needed a lot of chemo to keep my cancer cell count down, which is no way to live. If this second one works, I might be able to enjoy a long remission," Vashti explained. "How are you doing?"

"My bump is gone, and my checkup showed no sign of lymphoma. So I can go back to Germany now," he replied.

"What? I thought you were from Dallas."

"I grew up in Dallas and my parents are still living there, but I went to college in Germany and currently work there."

"You won't believe this, but my donor is a young man from Germany. Isn't it a coincidence? I asked my doctor for his name, but there is a waiting period before that information can be released. In the United States, it is one year. I have no idea what it is in Germany."

"My girlfriend is from Germany and works in the government. I will ask her and let you know."

"Cool. Thank you."

"Thank you for making me laugh after my transplant, when I was feeling so sick. You also helped my mother understand that she didn't have to be a drill sergeant. Good luck with this second transplant, Vashti."

"Thanks. Enjoy your life in Germany. Don't worry about the lymphoma. It is unlikely to ever come back, and if it does you can deal with it then. Life is too precious to waste on worrying about something that may or may not happen," Vashti said encouragingly. Once again he appreciated her advice to him.

Soon the nurse appeared and told Vashti they were ready to start the high-dose chemo. Vashti asked if it would be like the chemo for the first transplant. The nurse explained that it was similar but stronger. Vashti asked how patients lived through it, thinking the chemo for her first transplant had to have been as bad as it could get. When Vashti asked about the side effects, the nurse told her there could be burning both inside and outside her body, such as in the lining of her throat and possibly on her skin. When Vashti questioned how chemo administered through an IV could burn her skin, the nurse said the treatment was extremely strong in order to kill every myeloma cell in her body before the transplant. She added that other side effects were more typical, like nausea, vomiting, and hair loss. Vashti was glad Jeff would be in Houston soon so he could shave her head again. She called him and said she was eager to get the transplant over with, start her recovery, and go home.

That evening June left the hospital early, hoping to sleep as much as possible prior to the next day's transplant. Before going to bed, she called Conor and described the type of chemo Vashti faced this time around, which scared him because he had never heard of anything that toxic. June expressed her amazement at how courageous Vashti had been during the hell she had endured the last year and that she herself could not have tolerated it. She slept fitfully, feeling very unsettled. Early the next morning she left for the hospital highly anxious. As she approached Vashti's door, she heard wailing sounds then found Vashti lying in bed soaking wet and writhing in agony. The two nurses with her informed June that Vashti's throat was severely burned, making it painful for her to swallow, and that they were waiting for a medication that would numb it. June held Vashti's weak body close, rocking her back and forth, then asked the nurse to bring more pain medication immediately. The nurse explained that they had given Vashti so much pain medication it had caused her heart rate to drop to dangerously low levels, so they had to wait a while before administering more.

Finally, the medication for Vashti's throat was delivered and seemed to help a bit. Soon after, the donor's cells arrived by special courier, and the transplant began. Because the pain from the chemo was so excruciating, Vashti had no reaction to the infusion of cells into her body. At this point, June asked the universe for strength to help her witness Vashti's suffering and for Vashti to survive this hell.

When the transplant was over, Vashti's pain was still so severe that she didn't open her eyes. Gazing at the many pumps and monitors hooked up to her daughter and at the two IV stands covered with medical equipment, June felt utterly helpless, unable to relieve Vashti's misery. All she could do was provide love and hope.

June dialed Conor's number and whispered into the phone, "It is over. Vashti did well, but she is in unbelievable pain. Please call Jeff and let him know."

Conor passed June's message along to Jeff, who then berated himself for not being in Houston for the transplant. Although Vashti had told him she would rather have him visit after her discharge, he yearned to be there now to comfort her.

Vashti experienced more trauma when she went to the bathroom and discovered her private parts were also burned, making urinating exceedingly painful. The pain resulting from the chemotherapy caused June to worry that Vashti might not make it. By the third day post-op, however, Vashti could whisper, prompting June to keep her supplied with Italian ice to help cool her throat.

That evening June called Jeff and explained that Vashti could only whisper but would love to hear his voice.

"Jeff, I made it," Vashti murmured, reaching for the phone.

"I knew you would. It is over now, and you will never have to do this again. Last night I walked along the beach searching the skies for the green flash, but no luck. The sunset, though, was so beautiful it took my breath away. When you move here, we should watch the sunset every night on the beach until we see the green flash."

"Yes," Vashti whispered, remembering her awe at hearing Jeff's description of the green flash.

"Do you want me to come be with you through this rugged stuff? I would do it even if I could only stay one day."

"No, not now. Mom is here," Vashti told him.

"Okay, as soon as you feel better. Tonight I will call you back and read you some of our favorite Dylan Thomas poetry, so it can soak into your soul."

"I love you, Cookie."

"I love you, too. Forever and a day."

After hanging up, Jeff cried, wondering why this had to happen to the sweetest soul in the world and why God couldn't help her.

Soothed by talking to Jeff, Vashti was able to get her first good sleep since the transplant.

After a couple of weeks, Vashti showed more signs of life. She was able to walk around her room and converse for longer periods of time, June took the opportunity to relay some news to her daughter, telling her that on the day of her transplant a man and woman had come to visit but the nurse had not let them in to see her. So they had left her a message stating that in Germany the waiting time to find out a donor's name was two years. Smiling, Vashti asserted that she had to live for at least two years so she could track down her German donor.

One night more than three weeks after the transplant Vashti suddenly looked at June and said, "Let's walk. I think I will be able to do at least one lap around the unit." Since Vashti had never taken laps at night, June found the request curious.

Stepping into the hallway, they saw several nurses dash into the room of a woman with whom Vashti had walked before having their respective transplants. "I hope nothing is wrong," Vashti commented.

Soon a cart approached carrying the woman, who looked terrified. She grabbed Vashti's hand and said, "They think I might be rejecting the transplant."

Vashti bent down close to her face and replied, "Don't be afraid. You will never be alone. I will be sending healing energy your way." Then Vashti asked the nurse, "Where are you taking her?"

The nurse replied, "She is going to have some liver function tests."

Vashti told her friend she would see her after the tests, then kissed her gently on the forehead before the nurse wheeled her away.

June looked strangely at Vashti and asked, "Is this why you wanted to take a walk tonight?"

"I had a feeling something was happening. Do you think she will die, Mom?" Vashti replied.

"If she is rejecting the transplant, there is a good chance she won't survive," June answered somberly, thinking that Vashti's inspiring words must have comforted the woman.

Once back in her bed, Vashti sent June to the apartment to get some rest. Imagining how the scenario they had just witnessed could be Vashti's fate as well, June did not want to leave, but Vashti insisted, saying that she would call Jeff then go right to sleep.

June's phone conversation with Conor that night focused on the woman's situation. June concluded by saying, "The lady had a look of abject terror on her face. I felt deeply sorry for her and couldn't help thinking this could be Vashti's fate, too."

"Let's hope the woman is soon better and Vashti does not undergo such a rejection. Did the doctor say when she might be released?"

"He said possibly in a week or two. Vashti really wants to get out of here. Frankly, this has been almost too much to bear."

"I know you need a break, June. I will be there by the end of the week, and you can fly back here to handle your hearing. Why don't you stay here an extra day to rest and visit with the dogs? Juma and Lilly miss you terribly."

"I don't want to be away from Vashti too long, though she is looking forward to having you there with her," June said. She had been exhausted for so long that immediately after hanging up she fell fast asleep. Sleep no longer perked her up, however; it merely enabled her to get up the following day and carry on.

The next morning June found Vashti attempting to eat breakfast. Because her weight had dropped to a dangerously low eighty-nine pounds, she was now required to drink at least three meal replacement beverages every day, whether she ate or not.

June asked her to think of something yummy that could be brought into the hospital. Vashti retorted that she only had vague memories of experiencing food as yummy but would try to come up with something.

The doctor stopped by and told Vashti that if her white cell counts kept rising she would be discharged the following week. She was extremely glad to hear this news and, after the doctor left, remarked with determination, "I'm so tired of being confined. And I have kept Jeff from visiting for such a long time, not wanting him to make the trip until I was back in the apartment. I plan to will my cell counts to keep rising so I can get out of here next week."

Vashti and Conor's time together in the hospital, infused as it was with good humor and storytelling, made Vashti feel like she was at home. When Conor first appeared in her room, her face lit up. "Vashti, I've brought a small gift to lift your spirits," he said, handing her a tiny bundle, which she proceeded to unwrap. "I brought this antique pocket watch to reassure you that you will have a lot of time to enjoy life once you recover," he added.

"Dad, I love it. Set it to the correct time, and put it here, right next to me," Vashti urged.

"Remember, as you were growing up, how you refused to wear a watch and would ask endlessly what time it was?" Conor continued. "I recall exactly when your questioning pushed me over the edge. You, Mom, and I were sitting in a small restaurant in Siena, Italy. Annoyed by your question, I jumped up and shouted, 'Vashti, you simply have to start wearing a damn watch!' causing every patron in the place to stare at us."

"I remember," Vashti replied, smiling.

"We picked that restaurant because it was a prime spot for watching the Palio race, where representatives of the *contrade* of Siena challenge each other in a passionate horse race at the Piazza del Campo on July 2 and August 16 each year. I'm bringing this up to set the stage for a sincere apology for my outburst."

Vashti laughed at the thought that he had told a long story to make a little apology for getting angry in the distant past. But she loved him for his thoughtful gesture.

"Dad, I have been missing our family trips, which exposed us to so much history and so many sights," Vashti responded.

"I have another small gift—these silk roses," Conor said, handing her a dozen red silk blooms.

"Dad, they are beautiful."

Before leaving to catch his plane home, Conor embraced Vashti and assured her that she would soon be a free woman on outpatient status and that he would be waiting for her at the airport on the glorious day of her arrival.

CHAPTER 26

THE CELEBRATION OF VASHTI'S THIRTY-FOURTH BIRTHDAY in the hospital
on November 25 had both comic and tragic overtones. June made the day
as festive as possible by decorating Vashti's room with balloons, streamers,
and birthday signs. She had also bought kits, each of which contained a
pair of crazy-looking black glasses and a variety of flowers and peace signs
to glue on to them. The night before her birthday Vashti and June decorated their glasses, and the next day they asked the staff to vote on the
most outrageous pair, writing their choices on slips of paper to be dropped
into a hat.

That day June arrived with a huge ice cream birthday cake, insisting
that not even an allogeneic transplant could stop a proper Warner family
birthday celebration. Vashti smiled and said she hadn't expected such fan-
fare. The nurse caring for her told her that, coincidentally, it was also Dr. M's
birthday, which amazed Vashti. When Dr. M appeared and wished her a
happy birthday, she reciprocated then sat up in bed and gave him a hug.
June handed them both a piece of cake, and Vashti asked Dr. M how his
family was celebrating his special day. He replied that they were taking
him to his favorite Mediterranean restaurant that evening, then home for
dessert and presents. He explained that his two daughters, who always had
special presents for him, were like night and day, one studying at the university and considering medical school, the other in high school and wanting to become a comedian. At this, Vashti and June both laughed.

That evening, after watching a hilarious movie, June gave Vashti her
presents. The first gift was a framed picture showing a charming renovation
that Conor had made to her house, replacing a sliding glass door between
her bedroom and the veranda with two exquisite French doors on which he
had taped a festive bow. The next gift was a Chinese money card contain-

ing a hundred-dollar bill for every year of her life. At the bottom of the money card were several antique Chinese coins, which Vashti enjoyed examining. The last gift was a stunning white gold diamond necklace to match the white gold diamond earrings she had received for an earlier birthday.

Next Vashti and June tallied the votes from their ugly glasses contest, discovering that Vashti had won by one vote. June conceded graciously and told Vashti that she had always been more artistic, or maybe crazier. June hugged her and assured her that Conor would plan the surprise of a lifetime to mark her next birthday. Vashti countered that she'd had a delightful birthday *this* year despite being stuck in the transplant ward of a hospital, amazing June with her daughter's ability to appreciate positive experiences in the midst of the seemingly endless pain and anguish she'd had to endure.

As June gathered up her things to leave, Vashti grabbed her hand, saying, "Mom, I'm scared that after all the treatments they might still find multiple myeloma cells. What more could I possibly do to get a remission from this cancer?"

The thought also scared June, but she hugged Vashti and tried to reassure her, saying, "Don't worry about that until we get there. Remember, in six months you will likely have a strong immune system that will kill any cancer cells in your blood. Let's just focus on getting that immune system working."

Vashti's remaining days in the transplant ward passed quickly. On her last day there, Dr. M came by and told her, "Vashti, I am glad you are going to be an outpatient now. After a few weeks of outpatient monitoring, we will be able to send you home to New Mexico."

"That will be a happy day," Vashti replied as she envisioned going back to her house and seeing Bertie and Jeff.

"However, there is something I need to discuss with you," Dr. M continued more earnestly. "We have detected some myeloma cells in your blood following the transplant. We have a couple of options. We can wait and see if they increase. If they don't increase, I am confident that when your immune system is fully functioning it will kill any remaining cells. Our other option is to continue chemo and kill the remaining cancer cells now, after your recovery."

Vashti was devastated by this news, considering all she had been through. She turned white and her lips trembled. When she finally could speak, she said, "How could there be cancer cells in my blood after everything we have done to eradicate them? Now it seems these myeloma cells can't be killed and won't stop multiplying until they kill me."

"There isn't a large number of them, but we are aiming for zero. I would suggest chemo, and then we will be done with it," Dr. M said, reassuringly.

"It isn't the type of chemo that I just had, is it?" asked Vashti.

"No. I talked with an oncologist here, and there is a new drug we would like to try."

"Whatever you think is best," Vashti muttered softly, going suddenly numb.

"I will see you before you go home, and we can discuss it again. In the meantime, continue to recover," Dr. M stated, trying to sound as positive as possible.

"Dr. M, a woman whose room was across the floor from mine had her transplant on the same day I had mine, and we used to walk together. She is no longer on the floor, and I've asked the nurses what happened to her, but to no avail. Can you tell me?" Vashti inquired, concerned.

"Vashti, she suffered a rejection from her transplant and died. I'm sorry," Dr. M reported.

When Dr. M left, Vashti sobbed for a long time, both for the woman's death and for her own possible fate. She said to June, "That poor woman. These myeloma cells are also going to kill me. I can't think of any more toxic chemo in the world than what I have been given, and it couldn't kill them, Mom. They can't be killed."

June held Vashti close and tried to comfort her, assuring her that she needed to focus on her recovery and that they would deal with the few cancer cells as Dr. M had suggested.

But despite this encouragement Vashti whispered, almost inaudibly, "I just don't know how much more I can take, Mom."

A few days later Vashti was discharged from the transplant ward to outpatient status. It was getting close to Christmas, so June took her for a ride past the Christmas displays, pulling over twice for her to vomit out the car door. Once settled back in their apartment, Vashti asked for Keva juice, so June left to pick some up.

Right away, Vashti called Jeff and said, "Jeff, I'm in the apartment at last."

"That is the best news I've heard in a long time. I'll be in Houston early tomorrow and can't wait to see you."

"I want you to know that I'm in much worse shape than after the first transplant. Even so, Dr. M thinks I'm recovering at the rate he wants to see."

"Vashti, you need to remember that you have been through a procedure from hell. It will take time for your body to come back. And the handfuls of pills you must take each day probably also make you feel sick to your stomach."

"I've missed you so much, Jeff. I didn't want you to come to the hospital this time because I was hoping to spare you from seeing me during the procedure."

"I wouldn't have minded, but I want to be there when you want me there. I actually want to be with you every minute of the day, you know."

"I want that, too, but I'd love you to save your days off for when we can enjoy them together."

"I've explained to my boss that I want to take unpaid administrative leave so I can be with you when they let you go home."

"That would be fantastic. Can you afford to take time without pay?"

"I have been saving money, so I would not have to visit your dad to file bankruptcy."

Hearing his words made Vashti cry. Then she grinned and said, "Tonight I will dream about being in your arms. Then when I wake up you will be here and make my dream come true."

"I want to make all your dreams come true for the rest of your life."

"I'm so lucky to have you back at my side. I think I would have given up after the effects of my last high-dose chemo if I'd had nothing to look forward to. But the thought of having a future with you gave me the strength to willingly take my next breath."

"I'm glad you did because I can't live without you."

"See you tomorrow, Cookie."

"Love you, Vashti."

Vashti hung up and stayed perfectly still in her bed. There was no way she could have told Jeff about the multiple myeloma cells still in her blood.

June returned with two Keva juices, hoping Vashti could sip them during the night. She now weighed eighty-four pounds and was so thin and frail that June worried Vashti's bones might break if she fell.

"You look better than when I left. Let me guess. You talked to Jeff," June remarked.

"I did, and we are both so excited that we will be together tomorrow."

"I will pick him up, but I think you should wait here for him. You don't have much energy, and you should reserve it for seeing some of the festive Christmas decorations," June advised. Vashti agreed.

CHAPTER 27

THE NEXT MORNING WHEN JUNE LEFT FOR the airport, Vashti was still asleep. June was glad Vashti hadn't insisted on going with her because she wanted to prepare Jeff for Vashti's appearance and condition. As it turned out, once he was in the passenger seat June told him, her eyes filling with tears: "Vashti might sound good on the phone, but that poor girl is struggling to recover—to live. Dr. M tells us he is happy with her recovery thus far, but I'm not nearly as confident. She needs to take so many medications each day, and her appetite is not coming back. She is very thin and frail, and the light is gone from her eyes."

Alarmed and deeply concerned by June's revelation, Jeff could only respond with empathy for Vashti, saying, "I can hardly imagine what she had to endure going through this second transplant so soon after the first one."

When they arrived at the apartment, Jeff picked Vashti up in his arms and held her, worried about her frail appearance as June had warned. After June had prepared coffee and some snacks, she found the two lying on Vashti's bed discussing the second transplant. June set the coffee and snacks on a small table nearby and told them to call if they needed anything.

About forty-five minutes later, June heard Vashti scream. Then she heard her moaning from the bathroom, where she found Vashti sitting on the edge of the tub, her feet in bathwater with copious amounts of blackened skin floating on its surface.

"Everything is okay, Mom. Jeff is just helping me with my painful feet," Vashti explained. "I told him how, after the chemo from hell, my feet swelled up like two marshmallows that had been toasted in a fire until fully blackened. The sight made me recall how, when I was young, I liked toasting marshmallows but sometimes held them so close to the fire that they turned black, at which point I would let them cool for a minute, pull the black covering off, and eat the white marshmallows underneath. Thinking we would try the same approach, we began pulling the black, burned skin off. Then we came to a piece that was really stuck, causing me to scream."

Later Jeff walked Vashti around the pool area, and when they returned, Vashti had some color in her cheeks but was exhausted. Jeff got her comfortable in the recliner, covered her with a quilt, and said he would take care of dinner. Before long, a man delivered Vashti's favorite Indian food, butter chicken and rice. Jeff set it on a small table by the recliner, pulled up a chair beside her, and invited June to make a plate for herself. Then he sat down holding Vashti's plate and said, "I wanted you to have a special belated birthday dinner."

Tears welled up in Vashti's eyes. Jeff wiped them away then fed her a small amount of rice and chicken on a spoon. She closed her eyes and savored the taste. Next he fed her as much as she could eat. Only then did he prepare a plate for himself. Suddenly a beautiful bouquet of flowers was delivered, along with so many balloons they could hardly fit through the door. Jeff told Vashti that there was a different-colored balloon for every year of her life, emphasizing that he was going to have serious trouble in future years because they already had a hell of a time finding balloons in thirty-four colors, which made Vashti laugh.

Hearing another knock on the door, Jeff answered it and quickly disappeared into the kitchen with something before anyone could see what it was. Soon he returned carrying a gorgeously decorated chocolate cake—Vashti's favorite—with milk chocolate frosting, and candles lit on top. June and Jeff began singing "Happy Birthday," and Jeff told Vashti to make a wish. She kept her eyes closed for a long time and then blew out every candle on the cake. Vashti was only able to eat a few bites but said she wanted to have it for breakfast the next morning. Jeff looked at June and said, "This girl must be getting well. She sounds like her old self. Only Vashti would think cake is one of the best breakfasts a person could ever have." He then took a card and a small wrapped gift from his pocket. As Vashti read the card, tears came to her eyes. She then opened the gift, which was an elegant silver necklace with a small silver acorn hanging from the chain.

"Oh, Cookie. It is beautiful," she said, hugging him. "How did you ever find a necklace with an acorn?"

"I could not find one anywhere, so I hired a silversmith to make it."

"How precious. Put it on me, and let's see how it looks."

Jeff clasped the necklace around Vashti's neck and held up a mirror so she could look at it. "I love it and will always treasure it," she said. Then Vashti explained to June, "When we first came to Houston and I walked around the apartment complex, I kept picking up fallen acorns. I told Jeff they reminded me of him, because I would look up at the majestic, strong oak trees from which they had fallen and think of him. That's why this gift is so special. I can't believe Jeff remembered me telling him that." Then she noticed, hanging beside the acorn, a small silver circle engraved with the number 33, a multiple of her lucky number, three, and smiled in appreciation.

By now Vashti was exhausted, so Jeff carried her back to her bedroom. As they passed her, June thanked Jeff for the festive birthday party he had organized.

The next morning June tapped on Vashti's bedroom door and asked what they would like for breakfast. They shouted in unison, "Cake." June shook her head and told them she would put the coffee on and set the table for cake.

When they joined her, Jeff cut pieces of Vashti's birthday cake for them all to eat. Then June cleaned Vashti's port while describing the procedure to Jeff and also telling him when and how to give Vashti her medications. Having never seen so many medications for one person, Jeff looked horrified. Vashti hastily explained that they were necessary for now and that when her immune system was functioning she would only have to take one pill a day to prevent rejection. To cheer her up, Jeff offered to take her to a nearby art museum and asked June to come along.

Soon after arriving at the museum Vashti sat down to rest due to her low energy and ultimately opted to go home for a nap. On their way out, they stopped at the gift shop, where Vashti started paging through a book while Jeff put on a huge shark head mask with vicious teeth. When Vashti turned around and saw Jeff in the mask, she laughed, grateful to him for always making her smile.

Back at the apartment, Vashti lay down for a nap and Jeff read some of their favorite poems in a way that brought the images to life. She hoped she would be able to write more poetry herself when she felt better. Later Jeff invited Vashti on a drive to see the colorful Christmas lights, and she suggested they stop for ice cream cones.

After they had gone, June called Conor to tell him about their day. "Hi, Babe. What are you doing?"

"I just got back from court, so your timing is perfect."

"Jeff arrived yesterday and he threw an incredible belated birthday party for Vashti. She was so surprised and happy."

"I knew he wouldn't forget her special day because his birthday is the day before hers if I remember correctly."

"That's right. He was born about ten hours before Vashti, an amazing coincidence that seems to augur their close relationship. For her birthday, he had an Indian restaurant deliver some of the best butter chicken and rice I have ever eaten. Vashti surprised me by how much she was able to eat."

"I'm glad to hear that because she has to gain some weight. I'm worried that she hasn't put on any weight since the transplant."

"Me, too. All the medications she has to take suppress her appetite, so I'm glad she ate at least some of the food Jeff ordered. He also gave her a lovely silver necklace with a silver acorn pendant, along with a small silver circle engraved with the number 33. The acorn symbolizes a special memory Vashti has of Jeff, and, as you know, three is Vashti's lucky number."

"It sounds like Vashti enjoyed another meaningful birthday celebration."

"Yes, but I think Jeff was startled when he saw her looking so tired and frail."

"June, she is a strong woman, but it will take time to recover from this."

"I know. Yet I worry because she still has myeloma cells in her blood, and I can't imagine how that is possible when her treatments were so aggressive they nearly killed her."

"Dr. M doesn't sound very worried about it, so maybe we shouldn't be."

June told Conor she would try to be less anxious and allow for the time needed to assess Vashti's progress. While hanging up, June heard Vashti and Jeff return and found them in the kitchen, where Vashti was vomiting into the sink.

"I think the ice cream might have been too much for her," Jeff said.

Trying to be upbeat, Vashti added, "Nevertheless, we had a wonderful time, Mom." June left them alone to wind down before bed.

"Jeff, thank you for the amazing birthday party. I feel terrible that I can't throw you one this year," Vashti told him.

"Next year you can throw me a birthday party, something I'll look forward to because you definitely know how to throw a party. I'm sure you remember that we had the craziest parties imaginable."

"Well, some details may be a little foggy because of the tequila involved, but I agree all of them were wild and fun."

"We are going to set a new bar for parties with my friends in San Diego when you get there," Jeff promised, kissing Vashti softly on the lips and praying that he would never again have to be separated from her. Then he added, "Don't forget that I'll soon be returning to celebrate Christmas with you. I bet you'll be feeling much better then, and we can explore more of this city."

"Are you sure you want to fly to Houston for one day?"

"I couldn't not be with you on Christmas. I wish I could stay longer, but I'm saving up for when you can go home. Then I will be waiting at the Albuquerque airport for you, and we will have a solid month or more together."

"I can't wait. I may even have a discharge date by the time you come for Christmas."

"That would be the best Christmas present of my life," Jeff replied, hoping for that gift.

The next morning June found Vashti lying in Jeff's arms on a chaise lounge near the pool, and both of them smiling. The sight pained June because she would have to take Jeff to the airport in just a couple of hours, disturbing their joyous time together.

Later Vashti helped Jeff pack, and they left for the airport with plenty of time to spare. When June pulled up to the departure area, Vashti exited the car with Jeff and asked her to slowly circle the loop ahead and pick her up after she said a long good-bye to Jeff. Once Vashti was back in the car, she said, "Knowing Jeff will be back in a couple of weeks makes his departure easier this time."

"How about a hot fudge sundae?" June asked, thinking it would cheer her up.

"Not today, Mom. I'm tired and just want to nap. Maybe when I wake up Jeff will be with me and I will realize that driving him to the airport was only a dream," Vashti replied wistfully.

"That's a magical thought. In any case, it won't be long before we'll be picking him up for the last time," June stated.

"And I will have Jeff's Christmas present ready for him."

"What present is that?"

"My discharge date. He told me that would be the best Christmas present of his life."

Vashti's remaining days before Christmas were filled with tests and appointments. When the day came for her last appointment with Dr. M before discharge, she put on a dressy outfit in anticipation of celebratory news about her discharge. During earlier appointments, he had hinted at the possibility of her going home for New Year's, and now she hoped he would commit to that prospect for Jeff's Christmas present. To thank Dr. M for his care, Vashti also had a gift for him, a piece of pottery from Acoma Pueblo, known for its fine-line geometric and symbolic designs. Years earlier she had acquired a piece of Acoma pottery; and recently she had urged Conor to ask the artist, whose signature was on the bottom, to make an identical piece for Dr. M.

When Dr. M came in to see her, she handed him the gift. "Vashti, it is exquisite. Thank you," he exclaimed.

Vashti explained, "The Acoma Indians make pottery from a slate-like clay found in the hills surrounding their pueblo and typically decorate it with black-and-white geometric patterns that represent the cycles of life."

Dr. M closely examined the intricate designs with fascination. He then explained the chemo would be starting before Vashti's discharge on December 31, so she could celebrate New Year's Eve at home. Vashti could not contain her joy at now having not only a memorable Christmas present for Jeff but the best possible way to start the new year.

Since the area the large tumor had previously occupied on her spine remained extremely painful, she next saw some pain specialists. They advised her to have the nerves there burned. When Vashti asked one of the doctors if after the procedure she would be able to run, amazed at her spunk he responded, "To be honest, I don't know. Nor have I ever had a patient inquire about running after undergoing this type of procedure." Ultimately she decided in favor of the procedure. In response, the specialist pointed out that determining its effectiveness in decreasing her pain would take some time.

Early Christmas morning, in anticipation of seeing Jeff at the airport, Vashti put on a new outfit and a wig the color of her natural hair, but straight instead of curly because the wigs with curly hair looked nothing like her own curly hair. When she stepped up to hug Jeff at the airport, the sight of her looking much better immediately eased some of his worry. Hoping to make Vashti's Christmas especially joyful, Jeff turned to June and said, "We need to stop at the first place we see selling Christmas trees, so Vashti can pick ours out and enjoy the smell of a real pine tree." They soon found a place, and Vashti selected a healthy and strong little tree. Jeff then asked June to stop at a store where he could buy Christmas decorations. There he chose lights and ornaments, and Vashti felt good enough to pick out a star for the top of the tree, overjoyed with Jeff's Christmas spirit.

Back at the apartment, Jeff set up the tree and strung the lights. He then held out ornaments for Vashti to hang from the branches and the star to set on top. Finally, he lit the tree and they all admired its beauty in anticipation of spending a joyous Christmas together despite their concern about Vashti's condition.

June set out trays of cold meats, sliced cheeses, bread and crackers, fruits and vegetables with several dips, and Christmas cookies and candies. Vashti found Christmas carols on her phone to play as background music. Although Vashti was yet not permitted to drink, June okayed a glass of champagne for her, so Jeff poured champagne for each of them and made the first toast: "To Vashti, the most beautiful woman in the world—the woman who captured my body, heart, and soul many years ago—may she live a long and pain-free life."

June made the next toast: "To my beautiful daughter, Vashti, who has the cleverest mind I've ever known, the courage of a lion, and a heart of pure gold and who lives in the present, with the freedom to savor each moment of life, may her days be many and may she get to spend every one of them with the man of her dreams, whom she has loved for so many years."

Then Vashti toasted: "To Jeff, Mom, and Dad, who exemplify the adage "It is not *what* you have in your life but *who* you have," I am blessed to have the best people in the world in my life. Your love for me has never faltered and only amazed. I will love you forever."

They sipped the champagne in silence. Then Vashti, handing June a rectangular box, said, "Mom, Jeff helped me get this gift for you. When I first went to Boston with him many years ago, we tried to find you a special one of these but came back empty-handed. We have one now, that I hope you will use and enjoy for many years." Inside the box, June found a finely crafted antique metronome. She'd had one as a little girl studying piano, but not later, making it difficult for her to keep proper time when playing musical compositions. Touched, June thanked and hugged them.

Turning to Jeff, Vashti said, "And now I want to give a gift to you, something I didn't buy or even wrap: I get to go home on December 31 so I can celebrate New Year's Eve with you."

Overjoyed, Jeff held Vashti in his arms for a long time before speaking. "Thank you. This is the best gift I have ever received. I will be waiting at the airport with your dad on that day, and it will start a new chapter for us."

Jeff then fumbled for something in his pocket, knelt in front of Vashti, and said, "I want to marry you and spend the rest of my life with you. My divorce will be final on May 1, and I will be at your door on May 2 with a proper engagement ring and ask you to be my wife. I will speak with your dad in advance and ask for your hand in marriage. Until then, I want to give you a small token of my love to wear until I can replace it with an engagement ring that you help me pick out."

He slipped a white gold band engraved with infinity symbols interspersed with studded diamonds on Vashti's ring finger. Admiring the exquisite ring, she exclaimed, "It is so beautiful, Jeff. I love it."

CHAPTER 28

The morning Vashti departed MD Anderson for home she was very weak because they had restarted chemo two days earlier. But she tried to be joyous. As June pulled out of the apartment parking lot, Vashti looked toward the MD Anderson hospital and said, "I never want to return to this place again."

"I don't blame you, but how will Dr. M recheck you in six months if we don't return for a day?" asked June.

"Okay, maybe for one day," Vashti agreed. They then sped off without looking back.

After their plane landed in Albuquerque, June pushed Vashti in a wheelchair to meet Jeff. He was surprised to see her in a wheelchair, but he immediately rushed to hug her, carrying the biggest bouquet of fresh flowers that Vashti had ever received. She smelled each one and beamed with joy, although her face lacked all color.

Conor took June in his arms, swung her in circles, and said, "You're home." He then presented her with his bouquet.

Conor drove first to Vashti's house, where June offered to help her unpack.

"Mom, I want to just be with Jeff now and celebrate. Remember our discussion on the plane." Then, looking at Conor and Jeff, Vashti explained, "I told Mom that when we got back to Albuquerque she and I had to get a divorce." They all laughed.

Jeff said, encouragingly, "I can help Vashti put her things away. Then I'll stash her oversized suitcase in the very back of her storage room because she won't need it again until she moves to San Diego."

When Conor and June left, Jeff and Vashti sat on her leather couch close to the fire and gazed into each other's eyes for a long time. Then Vashti said,

"I've always believed that we make our own heaven and hell right here on earth. This is heaven."

Jeff replied, "I feel like Adam. He left the garden to suffer chaos, confusion, and woe, but the Merciful One guided him back to paradise." Jeff gathered Vashti in his arms and planted a warm kiss on the lips he longed for and loved. They kissed by the light of the flickering fire for quite some time.

Then, after making Vashti a special fruit smoothie, Jeff said, "I want you to tell me your life story, from your first memory until this moment."

"You have heard most of my stories," Vashti assured him, though she was touched by his interest in her life experiences, which she always loved sharing with him.

"I want to be reminded of everything you love or hate. I want to hear about the experiences that changed your life, for better or worse," Jeff insisted.

Vashti began, "I will just tell you about the many different emotions I felt today. When I opened my eyes this morning, the first thing I saw was Mom quietly packing my suitcase, and I felt a twinge of anger because I had wasted precious time in a city I hated, undergoing a procedure that not only didn't cure my illness but caused pain almost impossible to endure. Then I got up and, after showering, felt deeply grateful that I was alive to see another day. As we left Houston, the relief I felt was so pervasive I realized that in the deepest part of my being I must have thought I would never escape. Having to use a wheelchair today made me sad because I had anticipated much more progress in my recovery. Then being embraced by you caused all these emotions to fall away and leave me swimming in a glistening sea of love; the past had lost its significance, and my union with you had suddenly freed me to follow my heart. I felt the energy of love as the breath of life and knew I was connected to everything and everyone in the universe. There was no beginning and no end, no life and no death—because I saw them all as one."

Vashti rested her head on Jeff's chest and listened to his heartbeat. The more she loosened her grip on worldly things, the more acceptance she experienced flowing over her. She now felt complete freedom to act from her higher self, to serve others with love and compassion. She knew that this realization was the lesson she had come into this life to learn. Jeff stroked her head and felt her soft breath on his arm. He closed his eyes and surrendered to the love that had guided him into this union.

Sometime later Jeff asked Vashti if he should prepare Bertie's dinner. She nodded in agreement then explained, "Dad has been taking care of Bertie since I got sick. In the beginning Dad would prepare his dinner, call his name, and Bertie would come out of his house and race toward the food. But lately Dad has had to lift him from his house and set him by the food, then he would look around before taking a bite. So today I'd like you to prepare his dinner with lots of his favorite bok choy, but I want to take it to him and see if he remembers my voice and comes out of his house to get the food."

"If I were a betting man, I would bet you a hundred dollars that he does. I'm sure he's attached to you and has missed you."

So Jeff prepared Bertie's dinner, and Vashti set the tray down by his house and called his name. A few seconds later she called his name again. Then Bertie's head appeared in his doorway, and, keeping his eyes on Vashti, he dashed to the tray and buried his muzzle in the bok choy.

"Bertie," she said softly, "I knew you wouldn't forget my voice. I never forgot about you. I was too sick to come home, so I had Dad take care of you. That assured me I would find you in good shape when I returned. Look at how big you've grown. I know you're thinking I have gotten so skinny that you hardly recognize me. But I'm here with Jeff now, and he is an excellent cook, so I'm going to gain weight and look more like myself soon."

Amazed at Vashti's rapport with Bertie, Jeff remarked, "It's incredible that this prehistoric-looking creature can recognize your voice."

"Hey, watch your words. Bertie thinks he's quite the dapper dude and doesn't appreciate being described as prehistoric. He looks twice the size he was when I was first hospitalized and has become so handsome. Just look at the colors of his shell." They laughed, and Bertie looked up at them. "See, he knows I am getting after you for talking about him that way," Vashti observed.

When Bertie finished eating, Jeff thought up another way to test Bertie's attachment to Vashti. "Let's walk to the east wall," he said to her. "On our way back, you veer toward the north and I'll head south, and we'll see who Bertie follows."

As Vashti turned north, Bertie followed her. Jeff concluded, "I think he must smell you, and that's why he follows you and not me."

"I think you're jealous that I have such a faithful companion," Vashti joked.

They put Bertie back in his area and went inside. Jeff then carried Vashti to bed, they made love and, euphoric, fell deeply asleep.

The next day Jeff took Vashti by tram to the top of the Sandia Mountains, where they had hiked many times in the past. There they had a picnic, and when Vashti told him she wanted to stay to watch the sunset, he bundled her up in warm clothes he had packed for the adventure. They watched a breathtaking sunset. On the way home, Vashti said, "There are no green flashes in New Mexico sunsets, but wasn't tonight's sunset spectacular just the same?"

"It warmed my soul," Jeff agreed.

Back at Vashti's house, Jeff made her the best homemade soup she had ever tasted. "I think you are a better cook than I am," she commented.

"I think I'm divinely inspired when I'm with you," Jeff replied.

"When I get better, I want to prepare some recipes I have perfected. It's always heavenly to savor the final product, but why must the experience end poorly?"

"What do you mean by poorly?"

"Well, someone has to clean the kitchen. That is the part I don't like."

"You are thinking about it the wrong way. First, the best things in life are worth working for, so enjoying a savory meal can require cleaning up afterward. Second, the cook always gets to set the rules, one of which could be: 'If the cook prepares a delicious meal, the cook will not have to clean up.' The people who enjoyed the feast contribute by cleaning up. That is a good deal for everyone."

Vashti kissed him and said, "I like the way you think."

A few days after their Sandia Mountain adventure Jeff planned to take Vashti on a short trip to the Jemez Mountains and hot springs. Jeff knew she loved to soak in a hot mineral water tub and then get a massage. but he had to find a way to adhere to her restrictions. She was not allowed in a public bath or pool, or even a lake or ocean, for six months as any contamination could be life threatening for her. She had even been advised to take showers rather than baths during the first six months and to avoid massages since they might injure her spine or neck. Jeff solved the dilemma by secretly calling the hot spring bathhouse and requesting a private room with a small tub of mineral water for Vashti's feet and hands, as well as a shower so he could wash them after the soak. He also arranged for a massage therapist to work only on Vashti's feet and hands.

As Jeff started driving toward the Jemez Mountains, Vashti said, "I don't know if this is a good idea. I can't hike any distance, and I'm forbidden to have soaks and massages."

"This drive itself will be enjoyable, and if we put our heads together we might be able to think of something fun to do," Jeff replied.

As they drove, Jeff told Vashti more about the house he had rented for them in San Diego. "I think you will love the place. You take a two-lane road to the area and then a quiet, small road to the house. The house has beautiful views, and a cozy porch in the front. The living room has a west wall of glass exposing a view of the Pacific Ocean, which, a few steps to the west, takes your breath away. The house has only two bedrooms and one bath, but the main bedroom has two windows that look out to the ocean. At night, I open them both, and the sound of the surf is so hypnotic it puts me to sleep. Since moving there, I have become energized by the beauty and sounds of the ocean."

"Don't stop in the Jemez. Just keep driving west to California," Vashti urged in a dreamy voice, eager to be at the house in San Diego that Jeff had described. Jeff laughed, imagining them at the oceanside house.

When they arrived at the hot springs, Jeff got out of the car, extended his hand to Vashti, and said reassuringly, "Come with me. I promise there are no health hazards for you here today." A woman took them to a private room in the back of an adobe building. She advised Vashti to slip her shoes off and roll her pants up to her knees and her sleeves up to her elbows. The woman then lowered Vashti's feet into warm mineral water, placed a small table over her legs, set a tub of warm mineral water on the table, and submerged Vashti's hands in the water. Before leaving. she instructed Jeff to keep adding hot water to maintain the temperature that Vashti wanted.

Vashti rested her head against the back of the chair, closed her eyes, and said, "This is blissful, Jeff. Thank you." She soaked silently while Jeff kept adding hot water.

Eventually she fell asleep, and in a dream her spirit guide appeared in the form of a young boy with an angelic face. "You have nothing to fear. Release and melt into the water. Become the water," he said. Then he disappeared.

When Vashti woke up, the attendant turned on the shower. Jeff moved Vashti's chair close to the water and washed her hands and feet. The woman then slid a pair of disposable slippers on Vashti's feet and led her to a room with an overstuffed reclining chair. Jeff helped her settle into a comfortable position, after which a massage therapist arrived and massaged Vashti's feet and hands. Jeff watched Vashti's face, thinking she seemed fully lost in the wonder of the moment. Vashti slept peacefully with her head in Jeff's lap all sixty miles back to Albuquerque.

The thirty-three days Vashti and Jeff spent together were more extraordinary than they could have imagined, and they grew closer with every passing day. Jeff kept telling Vashti that he was sure he had fallen in love with an angel, as Vashti experienced wonder at even the smallest things.

June only stopped by a couple times during the month to deliver food she had prepared for them and groceries in case they didn't want to go shopping. June was happy to see her daughter's face glowing, but concerned that Vashti's hair wasn't growing out and she didn't appear to be gaining weight. After one visit, June called the oncologist, who told her that Vashti's most recent lab work, just received, showed no myeloma cells in her blood.

"Then we can stop the chemo right away?" June inquired, relieved at the news.

The oncologist replied, "Of the treatments ordered by MD Anderson, Vashti has only a few left. I thought I would examine her and determine whether we should finish the chemo cycle or not."

"Why would we finish the chemo cycle if there are no myeloma cells in her blood?" June asked.

"Although no cancer cells showed up in this report, some may be detected the next time her blood is tested," the oncologist replied ominously. June hung up, frustrated by the uncertainty of the test results and worried about what the future might bring.

CHAPTER 29

JEFF TOOK VASHTI TO THE BEST RESTAURANT in Albuquerque the night before his return to San Diego. But Vashti experienced extreme nausea and could only eat a small portion of her dinner. In bed that night, Jeff said, "Vashti, I'm worried because you don't seem to be recovering from this second transplant. What do you think about your recovery so far?"

"I don't know what to think. They never explained in detail what the first one hundred days, or even the first six months, would be like. I don't think I can take much more chemo, though. It is so toxic and draining that my quality of life sucks," Vashti replied.

"Do you think you should tell your oncologist that you want to stop chemo?" Jeff asked.

"I have confidence in her monitoring and believe if I became too fragile she would stop the chemo and change the treatment plan. I leave blood regularly, and she would never send me for a chemo infusion if my cell counts were too low. Still, with my body telling me to stop, it is hard not to."

"Please think about just stopping no matter what she says," urged Jeff.

"I'm scared to do that. If I refuse more chemo and the myeloma cells come rushing back, then everything I have endured will have been for nothing. I don't want to give up—I still have hope. My chemo cycle won't last much longer, and all but one of the other medications will be reduced until I no longer need to take them. As soon as the immune system suppression drugs are reduced, my new immune system will begin to function. Surely by that time I will be feeling much better and on my way to a remission that won't limit the things I do," Vashti affirmed.

"You've come so far. We just have to get you down the homestretch," replied Jeff, supportively. "Are you scared or bothered by anything other than the deleterious effects of the chemo?"

"Not really. After going through two bone marrow transplants, I have no fear. However, prior to the second transplant I worried about rejection because it almost always means death. I do pray every day that I will never again have to suffer like I did following the second transplant and that I will never be forced to say good-bye to you, Mom, and Dad," Vashti stated.

"What do you mean about saying good-bye?"

Vashti explained, "When I first started seeing my oncologist here, she told me there were many chemo drugs that could be used for people suffering from multiple myeloma. But in the past she'd had patients go through all the available drugs and run out of options. I asked how those patients died, and she told me they took care of their personal affairs, said good-bye to loved ones, and passed away when the cancer cells had pushed out most of the normal cells. I don't know if transplant patients die the same way. If they can get into remission, they have to hope it lasts a long time."

"Vashti, I believe with my whole heart that you are going to enter remission and that it will last a long time. You are so much younger than most of the patients suffering from this type of cancer that it must give you an advantage," Jeff observed.

"I hope you're right. I was in excellent health overall when I was diagnosed, which is why the finding was such a shock."

"I don't think I could leave your side unless we were close to having the worst horrors behind us. I will be coming back in March, less than three weeks from now, to celebrate your one-hundred-day mark. Can you believe you're almost over that hurdle?" Jeff commented.

"That gives me hope. To pass that mark will be a sweet victory," replied Vashti.

Jeff continued, "After being here for your victory celebration in March, I'll be back twice in April, for Easter and your six-month checkup in Houston. I know you will be feeling much better then. After that I will come back May 1 so that I can speak with your dad before asking you to be my wife on May 2. We can leave for San Diego on May 3 because three is your lucky number. What do you think of that plan, Vashti?"

"I've never heard of a better plan in my whole life," Vashti said, smiling.

Jeff kissed her, and then they made love in a way that left them breathless. Jeff could not tell where his body ended and Vashti's began, something he had never experienced with any other woman.

The next day when she took Jeff to the airport Vashti felt only slightly better. When she returned, she called June. While waiting for her to answer, she noticed that Jeff had left a brown bag for her filled with magazines. She dumped the contents out and laughed when she saw three bridal magazines with a sticky note that read: "Happy shopping! You'll be the most gorgeous woman ever to wear any of these dresses. Love you, Jeff."

"Hello, Vashti," June said.

"I just got back from taking Jeff to the airport."

"Dad and I were thinking about coming down late this afternoon and making dinner for all of us in your kitchen. How does that sound to you?"

"Mom, it would be fine to come by to chat, but I have no appetite."

"I know, Sweetheart, but we thought that your house might seem terribly quiet with Jeff gone."

"Mom, do whatever you want. I am enjoying the quiet now because it allows me to think and meditate. It is only while sitting in silence that I have even a slight chance of shoving aside my big fat ego."

"I feel the same way. If I had not meditated all these years, I'm sure I'd have gone over the deep end a long time ago," June agreed.

When Vashti hung up the phone, she realized how her weakness and inability to eat were weighing on her positive attitude and hopefulness. She had never known anyone who had gone through two bone marrow transplants, so she had no one to talk to about how she was feeling or when she could expect to feel better. She didn't know if her taste buds would ever function again. Everything she ate tasted like thick, awful paste.

Her thoughts then turned to Gabby, who had often texted her following the transplant procedure, giving her a lot of support. She had missed Gabby's graduation from high school because of her sickness, but she had told Gabby she would get well and be sitting in the front row at her university graduation.

Smiling at the thought of such a scene, she called Gabby to invite her to visit. "Hi, Gabby. It's Vashti."

"I've been waiting to hear your voice. How are you doing?"

"I've been better, but I'm hanging in there. I called to invite you to come see more of my new house. The last time you were here I didn't get to give you a full tour. Jeff came to stay when I first got home. It was great having him here for a month, but it was so hard to say good-bye to him at the airport."

"I can only imagine how hard it was."

"Would you like to come on Saturday around eleven?"

"I would love to. I'll bring some lunch."

After a while, Conor and June arrived with groceries and armfuls of fresh, colorful flowers, which made Vashti smile. "I thought we would arrange a large bouquet for your dinner table tonight then smaller bouquets for your bedroom, sitting room, bathroom, and by your bottles of pills so you will have lovely flowers to look at as you take them," June suggested.

"Mom, I'm so lucky to have you as my mother."

"I remember the book *Are You My Mother?* You carried it everywhere when you were little. In it a baby bird walked all over bumping into things and asking each one if it was his mother. Your favorite page was where he bumped into a crane and asked the crane if it was his mother," June recalled.

"Some nights when you said you were too tired to read I would cry and then you would read that book to me even if you were exhausted," Vashti reminded her.

"I remember. I always felt bad if my energy flagged before we read together or if I was too busy to do what you wanted," June confessed.

"Yes, and I sure let you know if I felt you should do something," Vashti continued. "Remember the summer I was in third grade and insisted on taking a swim class because my best friend was enrolled in it? I had already taken many summer swim classes, but when she told me about the races scheduled at the end of that one I was excited and wanted to sign up. You told me I couldn't because you were studying ten hours a day for the bar exam. I ran to my room and shouted that you were being selfish."

"I remember that day," June said. "You were so mad. I tried to explain that the bar exam wasn't some little test but a really big test that I needed to pass so I could get my license to practice law. But you still didn't think that was a good enough reason. You later talked to your friend, and her mother agreed to take you to the pool with her daughter. You loved the class and, during the races, discovered you were as fast in the water as you were running track on land. For a couple years, you talked about the races you won and that I hadn't seen any of them. It was years later, when you took the bar exam yourself, that you apologized for making me feel guilty about missing those races."

"I remember that day," Vashti replied. "You said I had nothing to apologize for because I was thinking and acting like the third grader I was then. You said you thought someday I would understand, never imagining it would be when I was taking the same insanely difficult bar exam. You said you thought I would understand when I became a mother with children of my own. Speaking of which, I was just remembering the cancer brochures in which doctors discussed with women patients the possibility of saving their eggs before starting chemo, in the event they someday wished to have children. No doctor ever discussed that with me. Why not?"

"I don't know, Vashti. Maybe because of the urgency of your condition. The day you were hospitalized you were deathly ill. Your pain was excruciating, and your kidneys were shutting down. I think they were focused on saving your life and figuring out what was wrong with you. By the time they knew what type of cancer you had, they needed to start chemo and radiation immediately because the tumor had already fractured your spine."

"I can understand that, Mom," Vashti conceded, though she wished she'd had more options then so she would have more options now. Then she added, "I want to meditate while Dad prepares dinner, then you and I can do the dishes." They walked arm in arm to the sitting room, shut the door, and meditated. Vashti then told June that while meditating she had rested in the arms of the Presence and forgotten that she was sick. June felt comforted knowing that her daughter had had some respite from her suffering.

That night they shared a delicious feast, although Vashti could only swallow a few bites. After dinner, Conor and June helped arrange Vashti in her chair by the window so she could read until Jeff called.

No sooner did her parents leave than Jeff called. "Cookie, are you safely home?" Vashti asked him.

"Yes, and the first thing I wanted to do when I got home from the office was call you. I want to be with you every minute of the day. I would love to hold you in my arms this very minute."

"I was in your arms this morning," Vashti reminded him.

"I know, but that was many hours ago. I want to hold you right now and talk to you all night long."

"Talk?"

"Well, talk and other things."

They laughed then had an animated conversation about their future now that Vashti was getting close to the hundred-day mark. Jeff asked her if she worried about taking the California bar exam. She told him she would take any exam to live with him near the ocean. She explained that until she passed the bar out there she could take a federal government job, which required only admission to the bar in one state and being in good standing in that state. She assured him she would not be working in a bankruptcy practice, however. Then she said she had to try to sleep and that talking with him had filled her with hope. She felt fortunate that he had found her after so many years and, against all odds, wanted to be with her for the rest of her life. She believed in karma and realized she must have done something right in this life to have captured his heart and have him by her side at this time.

Soon Vashti fell into a deep sleep and, in a dream, was visited by her spirit guide in the form of an ancient woman with a wrinkled face, stooped over and walking with a cane. Vashti couldn't understand her words because she spoke so softly. When Vashti asked her to speak louder, she looked up with eyes that appeared almost black, but then stooped over again and continued talking inaudibly. Vashti finally moved closer and heard her say, "You are able to love because you were loved before you were created." Then the old woman stretched her arms out to hug Vashti, but when Vashti moved forward to hug her the old woman disappeared.

CHAPTER 30

As Vashti waited for Jeff to come through security, she felt unusually better knowing it was her hundredth day since the transplant and grateful to God for helping her reach this point. As a result of her struggle, her appreciation for life had intensified so that even the smallest things filled her with wonder at the many ways in which all living creatures on the planet were connected to one another. Being in wonder, she concluded, was a beautiful way to live, something she curiously had not comprehended until becoming deathly ill.

The moment Jeff came out the of the security area, he lifted Vashti off her feet, saying over and over in her ear, "You made it!" When he set her back on the ground, he saw tears in her eyes.

"These are tears of pure joy," Vashti assured him. He kissed her gently on the lips, and they walked arm and arm to the exit.

On their way to her house, Vashti told Jeff that June wanted to take them to Vashti's favorite Indian restaurant for a celebratory dinner that evening.

"Do we have to go? I need to head back tomorrow, and I don't want to share any time I have with you," Jeff objected.

"Jeff, my parents helped me reach this milestone, too."

"I know, and I love them. I just don't want to share you today."

Vashti laughed and said, "I already told them that, and they agreed to let us dine and dash, but insisted on a brief meal together to celebrate."

Once inside her house, they made love on the couch in front of the fire. Then Jeff held Vashti in his arms for a long time, never wanting the moment to end, until she said they had to get dressed for dinner.

When they were seated at the restaurant, Conor ordered champagne and toasted: "To one of the happiest days of my life. My daughter has been through hell and back, and she still has the same sweet, loving smile she has always had. I applaud her strength and courage." They all enjoyed the meal, and Vashti ate more than she had in months.

Then Jeff and Vashti raced back to her place. There they took a long shower together and lay in bed talking about their love, the beach house in San Diego she would be moving into, and their dreams of a shared future. Vashti propped herself up in bed with pillows and appeared lost in thought.

"What are you thinking about?" Jeff asked.

Vashti replied, "Before getting sick, I figured I had come a long way for someone my age. Physically, I was in great shape. Mentally, I felt strong, having spent every year of my life since age five in school. I loved learning and the perspective it offered me, as well as the ability to analyze situations and make good decisions. I also assumed I was on a solid spiritual path, but I was wrong. I had taken only a few steps down that path. When I got sick, I began meditating several times a day, which was what saved me. It is shocking to hear you have a terrible blood cancer and may not be alive in three years. It turned my world on its head. Disoriented and seemingly, paralyzed, I fortunately had the love of my parents and close friends. They helped me navigate my way back to something resembling normal, given my circumstances.

"After that I had a lot of time to meditate, heal, and gain an understanding of what was in store for me. In the presence of the Divine, I started to comprehend that my cancer could be terminal, which prompted me to seriously consider my death. I never believed you die when you give up your earthly body; I believed you transition to life in a new form. You fear death only because of how the ego operates and the unwillingness to leave behind a life brimming with goodness and love. But then you realize you have always been surrounded by love, even before you took human form. When that awareness sinks into your soul, you begin to feel peace, and it deepens as you journey down your path."

"Vashti, those are the most beautiful words I have ever heard," Jeff responded. "Your peace transcends the horrors you have had to live through, and it affects all of us. My ideas about life have changed radically since we have gotten back together. Maybe thinking about death teaches us how to live."

"Absolutely," Vashti agreed. "It's like when you first learn to meditate and imagine yourself floating down a river. Although all sorts of objects pass by, you want to focus only on the river, so you don't engage with them. In letting your awareness of them go, you may even become one with the river—nothing else exists.

"Not long ago, while I was meditating with Mom, my consciousness left the physical plane, something I had never before experienced. When the ending meditation bell rang, it took me a while to come back to the present and to remember I was sick. This transformative experience profoundly changed me. I felt whole and free in a completely new way."

Jeff replied, "I am so happy for you. I can't imagine having that kind of experience."

They lay in silence a while, and when Jeff next looked at Vashti she was sound asleep in his arms. He covered her up and began thinking about all they had talked about. He whispered a prayer of thanks for having been led back to her and for his feelings of inexplicable joy and love.

The next morning when they woke up they lay in bed discussing Vashti's move to San Diego. Excitement danced in her eyes, and she grinned with joy at the thought of soon living by the ocean with Jeff. Thinking of his departure in a few hours, Jeff hugged Vashti and said, "Only one more time, when I visit you at Easter in just a few weeks, will I have to leave without you."

On their way to the airport, Jeff said he could hardly wait to come celebrate Easter with her. She will have had her last chemo that Thursday, and he would arrive the next day, Good Friday. Six days after their Easter together she would go to Houston with June for her six-month checkup. Five days after that he would be in Albuquerque to propose and help her pack, and the following day they would be on the road to San Diego. A new chapter would begin for them. Vashti would not have to face more chemo and would be taking fewer medications. They could both see the light at the end of the tunnel and delighted in the prospect of more happiness to come. The two embraced outside the terminal envisioning their future together.

After driving home, Vashti received a call from June, checking in after Jeff's departure and surprised to hear her daughter sounding upbeat. Vashti told her about the dates she had set with Jeff and confirmed that they were getting so close to being together forever that she wasn't nearly as sad as she had previously been when leaving Jeff at the airport. She added that the thought of living permanently with Jeff filled her with more joy than she had ever before known.

When Gabby arrived the next morning, Vashti gave her a big hug. "I haven't seen you in a while. You look pale and skinny. Are you sure you feel okay, Vashti?" Gabby asked, looking concerned.

"I guess so," Vashti replied "I see myself all the time, so I don't really notice anything unusual."

Gabby set down the lunch she had brought from Taco Bell, and they toured the place, beginning with the master bedroom. Gabby loved the new door leading to the veranda and asked, "Did your dad really tear out that old sliding glass door and install this one?"

"He did, and he gave it to me as one of my birthday presents. Let me show you the photo of it that he framed and handed me in the transplant unit, wrapped up with a bow."

Gabby looked at the framed picture and said, "Only your dad would think of such a great gift."

"Now let me show you my new sitting room and bathroom." Vashti described the decorating she had done in these rooms then added, "Dad installed a new shower with spray heads at different levels. As warm water is sprayed on your feet, knees, private parts, chest, and shoulders, the top shower head sprays your face and hair. It is the most invigorating feeling. You'll have to come for a sleepover and try it."

"I'd love to. I've never used such a shower."

Then Vashti showed Gabby the new skylights in the hallway and her arrangement of plants in an open area. Gabby loved plants too, and exclaimed, "Your array of plants on light-colored wood shelves looks fantastic!"

"Now come see the other two bedrooms," Vashti said. "This first one is the guest room, which I decorated myself in shades of gray. This last bedroom is my study. I put two of my large bookshelves in it, and then Mom and Dad found me this small desk so my healing recliner could go under the window, a perfect spot for reading."

"The study turned out classy," Gabby remarked.

"Thank you. Now come out to the kitchen and I'll show you the new appliances I picked out, then we can have lunch in the dining room."

After exploring the kitchen, Gabby said, "I really like the stainless-steel appliances you selected. You even have room in here for a small breakfast table. Cool."

"You know how it is when you get up in the morning to make that first cup of joe and need a place to chill till it's done," Vashti commented, grinning.

Then they entered the dining room, where Gabby unpacked the bag from Taco Bell. "I hope these are still your favorite tacos," she said earnestly.

"They are, but I don't know if I can eat two. I'll give it a hell of a try, though." They both laughed.

"Vashti, tell me about your second transplant," Gabby said as they started to eat.

"It was a lot harder than the first one. The high-dose chemo burned my throat and feet so bad that I thought I was going to die."

"Your feet?"

"Yes. My feet looked like toasted marshmallows that had caught on fire and turned bubbly black. When they started to heal, Jeff helped me peel the black burned skin off. We covered the bathwater with a layer of blackened skin."

"How did you ever get through such an ordeal?"

"With a lot of love from Jeff and my parents, and your regular texts. They revived my fighting spirit. I especially enjoyed hearing about your difficult classes at the university. I'm so proud of your determination, Gabby."

"It was hard to keep my grades up while taking college chemistry and other science classes, all of which had labs. The labs weren't hard, but they were at night and took time. I worried about losing my scholarship money."

"That would never happen to you because you are so smart," Vashti said, reassuringly.

After finishing lunch, they sat in the living room by the fire. "Gabby, Jeff has asked me to marry him," Vashti revealed.

"I'm so happy for you. Did you say yes?"

"It's a long story," Vashti replied. "Jeff filed for divorce, which, due to California's six-month waiting period, won't be final until May 1. So he can't officially ask me to marry him until May 2. He said he'll be coming back to Albuquerque on May 1 to ask Dad for my hand and officially proposing on May 2."

"He is not wasting any time, is he?"

"No. He told me that after he married his wife he realized he still loved me, so he started following me on Facebook. When he read about me being ill, he panicked and called around till he found out I was at MD Anderson. He phoned me one evening and came to see me the next day. We have been together ever since."

"His reentry into your life sounds like a fairy tale."

"Please look through these magazines with me and help me pick out a wedding dress." Vashti pleaded.

"It is thrilling to look forward to a beautiful wedding after all you have been through," Gabby exclaimed.

They sat on the couch for a couple of hours narrowing down the dress choices to ten styles. Then Vashti said, "I'm so exhausted that the dresses are all starting to look alike. Next time you visit we'll narrow the choices to three and then make a final selection."

"Deal," Gabby said, getting ready to leave.

They embraced at the door, where Vashti declared, "I love you so much, Gabby."

"I love you, too, and never want you to be gone for so long again," Gabby replied.

After Gabby left, Vashti stretched out in her sitting room and slept until her phone woke her up with a start. Hearing Dave's voice on the line, she smiled and said, "It's about time you called me. I thought you had completely forgotten about your best friend."

"I would never forget about my best friend, but I had a big assignment to complete before taking a break. You would love the design I created for this company. They were exceptionally pleased. I feel a bonus coming as we speak."

"That is great, Dave. I knew my best friend would go far."

"How are you feeling, Vashti?"

"Like I have been put through the wringer, but I'm still kicking."

"A simple thing like two bone marrow transplants couldn't knock you out."

"Only because I kept my faith and hope alive, which saw me through."

"I hear you."

"Dave, I have some good news. Jeff asked me to marry him. What do you think about that?"

"If you love him, I think you should marry him."

"That's all you have to say?"

"Well, that and the fact that when you do, my wife can quit worrying about you and me."

"Tell me she's not still worried."

"Let me just say not as much."

"Dave, you know what I'm going to ask you, don't you?"

"I don't have a clue, but after knowing you all these years I don't think anything you do or say would surprise me."

"Good, because I want you to be my maid of honor at the wedding."

"What are you talking about?"

"Women ask their best friend to be their maid of honor. You are my best friend, so I'm asking you to be my maid of honor."

"Well, okay. I can't ever say no to you. I'll be your maid of honor. But you aren't going to ask me to wear one of those long shiny dresses that match the bridesmaids' gowns, are you?"

"Yes I am, but your dress could be a few shades lighter than the others so you can stand out as the maid of honor."

"No, no, no. I draw the line at the long shiny dress," Dave insisted. They laughed hard, the way they used to, needing to wait a minute before going on with their call.

Then Dave remarked, "Vashti, you can't imagine how good it is to hear you laugh. I didn't know if I would ever hear that sound again."

"You can't imagine how good it feels to laugh again," Vashti responded.

"So did you say yes when Jeff proposed?" Dave asked.

Vashti explained the situation, then Dave asked, "When he proposes on May 2, are you going to say yes?"

"I'm going to say yes."

"Then I'm happy for you. I remember wondering, when you two broke up, if you would ever snap back to your old self. It took a long time."

"It did. After we broke up, I realized he was the one, and then I had to accept that he was the one who got away."

"Why didn't you tell him how you felt and that you had made a mistake?"

"Because by then he was married. Men are so strange. They get badly hurt, and, instead of taking time to heal, they go headlong into something new. Men must be emotional retards," Vashti opined.

"Hey, you're making a gross generalization. Not all men are emotional retards. I'm not."

"Dave, you are very different from other men I know, and that's one reason you are my best friend."

"That's better. I'm pleased to know that I'm not emotionally retarded."

They laughed and talked some more. Vashti's spirits were high, as they invariably were when she spoke with Dave. She knew he would always occupy a special place in her heart.

CHAPTER 31

On the Monday following Palm Sunday, Vashti woke up feeling weak and nauseous. She let June know but decided not to call her oncologist, preferring to wait and see if she felt better the next day—a plan her mother accepted. Vashti spent the day in bed, hoping to recover before Jeff's arrival in four days.

That night Jeff called, and she explained the situation to him. "If you aren't feeling good today, how are you going to do that last chemo treatment Thursday?" he asked.

"I'm hoping I'll feel better tomorrow, have the last treatment on Thursday, and be done with this forever," Vashti replied.

"If you don't feel better, promise me you'll refuse the last treatment," Jeff urged.

"Don't worry. I leave my blood there on Wednesday and see the oncologist Thursday morning before the chemo, so she will determine if I should have it or not. She is the expert, and I trust that she's carefully monitoring my condition."

"I can't help but worry, but I'll try not to drive myself crazy with it," Jeff said anxiously.

"Great. I want you feeling good when you get here."

"Remember, I have a flight to Boston at 10:00 a.m. tomorrow to go to a forensics conference. I'll call you as soon as I get there. I'll be at the conference all day Wednesday and Thursday, and leave for Albuquerque at 6:00 a.m. Friday. I don't want to miss one minute of our time together."

"I don't either. And after that the next time you fly to Albuquerque will be your last for a long time," Vashti replied.

"I'm counting on it. I have been searching for the best oncologist in the San Diego area who specializes in treating blood cancers," Jeff said. "I also have an Easter surprise for you,"

"Tell me."

"Then it wouldn't be a surprise."

"I want to know what it is more than I want a surprise."

"Okay. I know you asked your parents to hide Easter eggs for you until you were in your twenties because you loved the search. On Saturday night after you fall asleep, I'm going to hide Easter eggs filled with awesome treasures all over your house."

"I can't wait. I haven't been on an Easter egg hunt in years."

"But I won't be as easy on you as your parents were. I am going to hide the eggs in obscure places."

"I hate to break this to you, but you are starting at a great disadvantage. You'll be hiding those eggs on my turf. I know this house much better than you do, every little nook and cranny."

"Okay, Miss Smarty Pants. I'll think of a primo surprise, and if you find all the eggs you will win the primo surprise, too," Jeff quipped. They talked a little longer, then Vashti said good night, eager to sleep well and feel better the next day.

However, even after she meditated sleep eluded her, although she thought that the peace instilled by meditation was probably as good for her health as sleep. Finally, as the sun came up she dozed off for a couple of hours.

June called early in the morning to see how she was doing. "I can't say I feel better, Mom, but I don't feel much worse either," Vashti reported.

"I'm concerned, though, and I wonder if we should call the oncologist," June suggested.

"Mom, what would she do for me?"

"She would examine you and see if everything is as it should be."

"She is overbooked every day of the week. I would have to be squeezed into her schedule, and that would mean waiting for hours. Since I don't like that place, it would do me more harm than good to sit there waiting," Vashti objected.

"Okay, keep me posted on how your day goes. Dad and I will come by when he's back from the office."

"That sounds great. I'll see you later," Vashti replied.

After hanging up, she started journaling, eager to express her feelings about life as she saw it now, in case she became suddenly weaker and unable to write. When her parents arrived, Vashti told them she would be leaving blood for testing at the university lab the next day and if she felt worse she would ask for an appointment with her oncologist.

Vashti woke up the next morning feeling worse. She realized that her energy level was dropping and the nausea was intensifying with each passing day. She left her blood in the lab and promptly went to the oncologist's office to inquire about an appointment. The doctor was heavily booked, but the nurse invited her to wait. Vashti replied that she had an appointment with the doctor the next morning, as well as her last chemo, so she would wait till then.

Vashti drove home, lay down, then called June with an update and a request, saying, "Mom, I was just thinking that we haven't had a sleepover in a long time."

"Come to think of it, we haven't," June replied. "I'll pack my bag and be there in about an hour. How does that sound?"

"If you want to, I'd like that a lot," Vashti said, comforted by the thought.

June quickly packed and left a note for Conor. As she backed out of the garage, her heart was pounding. Vashti hadn't sounded like herself, and June feared her daughter was fading.

She found Vashti sitting in her reading chair wearing only a thin nightie that made her look like mere skin and bones. "Vashti, can I make us both something to eat?" June asked, hoping to convince her to consume something healthy.

"I would take a cup of tea, but Jeff has ordered dinner for me, and it will be delivered soon. I told him I now weigh seventy-eight pounds," Vashti revealed.

"Good lord, what is the oncologist saying about your weight loss?" asked June.

"I think I weighed eighty-four pounds last time they weighed me in her office," Vashti stated. "They want me to eat as much as I can to gain weight, but I can't eat, Mom. I have no appetite, and everything I try to eat tastes like either paste or cardboard."

"What did Jeff order for you?"

"We used to eat a lot of Cajun shrimp with dirty rice at Pappadeaux, so he ordered shrimp for me."

"He is such a sweetheart."

"I know. He would do anything for me."

"Let me make tea. And when the food is delivered I will serve you dinner."

June prayed that Vashti would be able to eat some of her favorite shrimp dish. She set the table and lit a candle, hoping to make the meal as inviting as possible. When the food came, June scooped some onto Vashti's plate, and they agreed on how delicious it smelled. Vashti struggled to eat three of the jumbo shrimp on her plate then said, "I don't think I can eat any more."

"I put one of your meal replacement beverages in the freezer to get super cold. Would you try drinking it?" June asked.

"I'll try. Then let's go back to the sitting room and meditate," Vashti requested.

They meditated in silence for a long time. When the ending bell chimed, it took a while for Vashti to open her eyes. As she did, she looked at June and said, "If I ever reach the point where I don't have the strength to go on, you wouldn't be mad or disappointed in me, would you, Mom?"

Distressed, June jumped up from her seat, planted herself on the arm of Vashti's chair, and asked, with tears streaming down her face, "Tell me what is happening, Vashti. I'm very worried and don't know what to do. Are you feeling so terrible that you think you might give up?"

"Oh, *Mamacita*, I'm weak and tired. I have felt terrible for so long that

I don't know if I'm worse or not. When I meditate, I can leave my suffering behind, and it feels good. Sometimes I don't want to open my eyes and come back."

June embraced Vashti and reassured her, "I would never be disappointed in you. I have watched all that you have been through, and you have amazed me. You've come so far, Love. We will see the doctor tomorrow and find out when you will start feeling better. You're going to make it across the finish line, Vashti, and then all of this will be behind you."

"Thank you, Mom, for running the whole race with me. I don't know what I would have done without you," Vashti said gratefully.

June helped Vashti into bed, propped her up on pillows, and covered her with her favorite quilt. Then Jeff called to say he was in Boston, about to rent a car, and would call back after checking into his hotel room. Vashti thanked him for the delicious shrimp dinner and encouraged him to go to sleep soon because the conference was to start early the following morning. He insisted on calling her later to hear more about her appointment with the oncologist the next day.

When June returned to Vashti's room, she found her asleep with the phone in her hand. She gently removed it and set it on the pillow beside her.

Jeff called back about an hour later. Vashti told him her insomnia had returned, that she could only sleep for short periods and then lay awake for hours. She promised to leave a message on his cell phone after seeing her doctor and having her last chemo treatment, and told him not to worry about calling her back until he was done for the day.

While Vashti was talking to Jeff, June called Conor and told him she felt strange after what Vashti had said about giving up. She added that things had to improve soon because Vashti didn't know how much longer she could take it.

June woke up at the crack of dawn feeling like she had hardly slept, having gotten up several times during the night to check on Vashti. When she woke her up, Vashti had a tough time getting ready to go.

During her appointment, the doctor examined her as she described the rough week she'd had. She explained that at times even taking a breath seemed to require more energy than she had. The doctor, concerned, asked Vashti if she wanted to skip the last chemo treatment for now and instead be admitted to the hospital for observation. Vashti didn't like the sound of that after spending so much time in the transplant unit and replied that she just wanted to have the last chemo treatment and be done. She thought if all they could do was observe her she would rather have Jeff observe her at home. The doctor asked Vashti to leave more blood at the lab before heading upstairs for the chemo and told her to come back the next morning for another evaluation. Finally, the oncologist asked her to stay at her parents' house through Easter weekend, which she promised to do.

Vashti and June stopped at the lab then rested in comfortable chairs until it was time to go upstairs for the chemo treatment. The infusion area consisted of a long row of little cubicles, each furnished with a reclining chair. The chemo nurses were assigned to specific patients for the day. Vashti was disappointed to learn that she was not assigned to her favorite nurse for this treatment. As her assigned nurse started the infusion, Vashti was too weak to do anything but lie still with her eyes closed. And while she usually talked and joked with her nurse during the infusion, today she was silent. She looked so pale and weak lying there that it broke June's heart. "God, we give thanks that this is the last treatment," June silently prayed.

Suddenly Vashti started to mumble. June lowered her head and heard her say, "I know the reason . . ."

June held her hand and asked, "What reason, Vashti?"

"The reason we are here," Vashti murmured. "We are pure souls, every one of us. Many are not able to understand or accept the infinite love of the One and the unearned mercy the One showers upon them. He sends us here to love." Vashti promptly fell asleep.

A while later her favorite nurse appeared in the doorway of her cubicle and asked, "Vashti, what are you doing here today?"

Vashti responded, without opening her eyes, "I always have chemo on Thursdays, and I'm terribly disappointed that you aren't my nurse for my last session."

"But I just saw your blood work, and you shouldn't have chemo today. Not by the look of the lab report."

"What?" Vashti asked, sitting up. Shocked, they all stared at the infusion bag, which was almost empty. "I guess it is too late to worry about that now," she added, and the nurse left shaking her head.

Vashti's assigned nurse came in a few minutes later and unhooked her because the infusion was complete, saying nothing about the lab report. Vashti and June had no idea what could happen from having chemo when it was not supported by the lab findings. They thought that surely if there were any risk of danger to Vashti the oncologist would have shown up immediately.

On the drive back to her parents' house, Vashti said, "Regardless of that promise to the doctor, Mom, I'll be going home in the morning because Jeff, arriving later in the day, can monitor my status."

"You just lied to the doctor, who was concerned enough to ask you to stay with us," June said.

"It was just a little white lie. She didn't want me to spend the weekend alone because I'm not doing so well. But Jeff will be with me," Vashti asserted.

When they arrived at her parents house, Vashti let June put her to bed. Conor appeared in the doorway and asked, "Is a celebration in order, Vashti?"

Vashti replied ruefully, "I wish I could celebrate, but I don't feel well enough at the moment. Maybe later." Then she asked for her cell phone, and June handed it to her, certain that she would be texting Jeff with the good news about the last chemo treatment being over.

June stepped into the kitchen thinking she'd better text Jeff as well, in case Vashti fell asleep before sending her message. After all, she reasoned,

Vashti was always tired after chemo, but today, having gone into it tired, she was exhausted. As June began texting, she felt a mysterious warm gust of wind rush in from the hallway, causing the hair on the back of her neck to stand up. It reached her and paused, completely enveloping her in a benevolent way. Then it passed over her and seemed to go out the kitchen window. Alarmed by this possibly ominous sign, June dropped her phone on the floor and ran to Vashti's bedroom. Vashti's foot was protruding from under the quilt, which June considered odd since her daughter had had chills when she tucked her in. She grabbed Vashti's foot and said, "Vashti, have you become feverish?" There was no response. She said her name louder and still got no response. She grabbed Vashti's wrist to check for a pulse but felt none and shouted to Conor to call an ambulance. Then she put her face next to Vashti's mouth to check for a breath but could not detect any. She lifted Vashti's eyelids; the pupils were dilated and fixed. Seeing this, she jumped on the bed, screaming, "No, no, no! Don't leave now, Vashti! You've almost made it!" She sobbed as she placed the heel of her palm on the center of Vashti's chest and, with her other hand over it, started doing compressions, counting, "One thousand one, one thousand two, one thousand three."

Conor rushed into the room saying the ambulance was on its way. June asked him to help her move Vashti to the floor because the bed was too soft for the compressions to work. With Vashti on the floor, June started compressions again. A voice on Conor's phone started counting, "One thousand one, one thousand two, one thousand three." June looked toward the ceiling and screamed, "I'm getting nothing! Stay with me, Vashti! Don't leave, Vashti!" Amidst the turmoil, she yelled at Conor, "Where are they? It is taking them forever." To June it seemed like an eternity before the paramedics arrived and gently lifted her hands from Vashti's chest, telling June they would take it from there as she screamed, "No, no, no!" Conor backed June out of the room and sat her down in the living room, where she became perfectly still, silent as a stone. Now in shock, she had no idea who was doing what. A fireman emerged from the bedroom and told her, "We got a heartbeat, but don't get your hopes up yet. We are transporting her to Presbyterian Hospital downtown."

June and Conor pulled up at the ER entrance directly behind the ambulance. As the paramedics lifted Vashti out, Conor and June leapt from their car and grasped the gurney carrying her. Once they were inside, the emergency doctor examined Vashti and shouted, "Code!" Medical personnel charged in to assist, pushing Conor and June aside. June knew the code procedure well from her years working in the ER but didn't want to believe it was her daughter coding. Then the medical personnel dispersed, and Conor and June rushed back to Vashti's side, with June pleading, "Stay with us, Vashti. Stay with us."

But within minutes the ER doctor again shouted, "Code!" The medical staff came rushing back in, once more pushing Conor and June aside. As the staff dispersed a second time, Conor and June again rushed back to Vashti's side. June attempted, between sobs, to tell the ER doctor that Vashti's fiancé was in Boston for a conference, a comment he acknowledged. Minutes later the ER doctor shouted for a third time, "Code!" This time Conor and June were pushed to the back of the room, where June collapsed in a chair with her head in her hands, sobbing, "She's gone," over and over again. The ER doctor approached them and told Conor, "We have coded her three times, and I'm advising that we not code her again. We have her on a ventilator that's breathing for her, and we're going to transfer her to a room in the ICU. I hope your daughter survives until her fiancé comes, but we don't know how long her heart will continue beating. I'm so sorry."

Conor had to almost lift June from her chair, and soon they were accompanying Vashti to the ICU, where they were met by two nurses, who settled Vashti in the room and checked the ventilator. Now June was finally able to call Jeff and explain that she had found Vashti unresponsive shortly after returning from her chemo treatment at about 5:00 p.m.

Jeff remained silent for a few seconds then said he would be in Albuquerque as soon as possible. June never hung up; instead, she dropped her phone, rested her head on Vashti's chest, and wept. Conor guided her to a reclining chair close to Vashti's bed, where she appeared to pass out. He stood motionless between Vashti and June, watching them both. Soon June started to moan and stir. Then she bolted upright, rushed to Vashti's side, and grabbed hold of her hand. Hearing a beep from the monitor, June said to Conor, "Her heartbeat is slowing. It will keep slowing until it stops." As June fixed her gaze on Vashti's face, Vashti's heartbeat slowed to only a few beats per minute. At this point, the nurse said it was time to unplug the monitor and ventilator and get the doctor. As she unplugged the machines, the air in the room became stone silent.

By the time the doctor arrived to examine Vashti, Conor and June were themselves hardly breathing. They felt as if they had been there for days. When the doctor completed his exam, he looked at his watch and said softly, "I pronounce Vashti Warner expired at 3:03 a.m. on April 3."

Upon hearing the three mentions of Vashti's lucky number, she threw herself on her daughter, saying, "Thank you for sending that message, Vashti. Now I know you are okay."

The doctor, looking confused, told Conor they could stay as long as they wished. Conor thanked him and informed him that his daughter wanted to donate all her organs, but the doctor explained that because of her cancer she could not. June, in support of Vashti's advocacy for organ donation, said, "She can surely donate her corneas."

But the doctor replied that they would be unable to accept even those. He then added, "We could take tissue samples for educational or research purposes, but it would require an autopsy. Let me give you time to discuss it, and if you decide to donate tissue samples I will get a form for you to fill out."

When the doctor left, June turned to Conor and whispered, "What do you think she would want?"

He replied, "I think she would want to donate whatever she could to help anyone she could."

"I agree," June said, intuiting that Vashti's love for others could indeed be expressed in this way. June recalled Vashti's mumbled words during her last chemo treatment about the reason people are on earth—to learn to love. Those words not only convinced June that tissue donation was aligned with Vashti's wishes but would remain a guiding principle in June's life.

June came back to the present moment when the doctor returned with the forms to fill out. After they completed them, Conor, still surprisingly unperturbed, told the nurse they were going to say their final good-byes and leave. Before he could utter another word, however, his shoulders started to heave. The nurse touched his arm and expressed sorrow for his loss.

June and Conor said their final good-byes to Vashti, each in their own way, then Conor gently guided June to the door. They left the room in disbelief that Vashti could be dead only eighteen months after being diagnosed with cancer.

When June and Conor left the hospital, June was so distraught that she faced the rising sun and silently prayed, "Take me with her, Holy One. I don't want to live my life without her." This prayer played over and over in June's mind till she and Conor were home, collapsed on their bed, when it morphed into Vashti's childhood voice saying, "We have to take care of Dad, Mom, because we are the only family he has." Then the words turned into Vashti's adult voice saying, "Take care of Dad, Mom. You are the only one he has." Those words pulled June back from the abyss, after which she fell into a kind of sleep she had never before experienced.

Conor felt frozen in time. Then he remembered the text from Jeff saying his flight was due to land in Albuquerque at 11:30 a.m. Conor set his phone alarm so he'd be sure to pick Jeff up on time because Jeff would need him as a son needed a father in times of trauma. Conor had first met him when

Jeff was no more than a kid, and even then he had thought Jeff would be a perfect match for Vashti and a wonderful addition to their family.

One of Vashti's remarks to Conor echoed in his mind: "You are the Rock of Gibraltar, Daddy. I don't know where *that* rock is, but you are my rock here, to take care of me." Tears streamed down his face as he silently vowed, "I'll always be your Rock of Gibraltar, Vashti, and I'll try to be Jeff's, too." Then he cried himself to sleep, something he had never done before.

CHAPTER 32

When Conor caught sight of Jeff at the airport, he inhaled sharply, clearly distressed. Jeff's eyes were red and nearly swollen shut; his face was white; and he looked like he might faint at any minute. As he approached Conor he said, "I came as soon as I could, but I'm too late." The two hugged and wept together.

While they disengaged, Jeff hollered, "Take me to her right now."

Conor replied, "Unfortunately, you can't go to her now because she is in necropsy, where they will be performing an autopsy."

"An autopsy? Are you out of your mind? Don't you think Vashti suffered enough in this life? Now you are allowing her physical body to be ripped open after her death?"

Conor patiently explained, "Vashti was a big supporter of organ donation. She wanted every viable organ of a person's body to be donated. After the doctor pronounced her dead, we inquired about having her organs donated, but he said that because of the cancer they would be unable to use any of her organs—even her corneas, which June had asked about. He told us the only items Vashti could donate were tissue samples for education or research, and to obtain the tissue they had to do an autopsy. We decided Vashti would want to donate anything she could, so we completed the paperwork to have tissue removed for both education and research. After that she was taken away to necropsy."

"I'm sorry for shouting. I just wanted to hold her in my arms one last time and tell her how much I love her. And since she wanted to be cremated, this seemed to be my only opportunity," Jeff said, apologetically, as tears rolled down his face.

"I think there is something we can do, Jeff," Conor said. "After the autopsy, she will be sent back to the mortuary handling the funeral arrangements. I will request that she be prepared for an open-casket funeral so you can see her and say good-bye. Then they can send her body for cremation."

"Thank you, Conor," Jeff whispered appreciatively.

On their way to Conor and June's house to rest before their afternoon appointment at the funeral home, the two agreed that Jeff would sleep at Vashti's house at night, which was what he wanted to do. When they arrived at Conor and June's house, Conor took Jeff to Vashti's old bedroom, where he had spent much time with Vashti in years past, so he could rest and reflect. Conor then went to check on June, who was now awake. He explained that Jeff was resting in Vashti's room and that he would make coffee and tea then come get her when it was time to leave for the funeral home.

When Conor had poured himself a cup of coffee and sat down at the dining room table, Jeff came out to join him. "I'd like to help any way I can. If you give me Vashti's cell phone, I can at least manage her phone messages. And if I can use your computer I'll get into Vashti's Facebook account and handle her timeline as well," he said. Conor thanked him and accepted the offer, emphasizing that he and June were in no shape to do such things. As June entered the dining room, Jeff embraced her warmly, but seeing Jeff's sad face made June sob all over again. Jeff tried to comfort them both, saying, "I know Vashti believed that death was simply a transition into new life. And now her suffering is over. He choked up as he finished speaking, and June held him close for a long time. Then Conor rounded them up to go to the funeral home.

When they arrived, Conor made the necessary arrangements, including voicing a request for Jeff to have time alone with Vashti before her body would be sent for cremation. The funeral director assured them that Jeff would have private time with her in a small chapel.

Next the director took them to a display of caskets, including some that could be loaned to them for Jeff's viewing and for Vashti's funeral if they wanted. Then he led them to an area teeming with urns and invited them to select one. They settled on a deep green marble urn. June asked Jeff to select a smaller urn he could use for taking some of Vashti's ashes to the Pacific Ocean, June then requested to see jewelry urns in which she could wear some of Vashti's ashes around her neck for the rest of her life so that Vashti would always be with her. She selected a plain small silver urn on a thin silver chain. As they walked back out to the lobby, Jeff asked the funeral director to call him when Vashti's body was delivered after the autopsy and ready for private viewing.

Soon after June, Conor, and Jeff returned to the house, Vashti's friends began stopping by. Jeff visited with them and helped Conor get them refreshments. June collapsed on the couch, where she sat weeping the entire afternoon. Jeff checked Vashti's cell phone and noted that she had received 233 texts since the previous day, while her Facebook news feed was filled with posts. As dusk approached, Conor got June comfortable in bed then told her he was about to drive Jeff to Vashti's house.

When Conor pulled into Vashti's driveway, he looked at Jeff and asked, "Are you sure you want to stay here alone?"

"Yes. I need to be alone now to figure out how I'm going to get through this."

"Will you call if you need anything, or even if you just want to talk?"

"I'll call if anything comes up."

Jeff entered Vashti's darkened house, walked to the center of the living room, and fell to his knees, shouting, "Vashti!" so loud it seemed to echo off the rough-cut ceiling beams. Then he walked into every room in the house shouting her name except for the last room, her bedroom, where he whispered her name and fell on the bed. Smelling her scent in the nightie strewn across the covers, he began to cry so hard he thought he might pass out. Then he felt a warm hand on his dangling arm and heard Vashti's voice whisper, "I'm okay." He looked up quickly but found no one present. Jeff felt that Vashti had given him a sign of reassurance that she was still alive, although transformed.

The next morning the funeral home called Jeff to arrange a time for the private viewing. Jeff decided on 3:00 p.m. then called Conor, who said he and June would meet him there. When Jeff arrived, he found them sitting in the lobby, having already viewed Vashti for several minutes. She looked beautiful in a new dress she had never had the chance to wear, which Jeff, with Gabby's help, had picked out for the viewing.

The funeral director led Jeff to the small chapel and closed the door. Seconds later they heard a ghastly howl. June, with a pained expression, asked Conor if he thought they should check on Jeff. He remarked that he didn't think anyone should intrude on Jeff's time with Vashti.

Jeff approached the casket slowly. He took Vashti's small hand in his and told her how much he loved her. He said that a part of him was going to heaven with her, and a part of her was very much alive in his heart here on earth. Then he kissed her gently on the lips, remembering her words, "When we die, we are not dead. Life and death are not two opposite things. Life and death are one and the same thing. We live, we die, we're transformed into new life . . . It is all one and the same." After one last kiss, he forced himself to leave her.

Rejoining Conor and June in the lobby, he dropped onto a nearby chair and sat in silence with them for several minutes. Then Conor asked Jeff to come home with them for a while, but he declined, saying he had something to do and would call them later.

Jeff drove to a tattoo shop where he had scheduled an appointment for himself and Gabby. He explained to the tattoo artist that his fiancée had just died and he wanted a quote from one of their favorite poems, written by Dylan Thomas in 1933, tattooed over his heart: "Though lovers be lost, love shall not; And death shall have no dominion." Over the next three hours, the artist completed the tattoo, working masterfully with the lettering. Jeff liked the result and felt the words would always link him to Vashti. Gabby, for her part, had a hamsa hand tattooed under her arm.

The funeral Mass for Vashti was at the Cathedral of St. John's, her parents' church in downtown Albuquerque, on Wednesday at noon, six days after her death. Conor, June, and Jeff rode in a limousine to the cathedral about an hour before the Mass. The priest escorted them to a sitting room off the left side of the nave. About five minutes before the Mass was to begin, he returned to usher them to their seats. He explained that the cathedral was full and people were standing in the side aisles of the nave. Jeff was certain that Vashti would not have liked the occasion to be so solemn. While she believed funerals should be respectful, in her opinion every occasion needed a little something to go wrong just to make it interesting—and thus far everything had gone perfectly.

However, when the priest led them to the first pew and instructed Conor, followed by the others, to go in and walk to the end, Conor tripped halfway there and almost flew headlong into the center aisle. People in the row of pews behind him gasped, but a fall was averted as June, startled because she had never seen him fall, quickly steadied him. Jeff, witnessing the incident, saw it as an indication of Vashti's presence and whispered to her in his mind, "I'm glad you are here."

After all three were seated, the pallbearers slowly wheeled Vashti's casket to the front of the church. As June watched them, she prayed, "Divine Presence, Vashti was pure existence, pure consciousness, pure love. May her laughter be heard, her smile radiate, and the love in her heart flow throughout the universe for all time. Precious Vashti, you are the universe now in ecstatic motion. My love for you is infinite, and you are close to me and in my heart, until we are together again." After her prayer, tears flowed down June's face.

Then Vashti's best friend Dave spoke, telling the congregation that he thought he would be returning to Albuquerque to be the maid of honor at Vashti's wedding, but instead he was playing a very different role today. The congregation laughed quietly. He said that he and Vashti had been friends for so many years that he had watched her go from being a crazy girl to a beautiful woman. He described her as loving and kind, fun with a sharp wit, passionate, at times crass but always real, intelligent, motivated, caring, and compassionate. She had once told him that every person was here on their life journey to lift their brothers and sisters up and to never hurt, malign, or bring them down. Over many years, he had seen her uplift countless people and never hurt anyone. By the end of his eulogy, people's emotions were ranging from amusement to sorrow.

Jeff spoke next, for the family. Stopping several times to compose himself, he emphasized Vashti's beauty and benevolent qualities and promised to remain close to her parents because he knew that is what she would want him to do. After concluding, he missed taking the step from the pulpit to the floor, tripped, and came close to sprawling in front of the altar. He heard a gasp from several congregants before regaining his balance and walking back to his seat, whispering under his breath, "Vashti, that wasn't funny!" Once Jeff was seated, the priest began the Mass.

Vashti's funeral was heartbreaking for everyone who had known her. They felt there was a little less sun in the day without her in the world, that they would miss her laughter, her hugs, and her joyful smile. But they also felt that the love and compassion she embodied would still radiate out into the world.

After the funeral, the congregants and others met at a nearby pub for lunch. Conor and June were pleased that their dearest friends, Mike and Cheryl, had flown in from North Dakota to be with them in their time of loss. June's grief counselor had also attended, which had given June enough peace of mind to survive the funeral. A few mutual friends of Jeff and Vashti's, from when they had first dated years before, came to the pub to offer their support as well. In the late afternoon, some of Vashti's ashes were placed in a niche of the columbarium in the garden of St. John's Cathedral during a private ceremony. Conor and June each placed a letter to Vashti in the niche, and Conor also put in the pocket watch he had given her, which he had stopped at exactly 3:03.

The next evening a group of Vashti's female friends gathered at her house for a women's wake. Jeff, since he had been staying at the house, offered to help if they needed anything, and June stopped by briefly to greet them. Seeing some of the women baking chocolate chip cookies—Vashti's favorite—others drinking wine as Vashti had enjoyed doing, and still others dancing across the living room to Vashti's favorite Josephine Baker record, she marveled at the palpability of their love for her daughter. She then silently prayed for each of the women and thanked the Divine One that her daughter had been blessed with such devoted friends, certain that Vashti lived on in their hearts. Spotting Gabby among them, she hoped this young woman knew in her heart that Vashti had loved her as if she were her own daughter.

When Conor called Jeff the next morning, Jeff informed him that the last friends had departed around 3:30 a.m. after smoking a cigar in Vashti's honor on her veranda, as Vashti had often done. Jeff said there had been so much laughter and tears that he knew Vashti would have loved the wake. Then he corrected himself and told Conor that Vashti did love the wake.

Jeff also reported that during the evening the women had gone to Vashti's bedroom to measure the height of one of her high heels after pondering how she could have run in such shoes. While sitting on the floor in front of her closet, they noticed a strong scent of vanilla suddenly permeating the room. Amazed at the presence of Vashti's favorite aroma, they had called Jeff in from the study to help them search the room, but there was no trace of vanilla incense or vanilla candles having been burned anywhere in the house. Returning to the study, Jeff could hear the women speaking to Vashti as if she were there, telling her how much they loved her and missed her. He explained to Conor that the experience had been so moving that he felt certain Vashti had been there with them.

The rest of the day was a blur for Jeff, Conor, and June. That evening there was a wake at a local pub on Central Avenue for those who could set aside their grief and do what Vashti loved best—party. Shots were provided by people making toasts. Stories were told about Vashti, some of which made Jeff laugh while others brought tears to his eyes. Judge Sanchez, Vashti's favorite judge, attended but didn't speak. When preparing to depart, he told Conor he would never forget Vashti, that she brought sunshine to the darkest days, but what he liked best about her as a prosecutor had been her fairness in dealing with criminal defendants and her sincere compassion for them. To him, it was clear that she loved working with people and had an uncanny ability to always remember them. The judge expressed his sincere condolences and told Conor that people lucky enough to have known her would always remember her.

June focused on Vashti's closest friends. She saw D-Chappy gazing intently at photos of Vashti that had been arranged on a poster board for the occasion. She made a mental note to get to know him so she could one day tell him how Vashti had admired him. Brittney was also present, appearing distraught but easing her grief with the help of a few drinks. She had recently given birth to her first child, as Vashti had predicted, and named her Kaia. June lamented the fact that Vashti had never gotten to hold the baby but knew that Vashti had seen her from afar.

The following day Conor took Jeff to the airport for his return trip to San Diego. When Conor hugged him good-bye, he thanked Jeff for loving his daughter for the remainder of her life, as he had promised to do, and expressed sadness that her life hadn't included many years of remission. As Jeff started to wend his way toward the secured area, Conor said, "She would want you to go on and live life to the fullest. She wouldn't want you to waste time mourning." Jeff nodded solemnly as he continued walking.

Conor drove back home to find June grief-stricken, with their greyhound Lilly at her feet, as if watching over her. Conor was very worried about June, who since Vashti's death had not left the house except to attend the funeral and the wakes, even refusing to accompany Conor and Lilly on their evening walks. That evening, when she again refused, Lilly stopped at the door and whined until June came to check on her. Conor tried once more, but Lilly refused to move and began whining again, quitting only when June approached her a second time. June finally joined them for a walk but stopped abruptly upon seeing a small heart-shaped rock on the ground. It resembled the special rock Vashti's friend had given her at his wedding and that Vashti had often held in her hand to reduce stress during chemo. June was amazed and, showing it to Conor, commented, "It looks like Vashti's rock."

"It does," Conor confirmed.

"I have her rock in my treasure box. I'll compare the two when we get home," June said.

When she held Vashti's rock beside the rock she had discovered, she found them remarkably similar. Her discovery, she concluded, was a sign from Vashti that Vashti still loved her though in a different form. "Thank you, Vashti. Now I know everything is okay. I love you so very much," June whispered under her breath.

On Jeff's first evening back in San Diego, he was devastated, hardly able to believe that Vashti—having come so close to a remission and to living with him near the ocean—was really dead. He doubted his legs would carry him along the beach to watch the sunset, yet he knew that if Vashti had come with him to San Diego, this was the first thing she would have done.

After meditating a bit to gain strength, he reached for the small urn containing some of Vashti's ashes and left the house, deeply saddened. On his way to the shoreline, he repeated Vashti's name over and over, telling her she was finally there with him. As the setting sun left just a sliver of its golden light above the horizon. Jeff waded out into the Pacific Ocean, scattered Vashti's ashes in the water, and declared, "I will always love you, Vashti, forever and a day." Then scanning the horizon he suddenly saw the green flash. Standing transfixed, with tears streaming down his face, he smiled slightly, in awe of the spectacle before him. He whispered, "Thank you, Vashti. I knew you would come here with me and we would see the green flash together, that harbinger of eternal happiness."

CHAPTER 33

June slowly started relating again to the people and events around her. One day while cleaning out Vashti's house she unexpectedly found Vashti's journal, awakening an immediate sense of her daughter's continued presence in her life. June recalled feeling that her heart had been ripped from her chest, leaving an empty hole, when Vashti had died, and that the Divine One had gradually filled it with the energy of love and compassion Vashti had embodied. Remembering Vashti's wonder at the paradox of autumn leaves turning vibrant colors prior to their death, June realized that Vashti had mirrored that mystery by turning her fear and disappointment into a seemingly golden aura of love and compassion for others and gratitude for the life she had lived. It was then that love and compassion started pouring out of June to others, particularly those who were sick or suffering. The more June let this energy flow to others, the more it healed her own deep wounds as well.

Opening the journal to an entry Vashti had written the day before her last chemo treatment, when she was so weak she thought she might die, June and Conor were stunned to instead discover their daughter's expressions of gratitude for life. The entry read:

> If you are reading this, Mom and Dad, things didn't go as planned. I'd do anything to take your pain away, but I know I can't. All I can do is tell you that you have been the very best parents anyone could hope for. You made my life complete, special, and meaningful. Mom, you were full of energy, vibrant and tireless. Dad, you were quiet and strong. You always made me feel safe. And no matter what I did I knew you would love me and be there for me. Always.

I want you to know that my life has been incredible. Every dream, every desire has been satisfied and enjoyed. My life has been so rich, so full, all that I ever wanted it to be. As I write this, I'm smiling. I can't imagine having had a better life. Every place I've been, every face I've seen, every experience I've had has filled my life with joy. I've traveled, I've studied, I've played, laughed, and loved. I've sworn and gotten into trouble. I've had a loving family, including parents who loved each other and stayed together. I've failed and made mistakes. I've had a career and been successful. I've enjoyed the arts, mouth-watering cuisine, and enchanting architecture. I've hurt people and healed them. I've been a best friend, a companion, an advocate, an enemy. I've felt sorrow and loss, love, envy, humiliation, joy, fulfillment. I've been a victim and a champion. I've seen oceans and mountains. I've touched greatness. I've been accepted and rejected. I've been religious and lost. I've been beautiful and ugly. I've done everything a person can do. I've seen everything a person can see. I've felt everything a person can feel. Most importantly, I've done everything I wanted to do in life and I have no regrets.

About the Author

Lesley Lowe has practiced law for over twenty-five years. Before becoming an attorney, she worked for ten years as a registered nurse in emergency rooms. She was inspired to write *Autumn Gold* by the verve, courage, and compassion her daughter, also an attorney, exuded in the final months of her life. This is Lesley's first book.

She and her husband, Rusty, live in Albuquerque, New Mexico, with their two greyhounds, Lola and Bimba. They spend summers in North Dakota, near the Canadian border.